Her instinct was to say: **No, no**
then Tilly thought of her dad, **:**
muttered to herself, "Dign
She took a deep breath. Okay. Let's do this.

She tried out the drum. "Can you hear me at the back?"

"Sure can, Captain!"

Captain, she thought. *That's a joke.* She twisted the beaters around in her hands. *All right*, she thought. Tentatively, she began to beat out a steady rhythm.

And the crew followed. *Wow*, she thought. *That actually works . . .* She increased the pace, and the boat began to move out into the open water.

"That's it, Tilly!" shouted Xoha. "You're getting it!"

She kept the beat, and called out instructions, and the little red boat lined up against the others. She looked down the boat at the crew, each one of them looking at her expectantly. Tilly found that if she breathed, slowly and steadily, they all began to fall in with her breathing. So when she started the drum, they were all already in synch . . .

On the side, they were waiting to start the race. Tilly lifted up the beaters, breathed with her crew—then the whistle sounded, and they were off.

Thud, went the drums, and the oars followed, slicing through the water. She saw that Xoha was a little behind, just a split second, and she called to her, "Keep the pace!" She was conscious of the blues-and-greens, to her left, inching ahead, but she didn't panic. Second by second, she upped the pace, chasing them. The purples-and-whites were soon far behind. It seemed to Tilly she could see the whole race unfolding in her mind's eye—how to use the strokes of the other team to help them, how to manage the distance between them so they weren't cut off . . . *Patterns*, she thought. *I'm good at seeing patterns . . .* At her instructions, they sliced through the water, keeping up the pace, though never quite catching up on the blues-and-greens. They came in second—but it was very, very close.

Risera was ecstatic. She hopped out of the boat into the shallows and splashed up to give Tilly a big hug.

"See!" she said. *I knew you'd like bossing people around!*

**Don't miss these other
exciting books in the world of**

DESPERATE HOURS

by David Mack

DRASTIC MEASURES

by Dayton Ward

FEAR ITSELF

by James Swallow

STAR TREK®

DISCOVERY

THE WAY TO THE STARS

UNA McCORMACK

Based on *Star Trek*®
created by Gene Roddenberry
and
Star Trek: Discovery
created by Bryan Fuller & Alex Kurtzman

G

GALLERY BOOKS

New York   London   Toronto   Sydney   New Delhi

G

Gallery Books
An Imprint of Simon & Schuster, Inc.
1230 Avenue of the Americas
New York, NY 10020

First Gallery Books trade paperback edition January 2019

GALLERY BOOKS and colophon are trademarks of Simon & Schuster, Inc.

For information about special discounts for bulk purchases, please contact Simon & Schuster Special Sales at 1-866-506-1949 or business@simonandschuster.com.

The Simon & Schuster Speakers Bureau can bring authors to your live event. For more information or to book an event, contact the Simon & Schuster Speakers Bureau at 1-866-248-3049 or visit our website at www.simonspeakers.com.

Manufactured in the United States of America

10 9 8 7 6 5 4 3 2 1

ISBN 978-1-9821-0475-7
ISBN 978-1-9821-0476-4 (ebook)

To Matthew and Verity,
my guys

Prologue

Some nights, Michael Burnham thought, you had to resign yourself to not getting any sleep. The trick was to accept your fate and not lie in the dark allowing your wakefulness to become fruitless and circular thinking. In other circumstances she would get up, move around, do some work or meditation. But nothing Michael could do would solve the problem of a roommate tossing and turning and sighing into the darkness.

Things went quiet. Michael found that she was holding her breath, waiting for Tilly's soft snores to start. But no—the moment passed, Tilly turned again, and sighed, deeply, into the night.

Michael pulled herself up onto her elbow. "Tilly," she whispered. "What's the matter?"

Her roommate did not reply, but the other side of the room went suddenly very quiet. Not the soft quiet of sleep—no, something more watchful, wakeful, cautious. Tilly on red alert.

"Tilly," Michael said again, more firmly, and in her normal speaking voice. "I know you're not asleep. What's going on?"

The lights were down. Michael sensed rather than saw Tilly sit up, a darker shape in the darkness. "It's nothing," said Tilly. A small voice, tiny, barely audible. She talked like that sometimes, Michael had observed, like a creature curling up into a shell, trying to shield herself behind some kind of protective covering.

"Doesn't sound like nothing," Michael said. "Sounds like kind of a big deal."

Tilly laughed—a nervous laugh, like a tightly coiled spring. "Oh, you know what it's like when you can't sleep . . ."

"Mm-hm." *I know*.

"Thoughts go racing around your head . . . You can't shake them . . ."

"So . . . what's racing around your head right now, Tilly?"

No answer. Just a sigh, dredged up from somewhere deep within. Michael waited patiently.

"Oh, you know," said Tilly eventually, in the small voice. "Big day tomorrow."

In the darkness, Michael nodded to herself. Now they were getting somewhere. "Tomorrow?"

"You know. First official day. Command Training Program!"

"That *is* a big day," Michael agreed. "Aren't you excited?"

Another sigh.

Michael took a deep, calming breath. Right now, it was her most ardent wish—the depth of which could only be understood by someone who has had a long and tiring day, with another on the horizon—that she could lie back on her bed, close her eyes, and be instantly asleep. But it wasn't going to happen. Some nights, thought Michael, you had to accept your fate.

"How about some lights?" she said. "Soft."

When the lights came up, Michael looked across to the other bed. Tilly was sitting up, arms wrapped around her knees, all curled up on herself, tight and small. Her heart went out to her. Poor Tilly.

"Hey," said Michael softly. "Are you okay?"

What a question. Of course she wasn't okay. She looked dreadful—face pale and eyes wide and red. "You're not really worried about tomorrow, are you?"

"Well, *yes*," said Tilly, as if that was the most obvious thing in the world.

Michael thought about this. "It's natural to feel nervous," she said. "It's a big step—"

"I'm not *nervous*—"

"Okay."

"I'm . . . *scared*."

"That's natural too," said Michael. "Helpful, even. But you know you have a right to be there, don't you? You know you've earned your place?"

Tilly didn't reply.

"Tilly?"

"That's the problem. I'm not sure I *have* . . ." She gave Michael a sad smile. "Sometimes, you know, I just don't think I'm good enough—"

"That's not true!"

"It's just . . . Starfleet was never the plan, you see. The plan was always something else. So I can't help thinking that way. Sometimes."

"Want to tell me why?"

Tilly sighed. "It's kind of a long story . . ."

Michael shifted around in the bed, making herself comfortable. Some nights are *big* nights, and you had to accept your fate. Michael smiled at her roommate.

"I'm listening."

Part One
Autumn

1

Sweet sixteen, thought Sylvia Tilly, glancing at herself in the mirror. Her mouth twisted at the sight. Pale face. Long red hair. Curls—stupid, impossible, annoying curls. She tugged at one, which promptly fell into her eye. *Did I mention stupid? What do you do with curls like this? They won't do what they're told. They have a mind of their own.* It wasn't like Sylvia hadn't tried . . . *Down, curls! Stay straight! Stay sensible! Do the right thing!*

Sylvia looked away from the mirror and back at the screen. She suppressed a sigh. There on the screen was her mother, Siobhan. Siobhan was talking. Her mother did a lot of talking. She talked for a living. She made speeches, and they were very good speeches, and they had taken her all the way up to the Federation Security Council, where she was the representative of the core worlds, and she was going to keep on making very good speeches until she was chair of the council, which wouldn't be long now. When people met Sylvia, they would say, "Oh, *that's* your mother . . ." and Sylvia would smile politely, and then they would say, "You don't look anything like her." And she would answer, "It's the curls."

But the point was that Mom talked, *a lot*, and she expected to be heard, and the problem with *that* was that Sylvia couldn't always bring herself to listen. It was kind of . . . relentless? Sometimes you had to tune it out, for your own good, but the problem with that was you wondered whether people on the Security Council did the same thing, *Oh, it's Siobhan, talking again*, and the problem with *that* was you might give yourself the giggles, and if there was one thing Mom didn't like, it was giggles, *particularly* when she was talking.

"Sylvia," said Siobhan, pausing for breath, *"could you do something about that ringlet on your face? It's very distracting."*

"Sorry, Mom," muttered Sylvia. She started tugging at the curl, trying to fix it.

"You know, sweetheart," said Siobhan, *"if you tried fiddling less with your hair, it would probably be less unruly."*

Gee, Mom, I'm so glad you called . . .

"That's better," said Siobhan. *"Now, let's take a look at these grades."*

It was near the end of term, and Sylvia's report card had come in. Her teachers had been more than happy, much more than happy, but the problem with Mom was that you couldn't always predict what she would be pleased about. More importantly, you couldn't always predict what she would be *displeased* about. Sylvia felt her shoulders tense. "Everything's okay, isn't it?"

"Let me take a look," said Siobhan. *"I only just this minute got it."*

Sylvia watched the frown form on her mother's face. *Well, hi there, frown!* Sylvia thought. She and her mother's frown were old, old friends, went back *years*, although Sylvia sometimes thought that maybe the friendship wasn't really flowing both ways. *Hey, frown, how about a few more smiles?*

"All right," said her mother, leaning back in her office chair. *"There are a couple of issues I can see here."*

Huh?

"Mom," said Sylvia warily, "did you see the marks for math and science?"

"What?" Her mom glanced across the marks again. *"Oh yes, yes, they're fine."*

Fine? They were more than fine . . .

"Mom, did you see the mark for the science project?"

"Yes, I saw that—I don't miss things, Sylvia, you know I don't miss things—"

Well, there's one thing you seem to be missing . . . About today? Remember, today? You know? It's my birthday? Remember that? Huh?

"But I'm rather concerned about the topic," said Siobhan.

"Astromycology is a growth subject . . ." Oh no, another giggle. Sylvia bit her lip to suppress it, bit hard. It wasn't that kind of Mom-conversation. "You know, that's actually quite funny, if you know the field."

Siobhan gave a tight smile, then shook her head. *"I don't pretend to know the ins and outs, darling. But . . ."* She sighed. *"It's these mushrooms again, isn't it?"*

"Well, yes, but that's not really the most important thing—"

But Mom wasn't listening. Mom, for some reason, wasn't convinced about mycology. *"I do see how good your marks are in math and science, sweetheart, but they're not the whole of it, are they?"*

Uh-oh.

"What do you mean?" Sylvia said carefully.

"Well, what else is there here? If we look down the list?"

"I did really well in literature," Sylvia said brightly. "Like, upper tenth percentile." She was surprised not to have gone higher there, to be honest; she'd loved *The Tempest*, gone out of her way to track down as many different productions as possible, including an incredible one done entirely in zero g . . . That had been something else.

The problem with the term paper was that the teacher was pretty *urgh*, to say the least, and for some reason she hadn't always liked Sylvia's classroom contributions . . . She'd gotten pretty touchy in one class, now that Sylvia thought back. Something about *Who exactly is the teacher here?* Jeez, though, some people were so *touchy* . . .

"*I suppose upper tenth is fine—but, Sylvia, this mark for French is terrible!*"

Sylvia took a deep breath. She'd seen this one coming, and she'd prepared herself. "Okay, I'm not saying the mark couldn't be better, but it's not *terrible*—"

"*You live in Paris, sweetie!*"

"Only since the start of this academic year! Which is, well, it's not even a whole year, is it, when you add up the holidays . . . And, also, I *study* in New York!"

"*You've holidayed in the Midi since . . . since before you were born!*"

"You know, there are actually several dialects spoken there—"

"*I know that, Sylvia, I lived there as a little girl.*"

"—and that really complicates things when you're trying to improve your *oral* scores—"

"*Your grandmother is a native French speaker!*"

"But we talk to each other in *English*!" Sylvia's voice became a wail. "It's not my fault Granna's English is flawless! She's had a *lot* more time to practice English than I've had to practice French!"

There was a pause. Sylvia swallowed. *Hey, Mom, how about those birthday wishes? They'd be really nice round about now . . .*

Siobhan was folding her hands before her. *Uh-oh, here we go . . .*

"*The issue is, Sylvia,*" said Siobhan, "*that we're working toward being the most well-rounded person that we can be.*"

Okay, so the birthday wishes definitely weren't coming right now. "I know, Mom," Sylvia said. Tiny voice. Really tiny voice.

"I'll be the first to say that a real understanding—a genuine understanding of science and mathematics is crucial for any diplomat. But that isn't going to be enough. Sylvia, we've talked about this so often! If you're going to make it in the diplomatic corps, everything matters. Everything! You can't afford to specialize so much, so early."

Teeny-tiny voice. "I know, Mom."

"Don't look so cross, sweetie. I'm just worrying that some things might be slipping. And we need to find out why to fix the problem."

The problem. I'm always a problem.

"You've missed a couple of flute lessons, haven't you?" said Siobhan.

"I'm just finding the breathing difficult. I wish I'd stuck with the viola—"

"You don't get solos with a viola."

Not technically true, thought Sylvia, but she didn't pipe up in defense of the viola. Sylvia had her own problems right now. The viola could take care of itself.

"Okay," said Siobhan. *"I think I'll need to look through these marks more carefully. You're right, there is some good news, but there are a few things I'm a little concerned about. We might want to revisit whether this experiment of living with Granna is working out."*

Sylvia sighed. She loved living with Granna, and Granna's husband, Quinn. It was so much more relaxing than living with Mom. She didn't mean that in a bad way. It just *was*.

Siobhan frowned. *"At the very least you could start speaking French at home."*

Sylvia did giggle then. Poor Quinn. His French was

worse than hers. Actually, that might be worth it, to watch Quinn struggle with the subjunctive.

Siobhan looked up sharply. *"I'm not joking around, Sylvia,"* she said. *"We're not at red flags yet, but some of these grades are definitely heading toward amber."*

"I'm sorry, Mom," Sylvia said contritely. "I wasn't joking either . . . It was just . . ." She shook her head. "It doesn't matter. I really am sorry. I hear what you say, honestly I do."

"All right. Good. Well, like I say, I'll go over this in more detail, and maybe you and me and Granna can sit down next week and talk through what we think is best." Siobhan's eyes darted away from the screen. Clearly, something else was going on in the room, and the good side of that was that she would want to stop soon and get back to work. The bad side of that was . . . Well.

"Hey, sweetie, I have to go. I love you. I miss you. I want you to be the best you can be. Don't forget that, darling." Siobhan blew her a kiss. *"Night, night! Don't let the bedbugs bite!"*

The channel cut before Sylvia could answer. Mom was gone and the room was quiet. Sylvia sighed and sat for a while, hunched over the screen. She glanced at the mirror. The curl had come loose again. She gave it a listless tug. It bounced up, then fell down again. Stupid, stupid curls.

There was a tap on the door, and Granna came in. She took one look at Sylvia's face and frowned. "Oh dear," said Adèle. She came to stand behind Sylvia, resting her hands upon her granddaughter's shoulders. "Should I ask, *chérie*?"

"What is there to ask? Mom was . . . Mom."

"Ah," said Adèle, and pulled a face.

"It wasn't that bad," Sylvia lied.

"Oh?"

"But the thing is," said Sylvia. "The thing *is* . . . that

I'm never quite sure what it is I've done wrong. I *think* I'm doing okay, and I *think* that I've listened to what she had to say, but it's never quite *right* . . ."

"I know, *chérie*," said Adèle, stroking the crestfallen girl's cheek gently with her thumb. "Your mother loves you, Sylvia, she really does. I know sometimes she is very exacting. I know that her standards are high. But it all comes from love. She can see how smart you are—we all can! She just wants you to excel, to be your very best self. You have so much promise, Sylvia . . ."

"I know all that, Granna," said Sylvia. "I really do. But . . ."

"But what, *chérie*?"

Tiny voice. Tiniest of voices. "It's my *birthday* . . ."

Her voice trailed off. Adèle's hands tensed for a second upon her granddaughter's shoulders. "Sylvia," she said carefully, "did she not wish you happy birthday?"

"I mean, it's *okay* . . ." Sylvia said quickly. "I know how busy she is, and she's got so much to remember . . . I honestly don't mind, really I don't—"

"Oh, Sylvia!"

"Honestly, Granna, it's fine!"

Adèle was gathering herself up. She was only five four, but what she lacked in height, she made up for in elegance, poise, and an imperious presence that a few centuries earlier would have brought the court at Versailles to its knees. "That girl! I shall have a word with her—"

Sylvia's heart plummeted. "Please, Granna! Please don't do that!"

"It's your birthday, *chérie*! Sweet sixteen!"

"And I've had a nice dinner with you and Quinn! Cake, candles, song, the whole kit and caboodle! And I got that mark for my science project! Granna, *please* don't speak to her, *please*—"

But her grandmother was already through the door. Sylvia sighed. "Sometimes," she said, to nobody in particular, "I wish people round here could do a little less talking and a little more *listening* . . . I mean, it's not that much to ask for, is it? Huh? Huh?"

But nobody was listening. That was the problem. Nobody was darn well listening.

Sylvia flopped back on her bed. She put on some music and soon Bowie was singing to her about the starman, and, gosh, that helped with everything, didn't it? That made things seem a little less awful all around. She closed her eyes, and thought about life, and the universe, and everything. She thought about her science project (practical applications of pathogenic fungi), and how good it was—which was way better than any of her family realized—and how her teacher was talking about contacting a couple of experts in the field to find out exactly how good it was. Sylvia smiled. Just thinking about that project made her happier. People, they were tricky sometimes. Sometimes Sylvia couldn't get the words out, couldn't make herself understood. She knew she needed to work on that, along with everything else she needed to work on. But sometimes she was happier just losing herself in her studies, seeing the beautiful world that mycology revealed to her, a world where everything was patterned, and connected, and made sense . . .

Then the song ended, and she thought of her mom, and she felt sad.

Sweet sixteen, Sylvia Tilly thought. *Happy birthday, dear Sylvia. Happy birthday to me.*

Gabriel Xavier Quinn knew from the way the door flung open that his evening's peace was unlikely to continue. In fact, he'd been expecting fireworks all evening, because

Siobhan, his stepdaughter, was calling. That was almost a guarantee of . . . well, if not a quarrel, then some seriously fervent emotions, conveyed in no uncertain terms to each other by some seriously strong women. Quinn stuck his thumb into his book and watched as his beautiful and much adored wife swept into the room, and he thanked whatever stars had aligned to bring Adèle into his life.

Her relations, not so much.

Well, Sylvia was a darling.

"That *girl*!" Adèle cried, throwing her hands up. She muttered something under her breath, Gallically. Quinn didn't try to translate. His own ancestors had equipped him sufficiently in that respect, thank you very much.

Quinn was Adèle's second husband. They had met fifteen years ago, at the opera, and embarked on a whirl-wind romance that had taken their respective sets of friends completely by surprise. Adèle was grand, stately, aristocratic; Quinn was rather raffish and unkempt. In other words, there was considerable appeal on both sides. They married after three months and were exceptionally happy. Their particular joy was in daily proving wrong every single friend who had said it would only last eighteen months.

Quinn frowned. "What? Sylvia? She's a grand girl—"

"Not Sylvia! Siobhan!"

"Ah," said Quinn. "Well. Siobhan." He looked back down at his book, which was about the adventures of a captain and a surgeon serving on the same ship during the Napoleonic Wars. Right up his street. There was a whole set of them, and he was eager to get back on board. Things were simpler there. Quinn, in general, tried to keep out of the fraught and tangled relationships that existed between his wife, her daughter, and her daughter's daughter. But that did not stop him from taking an interest in Sylvia. He had been the one, in fact, to suggest that Sylvia might come to live with them in Paris and commute each morning to her exclusive day school back in New York. He felt sorry for Sylvia. Weight of the world on her shoulders. Only sixteen. She could do with a lot more fun in her life. He tried as best as he could to inject it, insofar as a step-grandfather could without incurring the wrath of either wife or stepdaughter, but it was a tricky balance. "What's Siobhan done now?"

"She forgot her birthday!"

Something serious, then. Quinn put down his book. "Aw no," he said. "How is she?"

"Putting a brave face on things."

"Poor kid." Quinn studied his wife's face. "What now, love?"

"Now, I will have a word with her mother . . ."

Quinn's eyebrows shot up. "And are you quite sure that Sylvia wants you to do that?"

But Adèle was already hastening toward her desk and opening a communications channel. Quinn took a deep breath. These had been the preliminary fireworks. Now he must prepare himself for the evening's main event. Siobhan was formidable. Only Adèle came close, and she had the advantage of being Siobhan's mother. Sometimes it made for some remarkable conversations. Quinn slipped his bookmark between the pages and leaned forward slightly, preparing to eavesdrop, without shame.

Siobhan was usually in a meeting, or talking, or being briefed, or doing something or other of (to be fair to the girl) genuine importance, so it took a minute or two for her aide to get her on the line. "Maman," said Siobhan, voice crisp, *"this isn't a good time—"*

Adèle cut straight through, the only person who could do that kind of thing to Siobhan and get away without a roasting. "You forgot to say happy birthday."

There was a pause.

"You only had to remember to *say* it, Siobhan! One thing! One simple thing!"

A further pause. Then: "*Merde,*" muttered Siobhan.

"Quite," said Adèle.

Siobhan lifted up her hands. "*All right,*" she said. "*I'll fix this.*"

Adèle rolled her eyes in exasperation. "You do realize, *chérie*, that this is not simply a problem to be fixed. That *Sylvia* is not simply a problem to be fixed—"

But Siobhan was already busy with her diary. "*Okay, listen. I can clear some space at the start of next week. We'll go to London. She's always wanted to go to London, hasn't she?*"

"Yes, she has—"

"*Great! So you think she'll like that?*"

"I don't think it matters where you go, *chérie*, as long as you spend some time with her. She barely sees anything of you, and when you do you're berating—"

"*I said she could stay with me, Maman,*" Siobhan said, exasperation of her own creeping into her tone. "*She's the one who wanted to go and live with you—*"

"Let's not go through that one again. She's here now. And I do think she's happier—"

"*Happier, huh?*" Siobhan's eyes narrowed. "*Were you the one who encouraged her to do that project on the mushrooms?*"

There was a pause. From his seat across the room, out of the firing line, Quinn said, "Oh, did she do that in the end, then?"

Siobhan's lips pursed. "*Oh, so it was you,*" she said. "*I might have guessed. Quinn, I love you, if only for my mother's sake—*"

"Thank you, Siobhan!" he said cheerfully.

"*—but, really, Sylvia's education is my business.*"

Quinn eased out of his chair and came over to the screen. "All we did was chat about what she was reading.

Some interesting stuff there! Way over my head, of course. But she's old enough to make her own choices, surely—"

"*I'll be the judge of that,*" said Siobhan frostily.

Quinn removed himself from view. If Siobhan was now on the offensive, a tactical withdrawal from the battlefield was the only sensible option for an underling such as he.

"*Okay,*" said Siobhan. "*Here we are. I've shifted a couple of meetings. That frees up Sunday afternoon and evening. There's a reception that night, but I can send someone from the office—the experience will do them good. Okay! That's excellent! We can meet at the Ritz at fourteen hundred— that's GMT, Maman, don't forget—and I'll have her back to you by twenty-two hundred. That's early enough for a school night, and I can get a couple of hours of work in afterward— Maman, are you noting all this down?*"

"Why should I do that, *chérie*? Your aide will put it into my schedule anyway."

"*Oh, Maman, you know how busy I am. It's more efficient that way! Don't be cross with me!*" Siobhan was starting to get upset. "*God knows I'm trying my best! It's not been easy, with Iain away—*"

Adèle relented. "I know, my darling. You are doing splendidly. Truly you are."

"*Thank you, Maman. I really am trying—*"

"This is difficult for all of us, I know," said Adèle. "We have busy lives, and we all have different needs, and we're all learning how to lead those lives and respect and love each other. I'm proud of you, *chérie*. I will always support your work and your choices. But one piece of advice, Siobhan, if you're willing. Just you and Sylvia on this trip. Nobody else."

"*Well, of course!*"

"And try not to check in to work. Just . . . *be* with her."

There was a pause. *"I'll try. But you never know what comes up—"*

"I know, *chérie*. Trying is all I ask." Adèle took a deep breath. "Well, there we are. Today's crisis is averted, more or less, and may this be the worst of your day, my darling. I'll leave you to let Sylvia know your plans, yes?"

"I'll do that straightaway. Good night, Maman."

"Good night, *chérie*," said Adèle. "God bless. I love you. I'm proud of you."

The channel closed. Quinn lifted his book, ever so slightly. Shields up. Adèle turned to him with a dangerous glimmer in her eye.

"Quinn!"

"Mm-hmm?"

"Did you really tell her to write about those blessed mushrooms?"

Quinn shrugged.

"Quinn!"

"Well, why ever not?" he said. "She's interested in them, for heaven's sake! Hey, what mark did she get?"

Adèle's lips twitched. "Best they'd ever had."

"Well, there we are! Good girl!"

"But *mushrooms*, Quinn!"

"I like mushrooms. Grand for breakfast. Who knows what else they might be good for?"

"Sometimes," said Adele, pursing her lips and looking very like her daughter, "I think you do these things on purpose."

"My dearest love," said Quinn, "I have a much stronger sense of self-preservation than that." Peaceably, he went back to his book, but he couldn't help but smile down at the page. Mushrooms. It was all too magnificent. In his heart, Quinn was sure that Sylvia would go far, and he had a hunch about those blessed mushrooms. But not even he imagined how far.

—

Siobhan had gotten one thing right: Sylvia had always wanted to go to London. Longed for it, in fact. The good thing about having a diplomat for a mother was that you got to go to some really interesting places. Sylvia had traveled a lot as a kid, particularly after the divorce, when Mom had been doing tours of various worlds, building up experience. The travel was a mixed bag, though. Because the bad thing about having a diplomat as a mother was that often you didn't see much more than a drinks reception, or a photo opportunity, or the inside of your (admittedly very nice) rooms, and that you were always hampered by where security would let you go. But London had never quite gotten onto their itinerary, and, besides, this wasn't for work. This was a proper day trip, just her and Mom, no officials or hangers-on, or, shudder, stepsisters . . . just the two of them. Plus security, of course.

With her term papers out of the way, Sylvia had time to spend the rest of the week reading up on the city. The Science Museum. The Natural History Museum. The British Museum. She hugged herself with excitement. These places—they weren't just world class, they were *galactic* class. Nowhere did museums like London. Rome, maybe. Okay, yes, Rome. But they weren't going to Rome . . . Her main worry was whether they would fit everything in. Would her mother want to look at some art too? Sylvia didn't mind looking at a few old pictures. Maybe the Portrait Gallery. A whole room of scientists and inventors, staring down at her: *Stand on the shoulders of giants* . . . Okay, she'd go and look at some portraits. But that was her limit, really. She studied in New York and lived in Paris, okay? She could look at some pretty good pictures any day of the week. But you didn't get museums like that every day . . . It was just a shame that Dad couldn't be there; it would be amazing to go around the British Museum with Dad, with his expert knowledge, but Dad was far away right now . . . Still, Sylvia intended to enjoy herself.

Two minutes into the afternoon, Sylvia realized that the outing wasn't going to go along with her itinerary, and she kicked herself that she had even imagined that such a thing was in the cards. Whose birthday was it, anyway? Siobhan was waiting for her inside the Ritz, looking stunning, and sitting behind teacups and scones and cakes and teeny little sandwiches of exquisite proportions. Sylvia's eyes widened in delight. Afternoon tea! Her mother stood up, came over, and put her arm around her. Sylvia found that when she was near her mother, she had this annoying habit of becoming awkward, like she grew an extra arm or something. She hugged her mom, harder than she'd intended. The table shuddered, nearly knocking over the teapot.

"Careful, Sylvia!" Siobhan disentangled herself from the embrace and reached to steady the pot. "Come and sit down, darling. Help yourself—isn't this all *beautiful*?"

Sylvia plopped down into one of the seats and began to fill her plate. Mom was right. It was all lovely, absolutely lovely. She had just taken a nibble from a little chocolate-and-orange macaron when her mother said, "Now. Here's what I've got planned."

Sylvia's eyes narrowed. *Red alert! Red alert!*

"First stop, it just so happens that my stylist is in town today, and so I've got us an appointment there. Oh, Sylvia, you're going to love him, he's a riot."

"Okay . . ."

"We'll get some fabulous outfits for you. He's a genius. There's a hair appointment booked for you at four, and then someone is going to come in to help with your makeup."

Clothes shopping. They were going clothes shopping? *Mom*, thought Sylvia despairingly, *have I ever given you the impression that I liked clothes shopping?*

"I've booked an early dinner," Siobhan said, "and then maybe we could think about a show. How does that sound?"

Sylvia perked up slightly. Well, a show sounded like it might be all right. Hey, wasn't the Globe right across the river, and, whaddya know, there was a production of *The Tempest* on right now, and by golly if she wasn't going to pay attention to every last second and take that into school on Monday . . .

"There's a new musical just opened," Siobhan said. "I thought it sounded fun!"

A musical. Okay, so it wasn't that Sylvia didn't like musicals, but, you know, Broadway? In New York? Where she went to school? Pretty good for musicals. And right now they were in London? Which, okay, the West End, but you know, also—did I mention the freakin' *Globe*?

She didn't say any of this, obviously. She didn't dare. Instead, she nibbled around the edges of her macaron. Her appetite had gone. She realized her mother was watching her, and she began to flush red.

"You're very quiet, Sylvia. Is this all okay?"

The museums had long since receded into the distance. She wasn't even thinking of them any longer—well, not much. Perhaps she and Dad could do them together after all . . . One day, when he wasn't half a quadrant away . . . "Sure, Mom," she said brightly, "sounds wonderful!" She finished her macaron and smiled. "These are delicious!"

"They are, aren't they? Not too many though, please, darling."

The afternoon was slightly less appalling than Sylvia had thought it might be, chiefly because her mother's stylist had realized the moment Sylvia walked through the door that

she didn't want to be there. "Hey," he said softly as he mea-
sured her, "trust me. I'm a magician."

He was as good as his word, although it wasn't the fast-
est conjuring trick Sylvia had ever seen. Two long hours
and about several million changes of clothes later (not to
mention hair, nails, and makeup), Sylvia looked in the full-
length mirror and nearly gasped out loud.

"Told you," he said smugly. "A magician."

He hadn't lied. Sylvia looked . . .

Exactly like her mother. Hoo boy, now that *was* some
party trick . . .

"Oh my goodness," Sylvia said. "That's . . . a little unnerving."

Her mother was standing behind her. Sylvia saw the
frown appear (*Oh! Hi there, frown! I was just wondering how
you were getting on today!*) and quickly covered her tracks.
"I mean, I look so grown-up!"

Her mother beamed. "You really do, darling! You look
incredible!" She squeezed her shoulders. "My little girl!
How did you get to be so big?"

Sylvia tottered out into the street after her mother. The
shoes . . . The *shoes* . . . Did her mother really go around
in shoes like this all day, every day? No wonder she was so
touchy . . . Her mother's car rolled up, and they clambered
in, trailing bags behind them.

Siobhan smiled at her daughter. "Sweetie," she said.
"Do you know how wonderful you look?" She opened her
handbag and took out a compact mirror, handing it to her
daughter. Sylvia held it up, tilting her head this way and
that. Yep, exactly like Mom. She could turn up at some
reception right now and sell a trade agreement with the
best of them. Except being who she was, she'd probably
trip over her heels and land face-first in the profiteroles. She
tried not to giggle. It really had been a very long afternoon,

and by now hysteria was mere *centimeters* away. She didn't want to laugh. She was scared her face might crack.

"I don't know how that hairdresser did it, but she's certainly got your curls under control," Siobhan said. Sylvia wasn't sure how it had been done, either, although there were an awful lot of pins involved, and possibly an actual antique *iron* had been brought out at some point. It felt like something was tugging at her scalp from every direction. It *hurt*.

"And the dress is gorgeous. Wonderful color for you. That kind of red isn't easy to match."

Yep, gorgeous. Felt like a suit of armor, but at least it was gorgeous . . . *When*, thought Sylvia wearily, *when oh when will this endless day end?*

But there was dinner first, and, yes, the restaurant was amazing, and the food spectacular too, but by this time Sylvia felt bone-tired. Her feet hurt, her head hurt, and a little bit of her soul hurt too. Once again, things hadn't worked out as she'd wanted. The worst of it was that it wasn't for want of trying, on both sides. She'd noticed that her mother hadn't looked at her communicator all day—hadn't checked in with her staff, hadn't even checked the news feeds once. She'd been completely, utterly, *terrifyingly* focused on her daughter . . . *Love bombs*, thought Sylvia. *Watch out for shrapnel.*

She chewed her way through dinner and managed to say some reasonably intelligent things about the sauces and the cut of meat and the wines, just to prove that Granna wasn't completely neglecting her wider education. When they got to the petit fours and the coffee, her mother sat back and looked at her fondly. "I've had such a good day, Sylvia," she said. "I do miss you, you know."

"I know, Mom. I miss you too."

They smiled at each other. Some regret on one side; some apprehension on the other. But also a great deal of love.

"But we have to make sacrifices if we want to achieve our full potential," said Siobhan.

Well, that moment passed quickly, Sylvia thought. She watched her mother carefully. She had the feeling that some big announcement was coming. She was pretty certain that her mom was going to say that living with Granna wasn't working, and she had been planning her responses to that. The important thing was not to get *swamped*, not to let her mother's reasoning make what she wanted seem childish, petty, *unreasonable*. It *wasn't* unreasonable to want to live with Granna. It wasn't unreasonable to want to be herself.

A bottle of champagne arrived. Sylvia oohed and aahed appropriately as the cork was popped. She could pass on champagne, if she was honest; the bubbles didn't agree with her. But Mom liked it, and so from an early age Sylvia had often found herself glass in hand. People seemed to think it was a treat for her. Usually she had a sip or two and then put the glass aside. She wasn't sure how she'd manage that here, under such scrutiny. *Check your messages, Mom*, she thought weakly. *I could do with a break.*

"So," said Siobhan. "I have some good news, darling."

Here we go. Sylvia braced herself.

"I've found a school for you, Sylvia. It's perfect, absolutely perfect!"

Okay, Sylvia thought cautiously. *I didn't see that one coming.*

"It's off Earth," Siobhan went on, "which, obviously, isn't ideal, but the curriculum! Sylvia, wait till you see it! It's exactly what you need to take the diplomatic route. I'll send you the brochure—I couldn't believe it when I saw it. I would have loved it at your age!"

Siobhan had never forgiven Adèle the strict convent school to which she had been banished for what she referred to as her "interminable and *blighted* adolescence" and "tantamount to forced claustration." When she complained, Adèle would shrug and say, "You've done all right, haven't you?"

Sylvia was catching up. "This school . . . you said it's not on Earth?"

"No, it's on Talaris IV."

"I've . . . never heard of Talaris IV."

"I have to confess I hadn't either. Very quiet. But the point about that is that the security is excellent. Sylvia"—Siobhan reached out to take her daughter's hand—"you know how seriously we have to take that. More so, as my role becomes higher profile."

Sylvia, instinctively, clutched her mom's hand. Of course she understood. It had been drummed into her from an early age. Her mom's work brought the attention of some pretty nasty people, people who wouldn't hesitate to use her children to get to her. Sylvia had gotten used to bodyguards, security; she barely even noticed it anymore. It was the water she swam in. So, yes, security was fine, of course—but off Earth?

"Mom," she said, "let me get this right . . . This school . . . Am I going to be boarding there?"

Siobhan blinked at her. "What a silly question. Of course you'll be boarding! You can't get back to Granna every night from Talaris IV."

"But Granna, Quinn . . ."

"Can take good care of themselves." Her mother tutted. "Honestly, Sylvia, I thought you'd be more excited. I know how much you love Granna and Quinn, but surely you have to admit it's fairly dull living with them. This way you get to be with people of your own age, make friends your own age—"

"I already have friends. *Tons* of friends—" Okay, that was something of an exaggeration, but that wasn't the point.

"You'll make more friends," her mother said, with more confidence than Sylvia felt. "That's a good thing, particularly as you get older. It's good to network as widely as you can."

I don't want to network, thought Sylvia. *I just want a couple of pals. How can I make pals when I'm being shunted halfway across the quadrant . . . ?*

"Playtime has to stop soon, darling. If you're going to be a serious person, you have to start thinking seriously. You're so privileged, Sylvia! People like us—we get to shape the Federation! We wield power and influence. We get to make things happen. We *make* a difference. And so we have a responsibility to learn to use that privilege as wisely as we can."

Yes, thought Sylvia wretchedly, *I know all that, and it only makes me feel selfish, and ungrateful, and wrong . . .* "Mom," she said desperately, "have you talked to Dad about this?"

"Dad? No, he's out of reach. But I know he'll see the sense of this."

"Perhaps we should wait to talk to him? I mean, it's a big decision all round—"

"Well, we'll talk to him when we get the chance. But I've had to pull some strings to get you in so quickly, and so I don't think he's going to disagree."

Sylvia sighed. Dad tended to defer to Mom when it came to her education, and right now he was so far away that it would be a done deal before he got his say.

Siobhan was frowning. "Oh, do cheer up, Sylvia. This is an incredible opportunity! It's a great school, full of fascinating people. You're going to have a ball!" Siobhan reached for her champagne glass. "Come on. Let's have a toast. Happy birthday, dearest Sylvia! Here's to your future. Your wonderful, wonderful future!"

But what future? Sylvia felt glum just thinking about it.
A diplomat? Really, Mom? Me? She reached for her glass,
missed, and sent champagne flooding across the crisp white
linen of the tablecloth. Waiters appeared from nowhere and
cleared it away in seconds, but her mother was sighing and
rolling her eyes.

And Sylvia resigned herself to her fate.

The day ended at last. Siobhan gave her a quick peck on
each cheek, and squeezed her tight, and then the transporter took hold, and Sylvia was back in the garden of
Granna's house. Paris twinkled beautifully around her. *I
don't want to go*, she thought sadly. *I don't want to go to yet
another dumb school. No Granna. No Quinn . . .*

She clumped inside. Granna was waiting, and when she
saw Sylvia, she came to fold her into a hug. "How was it?"

"Oh, you know. We did a lot of . . . things."

Granna held her at arm's length. "So I see."

"The show was fun."

"Oh yes?"

"There was a butler who was very clever, and a sort of
posh lord who was very dumb . . . It was really, well, *English*,
I guess . . ."

"But not Shakespeare."

"No, Granna," said Sylvia wryly. "It was definitely *not*
Shakespeare."

"That's a shame."

"It was okay."

Adèle led her toward the drawing room.

"Granna," said Sylvia, "did Mom mention the school?"

Granna sighed. "She did."

"And?"

"She's your mother, Sylvia. It's her decision."

Sylvia stopped still. Her grandmother turned to look at her.

"Sylvia?"

"Could you maybe—just a thought, putting it out there, just in case—maybe not give me up without a fight?"

Adèle pulled her granddaughter into an embrace. "Oh, my darling girl!" she said. "You always have a home here. But what can I do, *chérie*?"

Sylvia nodded. She'd known that was what Granna would say, but it had been worth a try. They went into the drawing room. Quinn, who was sitting in his chair, looked up and goggled at the apparition swaying toward him. "Good god, girl!" he cried. "Get those shoes off immediately! They look like hell!"

Sylvia kicked off the appalling shoes. She went over to Quinn and threw her arms around him. "I do love you, Quinn," she said. "You're such a pal."

Quinn smiled, and gave her a hug. "Back at you, darling."

"He has his moments," said Adèle. "Now. Bed. School in the morning."

When Sylvia got to her bedroom, there was a message waiting for her. A Starfleet seal, and then a familiar face. Short red hair—very short, to keep the curls under control—and a thoughtful, calm face. Lieutenant Iain Tilly, one of the quadrant's leading xenoarchaeologists, currently serving on the science vessel *Dorothy Garrod*, and about a hundred million billion light-years away from his only child, who right now was missing him more than anything else in the world. He'd taken this posting last year, and they'd all known that it would take him out of contact for long periods of time, but Sylvia thought now that perhaps if she'd understood better what

that would mean, she might have asked him not to go . . .
No, she would never have done that. This posting was a once-
in-a-lifetime opportunity for Iain, and she wouldn't have
dreamed of stopping him. Still, though, she couldn't help
wondering sometimes if he would have stayed, if she'd asked.

"*Hi, Sills,*" Iain said. "*Sweet sixteen. Happy birthday, my
amazing girl.*"

"Hi, Daddy," she said, and smiled.

Iain reached under the table, pulled out a party hat,
and perched it on his head. A tiny golden cone with a pink
tassel, and elastic that went around his chin. He looked preposterous. Sylvia started to laugh. "*Hang on a minute,*" he
said, rummaging around his desk. "*There was a party popper
here a second ago . . .*" He found it. He popped it. The paper
went all over him. He pulled a face and looked even more
preposterous. Sylvia kept on laughing.

"*Well,*" he said, "*I hope it's your birthday still, or close
enough. We've been off the beaten track for a while.*"

"Nearly a week late, Daddy, truth be told," said Sylvia
sadly. "But don't worry. I understand."

"*We're having an amazing trip out here, Sills. I can't
wait to show you what we've found. I think we can backdate
the start of the second Emmessinian Empire by nearly fifty
years, based on what we're finding.*"

"Hey," she said. "That's *big* news. Wait till I tell you
about my science paper!" Dad loved hearing about that
kind of thing. Dad was her pal.

"*I wish I could talk to you in person, Sills. I miss you so
much. Sixteen! I can't believe it!*"

"You and me both, mister," Sylvia said fervently.

"*Okay, I don't want to miss my chance to send this. I love
you so much, Sills. I know I've not been around much this past
year. But I'm here for you. I love you, little girl. I really love you.
I think you're incredible.*"

The message ended. Sylvia took off her new dress and hung it up as per instructions, and shook out her hair, and carefully removed her makeup. She put on her pajamas and watched the message again. When she was done, she lay down on her bed.

"I love you too, Daddy," she said to the ceiling. "But I'm not really a little girl anymore, you know? And I wish— oh, I *wish*—I knew what it was I did that made you go away."

2

The journey out to Talaris IV took over a week. Nope, thought Sylvia, no chance of popping back to see Granna, no chance of zipping between New York and Paris to enjoy both cities, in the way she had become accustomed to. Instead . . . Well, what? What were boarding schools like, really?

Sylvia had read some boarding-school stories as a kid. And, like most kids, she had fantasized briefly about being whisked away to one, suddenly free of her mother's over-bearing presence. Be careful what you wish for, huh? Still, she was smart enough to know that those books probably weren't going to be good preparation for this school. There weren't just girls there, for one thing, and she doubted things would be so formal as those schools. There probably wouldn't be all that much in the way of wizards, either . . . Still, she thought cautiously, it *might* be fun. Perhaps, thrown in with other people like this, there would be a chance to make some good friends. Sylvia had found in the past that when she started to get close to people her own age, when she started to relax and speak her mind, they tended to drift away from her. People really could be very touchy.

Siobhan couldn't get away from her work to make such a long journey, of course, so Adèle traveled out with Sylvia to school. Wherever Adèle went, Quinn followed, and that made the voyage particularly cheerful. Sylvia always remembered this as a time of great laughter and happiness. They lounged around the passenger liner, swam, read, ate good food, and generally had a great holiday.

"Going to miss having you around, love," Quinn said to Sylvia the last night on board ship. "You brighten up the place. Without you, me and your Granna will be a real pair of old duffers."

"I'm going to miss you too, Quinn," she said, and sighed.

"Are you nervous, love?" he said.

"Yes," she said, "of course. I just don't know what to expect . . ."

"Hockey sticks and midnight feasts?"

Sylvia laughed. "Oh, I don't think so. They're all going to be serious people, aren't they? Serious about study, serious about their plans . . ."

"You're serious too, you know," Quinn said.

Who? Me? Silly Tilly, that's me. She pulled a face.

He must have caught her expression. He leaned in, put his hand upon hers, and said, "You'll find your way, Sylvia. But it might not be what you think it's going to be."

"Well," she said, "whatever it is, it's sure taking its time making itself known."

"There's no hurry, love," he said.

Their ship made orbit, and they transported down to the surface of Talaris IV, to a public transporter a little distance from the school. The school had sent a groundcar to pick them up. Sylvia's nervousness was returning now that the moment approached when Granna and Quinn would say goodbye. When they reached the school boundary, they had to come through security. Even just to enter the school grounds was a huge task, a process as rigorous as those at

some of the official buildings Sylvia had visited accompa-
nying her mother. There were ID and genetic checks for
all three of them, and then a brief delay while Sylvia was
equipped with a tracker to locate her within the grounds.
Both Granna and Quinn looked thoroughly approving.
Quinn did nudge her, though, and point down to the little
mark on her wrist where the tracker now was. "There'll be
no sneaking off from here," he said, and chuckled.

Once they were let through, the car took them up the
long drive to the school. Tall trees with bright red leaves
lined the avenue so thickly that Sylvia, peering out, couldn't
see anything beyond. And then the trees stopped, and the
road opened out in front of a big house, built from the local
yellow stone. Sylvia had skimmed the brochure that her
mother had sent across, and so knew that this had been the
country house of some kind of minor aristocrat back when
Talaris had that kind of thing. It was very sensibly repub-
lican these days. The house was the only historical part of
the school, though, and it was where the teachers had their
offices and studies. The rest of the brochure boasted of the
brand-new facilities available to the students in the rest of
the complex.

The grounds were pretty, Sylvia had to admit. This
part of the planet was temperate, a mild climate with good
rainfall. The lawns in front of the buildings were green
and well kept, the flowerbeds bright and orderly. Adèle
made approving noises, but Sylvia was less impressed. It all
seemed . . . well, dull, to be honest, like every embassy she
had visited over the years. And so quiet . . . Where were all
the students?

The car stopped in front of the big main doors, which
were standing open. The little party got out. Quinn, looking around with a keen eye, noted the unobtrusive security
scanners all over. As they unloaded their bags, an imposing

Vulcan woman emerged from the house. "That's the head," Adèle whispered in her ear. "Stavath. Try to stay on the right side of her."

Stavath greeted Adèle and Quinn, and then turned to Sylvia. "Good morning, Miss Tilly," she said. "And welcome to our academy. We hope you'll be happy here, and successful."

She stood openmouthed. "Sylvia," Adèle murmured gently, prompting her to remember her manners.

"Thank you. Thank you very much. I hope so too."

"I've arranged for one of our students to show you around," said Stavath. At this, a girl stepped forward, about Sylvia's age, although smaller, rather slight, in fact, and with playful brown eyes that crinkled into a smile when she saw Sylvia. "Hello," she said, offering her hand, rather formally. "I'm Miss Igova."

Jeez, thought Sylvia, *is it all titles and surnames around here?* She put out her hand nonetheless. "Tilly," she said. "You can call me Tilly." She wondered to hear herself say it. *New place, new name*, she thought. *Let's go with it.* The other girl's brows knitted briefly in confusion, and then she smiled again, and said, "I'm Risera. I'm really pleased to meet you, Tilly. I hope you'll enjoy it here."

The introductions over, Stavath withdrew, inviting Adèle and Quinn to join her later at a reception for all new parents and guardians. Sylvia looked anxiously at Risera, who had turned to Adèle. "*Je suis heureuse de vous avoir rencontré et j'espère que vous pourrez nous joindre pour notre tournée aujourd'hui,*" Risera said. Her accent was flawless.

Adèle almost melted. "*Je serais ravie!*"

Adèle and Risera went on their way, Quinn and Sylvia following. "Damn," whispered Quinn in Sylvia's ear, "she's something else, isn't she?"

Sylvia nodded. She wouldn't admit it on pain of death,

but she felt somewhat awestruck by this girl, so poised and confident and competent. *I hope she'll be friends with me.*

They went on through the school, Risera chattering away to Adèle in French, describing the various rooms and buildings that they passed. Sylvia saw spacious and well-equipped classrooms and music practice rooms to die for; she shuddered slightly at the sight of tennis courts and fields for ballgames. The conversation ahead went on. Quinn winked at Sylvia, who rolled her eyes. *Maybe Granna should come here instead.*

Risera turned suddenly, and with a big smile, said, "I'm sorry, Tilly, I so rarely get a chance to practice my French. But today is about you, really, isn't it?" Before Sylvia knew what was happening, Risera had put an arm through hers, and was pulling her on ahead. "We're going to head up to the rooms now. *Madame et Monsieur* Quinn, may I escort you to the reception?"

"Don't you worry about that," said Quinn. "We can find our way. You girls run along."

"Are you sure?" said Risera.

"Of course," said Adèle. She tucked her arm around Quinn's, and the pair went on their way.

Risera turned to Sylvia. "Come on," she said. "I'll show you the room."

She led Sylvia down the hall, and then up a big staircase. As they went along, Risera kept up the conversation with ease; Sylvia was grateful: there was so much that was new that she was starting to flag.

"I guess your mother couldn't get away for long enough to bring you?" Risera said.

Sylvia went on the defensive. "Work, you know? It's hard for her to get away."

Risera nodded seriously. "Well, of course! We've all got parents in the diplomatic corps, we understand what it's like." She glanced at Sylvia. "I don't know about you, but I got fed up trailing around after the parents. It was such a relief to get here. Spend some time in the same place. Be able to put books on shelves and clothes in closets and not feel like I always had to be ready to pack."

Sylvia nodded slowly. She had felt the same way—but that was why she had asked to go and live with Granna and Quinn. She didn't just want to stay still—she wanted to stay at home.

"Everyone's really looking forward to meeting you, Tilly. We all think your mom is a great role model."

Sylvia gave a rather forced smile. "Sure, she's great."

"Maybe she could come and speak to us at graduation. People would love that."

"Are these the rooms?" said Sylvia.

"Oh! Yes! You've come pretty much at the right time," Risera said. "Last year we were all still in the dormitories—ten to a room. This year—pairs. I think they're trying to signal to us that it's time to get down to really serious study."

Yes, thought Tilly. *Playtime's over.*

They walked down a plain corridor lined with doors. There were a handful of other students around, unpacking and organizing their stuff. One or two looked curiously at Tilly. "I'll make introductions later," said Risera. "For now—let's take a look at the room."

She stopped a little way down the corridor and opened the door. "It's not much," she said, "but it's home!"

In fact, it was rather a pleasant room, with white walls, and a bay with a window seat that would face the sunset going down across the grounds. Four armchairs were gathered around this, and a little table, waiting for guests. On either side of the room there was a bed. The closets were in the wall behind the door. Tilly's trunk and cases stood in the middle of the room, waiting for her to start unpacking.

On the other side of the room, two desks faced each other, with shelves on the walls beside them.

"Hey, I didn't pick a side," said Risera. "I thought you might like to choose. Make yourself at home, you know." She smiled, with genuine warmth, and Tilly fell a little more in love with her.

"That's really kind of you. I don't mind, not really . . ."

"Really? I'll take this one over here, then. It's good luck to be on the left-hand side." She jumped on the bed. "It's good to be back!" she said. "Tilly, I think we're going to get along famously."

And that was Sylvia's fondest wish too.

Later that afternoon, Adèle and Quinn said their goodbyes and went off to the groundcar that would return them to the public transporter and then their hotel. They turned and saw Sylvia on the step by the big doors. She lifted her hand, and waved forlornly. Quinn waved back, and Adèle blew a kiss. And then Risera drew her inside, and she was gone.

"Poor kid," said Quinn.

But Adèle shook her head. "There's more of her mother in her than she realizes. I know she'll find her way."

In their room, Tilly looked at her trunk and cases and thought she'd better make a start. She'd barely opened them when there was a tap at the door, and a Bolian girl poked her head in. "Hi, Risera," she said. "How was the holiday?"

Risera jumped off the bed. "Xoha!" She pulled the girl into the room and gave her a hug. "It was okay. The usual. Hotels."

"Tell me about it," said Xoha, and flung herself on the nearest armchair. She and Risera immediately fell to gossiping. Tilly hung back, not wanting to interrupt, until Risera waved her over. "Tilly! Don't be shy!"

Xoha, turning, said, "Oh, I'm sorry, didn't see you there! Wow, amazing hair . . . Are you the new one?"

Tilly nodded. "That's me." She stood up from the bed, and she and Xoha took stock of each other. "Tilly," she said. "Sylvia Tilly. Tilly by preference, please."

"Oh," said Xoha, realization dawning. "I know who you are! Isn't your mother—"

"Yeah," said Tilly. "She is."

"She's great!"

"She certainly has her moments," Tilly said brightly.

"Do you think she'd come and talk to us?" said Xoha. She turned to Risera. "Sera, it would be such a coup. The seniors won't get anyone so well known."

"There's a sort of informal competition between our year and the upper year," Risera explained to Tilly. "For speech day. They always win—they've done placements by then and someone usually manages to get a big name to come along. But your mother . . ." She eyed Tilly thoughtfully. "Would she come?"

Tilly's heart sank at the thought. It would be just typical if Mom ended up more popular here than her. "She might," she said. "She's kind of busy . . . Can I take one of these closets?"

"Sure!" said Risera. "I started using the one on the right, but only because it's nearest. We can switch if you like."

"No, that's fine," said Tilly. She opened her chest and started to pull out the contents systematically. Risera and Xoha, sprawled on the armchairs, watched with interest. "Wow," said Xoha. "You're really tidy. You're gonna have to raise your game, Sera. She can be a real slob, Tilly. Don't let her leave unwashed cups around."

Risera, meanwhile, was studying each piece of clothing as it came out. "Tilly, are those pajamas *silk?*"

Tilly flushed. They were brand-new. She hadn't seen them before and definitely hadn't known they were in the trunk. She guessed her mother had bought them and instructed Granna to put them in her chest. Typical Mom gift. She shook them out. They were absolutely gorgeous, white with big bold violets on them. "Yup," she said. She folded them up, carefully, and put them away in the back of the closet. "But these," she said, pulling out her old favorites, blue cotton, softened with age and washing, "are *comfortable.*"

The two other girls laughed. Tilly carried on unpacking and listened in to their conversation. Most of it was about people she didn't know, dramas and jokes from before she had arrived, but every so often Risera would stop and explain. Tilly was grateful. It would be good to have someone sensitive as a friend. Tilly would be the first to admit that sometimes she had some funny little ways. She worked out in the course of the conversation that Risera was from Arixus. A small world; one she didn't know much about. She could learn.

There was another tap on the door, and two more girls arrived. The room was now full of laughter and chatter. Someone made a pot of spicy tea, and someone else produced some very pleasant little nutty pastries. Tilly, who had now gotten everything put away to her satisfaction, sat on the edge of her bed, nibbling a pastry, swinging her legs, and listening. She soon had their names worked out, and a little of their background. As well as Xoha, whose mother was a senior official for the Bolian Export Office, there was Erisel, from Risa, whose family, somewhat unexpectedly, weren't involved in promoting tourism, but were concerned with environmental policy, and, last of all, there was Semett, a quiet and pleasant Trill who was specializing in languages. ("She's amazing," said Risera. "It's unnatural," said Xoha. "Like witchcraft or something." Semett simply smiled and carried on listening to everything going on around her.) Tilly also realized, as other people popped their heads around the door to say hello, that Risera's room was a hub, a place where people dropped by to hear the news and find out what was happening. And at the core was this little group of friends.

Oh my goodness, thought Tilly, with growing delight. *I'm in with the in-crowd!* She hugged herself. Now, *that* was a first! Perhaps this wasn't going to be an unmitigated disaster after all. She imagined tea parties, study groups, confidences and jokes and shared histories. She realized she was excited about what lay ahead. *Maybe it's all going to be okay . . .*

Suddenly, a bell rang, and the gang of girls groaned.

"What's that?" said Tilly.

"First warning," explained Risera. "Five more minutes till bed; five minutes after that—lights must be out."

Tilly stood up to brush her teeth. None of the others made a move, staying comfortably in their seats and carrying on their conversation as if nothing had happened. When the second bell rang, the girls at last started to rouse themselves from their chairs. The visitors all grabbed their own mugs as they left, but there were still a few plates and Risera's and Tilly's mugs. "Where do we do the washing up?" said Tilly.

"The what?" said Risera, who was already heading toward her bed.

"The, er, *dishes*?" said Tilly.

"Oh, leave them till morning!" said Risera, waving her hand.

"It's okay, I'd rather do them now. I hate having dirty things around the place."

"Well," said Risera, by now snuggling up under the covers, "if you really want—there's a kitchen down the hall. But second bell means bed—you don't want to get into trouble on your first night."

Tilly hesitated, dishes in hand. Risera raised an eyebrow. "It's okay," she said. "They cut us some slack first night back."

"Okay, I'll do them real quick," said Tilly. "I'll remember next time—first bell means dishes."

Risera gave her a funny look. "You really can leave them till morning—"

"Ugh, no! I couldn't *bear* to think about them sitting there all night!" Tilly scuttled down the hall, found the kitchen, and was back in their room within five minutes. Risera's light was off, so she tiptoed in, putting away the crockery as quietly as she could.

"There's a message for you," Risera mumbled from her bed. "Your comm was beeping."

"Sorry! I'll set it to silent."

"'S'okay. Night, Tilly. Nice to have you here. Thanks for doing the washing up."

Tilly glowed with pleasure. She slipped over to her desk, put in her earpiece, and opened her message. *Daddy!*

"Hey, Sills," said Iain. *"Hope your first day has gone well. Hope you've got your first invite to a midnight feast. I'm sure you'll be selected for the lacrosse team and score the winning goal."*

"Yeah, yeah," she muttered. "Funny man is *so* funny."

"Seriously though, Sills, I hope you're going to have a good time. I know you weren't sure—and I wasn't sure either, to be honest—but Granna Adèle said it was a great place, really beautiful, and great kids, and I just want you to have the

time of your life. Happiest days of your life, you know?" He frowned. *"I don't know why they say that. When I was your age, I was in love with a college girl, and you can imagine how well that turned out. Ah, the pangs of unrequited love! Fiona Mackay, where are you now? How many hearts lie broken in your wake across the vast chasm of time?"*

"Silly Daddy," whispered Tilly, laughing softly to herself.

"Anyway, Sills, I just want to say—grab what's on offer. Give it all a go! What is there to lose?"

"Um, my *dignity*?"

"Apart from your dignity, but, to be honest, Sills, we of the red curls are starting off on the back foot there . . ." He ran his hands through his short hair, mussing it up. *"So—forget about dignity. Forget self-consciousness, and just go for it, little girl."* He blew her a kiss. *"I love you. We'll speak soon, I promise. Night, Sills. Have fun."*

The message ended. Tilly turned off the screen, but sat for a while at her desk, looking around the dark room. Risera was fast asleep now, a dark hump in her bed, snoring slightly. Tilly smiled. A roommate, and a really nice one. Maybe Daddy's advice was good. Maybe—maybe she would give everything a go after all. What was there to lose?

The first few days passed in a whirl. Tilly had to learn new names, new places, new schedules. There wasn't much time left at the end of the day to do more than get preparation done for the following day's classes, and then to fall with a groan exhausted into bed. She found, as she had expected, that she was way ahead when it came to math and science, but that her language skills were behind the others. Risera, she found out ruefully, could hold her own in nearly thirteen different languages, including three from Earth, and she didn't seem to think she was doing anything special. The language classes were a chore, not least because they didn't let the students use the universal translators.

Tilly thought this was ridiculous. "We went to all this trouble to *invent* this darn technology," she grumbled. "Why can't we just *use* it?"

Risera laughed. "What if it broke down, Tilly? What would you do then?"

"I'd *fix* it," said Tilly doggedly. "Math, that's the real universal language." She saw Risera's face, and said, "Have you never opened one up, Risera? They're not complicated, once you've got the hang of them."

Risera laughed. "I'll take your word for it, Tilly!"

Funny, though, Tilly thought. *Why not simply teach the students how the translators work?* They were going to be hugely reliant on them in their careers. All it would take would be one quick class, and they'd be equipped for life. And they could free up all the hours wasted by language classes.

By the end of the second week, Tilly was tired, and more than a little grouchy. The weather outside was glorious, the turn between late summer and early autumn, and the huge trees that formed part of the boundary around the school's grounds were vibrantly red. But it seemed to Tilly that she was hunched over books all the time, trying to catch up with the others while staying ahead on her own subjects and interests. One evening, the gang came around to hang out and drink tea and shoot the breeze. It nearly drove her mad. She picked up her books and went off in a huff to the library.

When she got back, just before first bell, only Risera was there.

"Hey," Risera said. "Sorry we disturbed you."

"It's okay. I was just trying to get ready for tomorrow." Tilly put her books down with a sigh. They had an economics test in the morning, and she didn't feel anywhere near ready. And economics was supposed to be one of her better subjects. She rubbed at her temples.

"You know, Tilly," said Risera, "it's okay to take a break sometimes."

"There's just so much to do!" Tilly said unhappily.

"Part of what we're learning to do is not to get over-whelmed. Staying inside all the time isn't good for you, you know."

"I can't work outside," wailed Tilly. "The pollen trig-gers my allergies. And there's insects, and the seats aren't comfortable—"

"I'm not talking about working outside. I mean, get-ting some exercise."

Tilly's eyes narrowed. "Excuse me?"

"Look, me and Xoha, we go rowing. It's really fun. Why don't you come along tomorrow and try it out?"

"Rowing?" said Tilly doubtfully. She pictured a small boat, with big oars, and huge muscly athletes straining away till it looked like the veins in their heads would pop . . . "Uh, no, I don't think that's my kind of thing—"

"No, really, come with me! It's not what you imagine!" Risera put her arm around her shoulder. "Come on, Tilly! Come and have some fun!"

Fun, thought Tilly as her alarm went off a good *hour and a half* earlier than usual. *In what universe is this fun?* Risera was already up, fresh faced and smiling, a picture of youthful health and energy. Wearily, Tilly pulled on her clothes and followed her out. They jogged down to the lake. Tilly's eyes widened. "Okay," she said. "You're right. This *wasn't* what I was expecting."

There were about fifteen girls there, some of them car-rying drums. As for the boats—they weren't the sleek, low things that Tilly was expecting, but wooden, rather ornate, painted bright colors, and with flags and bunting all over them. "What *is* this?" said Tilly.

"Arixxian rowing," said Risera proudly. "You haven't seen half of it, Tilly. Wait till the end of the semester, when we put on the whole show. There's *pipe* music!"

"Okay . . ."

"Here's an oar. Come on, let's give you a go."

She led Tilly over to a scarlet-painted boat, bedecked with yellow and orange flags and ribbons. The teams were four-person, with a drummer up front. Risera put Tilly at the back, where she could watch the rest of the team. "Listen to the drum," she said. "Watch the others. You'll soon get the hang of it."

Perhaps predictably, Tilly didn't get the hang of it. The boat she was in didn't exactly sink, but they came in some distance last, way behind the blues-and-greens and the purples-and-whites. She just *couldn't* get the timing right . . . No matter how she tried, she couldn't bring the oar down at the same time as her partner, and when it landed, it whacked the water like a diver belly-flopping into a pool.

"Okay," said Risera, after they'd clambered out of the boat. "Right. That wasn't bad for a first attempt—"

"Risera," said Tilly, who knew her limits. "I was *terrible*."

"You've never done it before! You just need practice!"

Tilly shook her head, a firm no. "No matter how much I do this, I won't get better. Look, it was nice of you to invite me, but I don't want to ruin things for the others . . ."

Xoha came past. "Tilly! You were *terrible*!" She was laughing, and she didn't mean anything unkind by it, Tilly knew, but still, did she have to be so plainspoken *all* the time? "Hey," Xoha said, a gleam in her eye, "why don't you try one of the drums?"

"Oh yes!" said Risera. "That's a brilliant idea!"

"Oh, I don't think so . . ." said Tilly.

"No, come on!" Risera pulled her back over to the water and made her sit in the prow behind the two big drums. "Okay," she said. "You're in charge."

"Risera, I really don't think this is a good idea—"

"Come on, Tilly, you're the boss now!" She shoved the beaters into Tilly's hands.

"Honestly, I don't think I can do this!"

But the others were all clambering into their seats and calling out their enthusiastic support. "Come on, Tilly! Yes, you can! You can do it!"

Her instinct was to say: *No, no, no! I really can't!* But then Tilly thought of her dad, saying *Give it a go!* She muttered to herself, "Dignity. Who needs it?" She took a deep breath. *Okay. Let's do this.*

She tried out the drum. "Can you hear me at the back?"

"Sure can, Captain!"

Captain, she thought. *That's a joke.* She twisted the beaters around in her hands. *All right*, she thought. Tentatively, she began to beat out a steady rhythm.

And the crew followed. *Wow*, she thought. *That actually works . . .* She increased the pace, and the boat began to move out into the open water.

"That's it, Tilly!" shouted Xoha. "You're getting it!"

She kept the beat, and called out instructions, and the little red boat lined up against the others. She looked down the boat at the crew, each one of them looking at her expectantly. Tilly found that if she breathed, slowly and steadily, they all began to fall in with her breathing. So when she started the drum, they were all already in synch . . .

On the side, they were waiting to start the race. Tilly lifted up the beaters, breathed with her crew—then the whistle sounded, and they were off.

Thud, went the drums, and the oars followed, slicing

through the water. She saw that Xoha was a little behind, just a split second, and she called to her, "Keep the pace!" She was conscious of the blues-and-greens, to her left, inching ahead, but she didn't panic. Second by second, she upped the pace, chasing them. The purples-and-whites were soon far behind. It seemed to Tilly she could see the whole race unfolding in her mind's eye—how to use the strokes of the other team to help them, how to manage the distance between them so they weren't cut off . . . *Patterns*, she thought. *I'm good at seeing patterns* . . . At her instructions, they sliced through the water, keeping up the pace, though never quite catching up on the blues-and-greens. They came in second—but it was very, very close.

Risera was ecstatic. She hopped out of the boat into the shallows and splashed up to give Tilly a big hug.

"See!" she said. "I *knew* you'd like bossing people around!"

Tilly, still recovering from the thrill of the race, burst out laughing. "Sera, that was *amazing*! The *power*," she laughed. "All of you, at my command!"

Risera laughed and squeezed her arm. Tilly felt like she was walking on air. One of the blues-and-greens came over and patted her on the back. "Is today really your first time on the water?"

Tilly nodded. The boy laughed and called back to his crew. "Hey, I think we've got some competition!"

It made a difference. Sure, the early mornings *stank*, but there was something about being out there on the open water, with the cool air whipping past, setting the rhythm and calling out to the team—*her* team. Tilly loved the freedom of the open water, but most of all, what she liked was knowing that she fit in at last. That she had a team, a gang, a set of pals, and that they were all pulling together and working together and looking to her for leadership. It was fun reading up on the subject too, and talking to Risera about it, and finding out what the colors symbolized, and planning the tunes and the display for the pageant at the end of the term . . . *A team*, she thought. *I've never been part of a team before.*

Heartened by all this, and wanting to find some more like-minded souls, Tilly came up with a new idea. Students were in general encouraged to set up their own clubs, the idea being that they would learn from promoting them and administrating them, not to mention from managing the inevitable conflicts and squabbles that came with any small group or society. Tilly knew what she wanted more than anything else. One evening, Risera came back to their room to find Tilly hard at work putting together some posters. "What's this?" she said.

"Okay, so you know that I'm not convinced we have enough science and technology on the curriculum," said Tilly. It was something she complained about all the time, to the amusement of the rest of the gang, who rolled their eyes and begged her not to make their lives a misery. *What if you succeed?* they wailed.

Risera laughed. "There's enough for me!"

"And every time I raise it with the teachers, they tell me that the timetable is full."

"They're right," said Risera. "I can't fit anything else in, and we haven't even started thinking about the exams and presentations at the end of the term—"

"Okay, so I've given up on changing the curriculum. Instead, I'm going to start an engineering club."

Risera blinked. "A what?"

"Engineering club!"

Risera frowned. "Is that a *thing*?"

"Sure!"

"But what will you do? Sit around building bridges?"

"Well, *maybe*," said Tilly. "Why not?"

"Where?" said Risera in bewilderment.

"Oh, don't be silly, you use construction programs. Anyway, I was thinking of something more relaxed. You know, share any programming or research projects we have going on. Maybe some short presentations about new scientific developments or breakthroughs that have caught our eye . . ."

Risera shrugged. "Okay. Well, if that's what you want to do in your free time."

Tilly felt slightly crushed. "You'll join, won't you?"

Risera glanced at her, and Tilly had the sense that her emotions were being read. She pursed her lips. Sometimes, this sensitivity was *annoying* rather than supportive . . .

"I honestly can't fit in anything else," said Risera.

Tilly sighed. She knew that was completely true. If she was being honest, she probably didn't have enough time for this either, but she was doing all the reading anyway, and it would be nice to have other people to talk to. And it would only be one evening a week . . .

"Tilly, are you quite sure about this?" Risera said.

Tilly looked up from her poster. "Of course! Why wouldn't I be?"

"Well, you're doing a lot already, and, you know, it's not really core to what we do here."

Tilly sat back on her heels. "Core? What do you mean by that? What's more core than science—"

"Oh, I don't mean to put your interests down. I know we need a good grounding in science, to be able to make good policy, but . . ." Risera shrugged. "We'll have expert advisors for all this stuff, won't we? When we're in the corps, or the civil service, or wherever . . . It's just not possible to be a specialist in subjects like this, is it? It takes people a lifetime to become specialists in some subjects. We're aiming to be good generalists."

Tilly looked at her uncomprehendingly. "But what about doing something that you really love?"

Risera was puzzled. "But I love all this . . ." She frowned. "Tilly, don't you?"

"What? The diplomatic corps? You know, and I'm speaking from experience here, Risera, but it's not that much fun. There's a lot of standing around holding champagne glasses and chatting—"

"I know," said Risera. "My parents are diplomats too. And what you call standing around chatting, I call talking to people from different backgrounds and cultures, visiting new and fascinating places—"

Tilly pulled a face. "One embassy is very like another, Sera."

There was a pause. "But the *work*," said Risera. "It's important. When we're out there, we make a genuine difference. Solving conflicts, maybe even stopping wars!"

"Oh, sure, yes, but, you know, there's also a lot of time spent making really annoying people feel like what they have to say is important so that they don't go off in a huff. You know? An awful lot of chitchat and time wasted. Protocol, they call it. I think we could all do with a lot less messing around and a lot more getting on with things."

Risera didn't reply. She sat down at her desk and opened her notes. She was chewing her bottom lip. Tilly had the vaguest feeling that maybe she had offended. "I'm not saying that it's not important," she said awkwardly. "It's just . . . I think lots of other things are important too."

"Sure," said Risera. She picked up her pen. "Hey, I think I'm just going to be in your way. I'm going to head over to Semett's. She's got some notes from the last sociology class that I'd like to take a look at. Come and join us later, if you like." She gave a wry smile. "It'll save on the washing up."

Tilly, confused, watched her go. *What just happened?* She shook her head and turned back to the posters. People were weird sometimes. People were *touchy.*

The first meeting of the engineering club was a quiet success. There were four of them altogether, including Tilly, which was smaller than she'd hoped, but it was good that there were at least some like-minded souls who wanted to geek out for a couple of hours a week. Tilly had booked one of the classrooms, but the group was so small that she decided it would be easier simply to hold the meeting in her room. The first session was fine, although Tilly wasn't sure that they followed her presentation on astromycology, but then there was a talk on binary stars, and someone had brought along a board game they were developing, and they had fun beta-testing it.

They all agreed to meet in Tilly's room again the following week. It wasn't as if they'd be disturbing Risera with their noncore discussions, Tilly thought. Risera was working on a sociology paper with Semett and had been hanging out in her room in the evenings. The rest of the gang seemed to have migrated over there too, so there was no chance of them interrupting the discussions either. Tilly was very disappointed that none of her gang had shown any interest in coming along to the club, but not everyone had to enjoy the same things, did they? Besides, it was nice to have a little peace and quiet in the room. The others did get very noisy, and they weren't great about keeping the place neat and tidy.

She still saw Risera every morning at the lake. The

Arixxian rowing had really taken off, partly because of Risera's sterling promotional efforts, and partly because it was genuinely fun. There were eight teams out on the water most mornings. Tilly had helped Risera design some posters and then had gone around with her, putting them up all around the school. (*Huh*, she thought. *All that work I did for her. You think Sera could have helped publicize my engineering club!*) The teachers were starting to ask questions about the rowing, and Risera was pushing for it to be recognized as an official school sport. It was all getting pretty serious out there, and very competitive. Some of the seniors were muttering about getting a team together and showing them how it should be done. Tilly didn't mind the upsurge in interest in the sport: in fact, she was loving it, not just because of the pleasure of the open water, but because it brought her and Risera into close contact. They were both ambitious for the reds-and-yellows, and when they were working together it felt like they were still close.

One morning, after a particularly grueling session, the team downed oars at the far side of the lake. They pored over their timings, and Tilly issued a few pointers as to how she thought they could improve. In the distance, the bell rang to tell students it was fifteen minutes until they were expected to be down for breakfast. They scrambled into the boat and Tilly started the motor. They didn't waste time and energy rowing back—they used as much time as they could for practice, and then got to the school as efficiently as possible. This morning, however, the motor wouldn't start. There was a gasp and splutter, and then nothing.

"What's going on?" said Risera.

"Motor's dead," said Tilly shortly.

Everyone groaned. This meant they would have to row back, and dash to the showers, and hurry through breakfast—if they still had enough time left for breakfast—or risk being late for the first attendance and getting into trouble for that . . .

"Don't worry," said Tilly cheerfully. "I've got this."

She got to work. The team looked on, some sighing, some rolling their eyes. "Tilly," Xoha said. "Can we just get rowing? We don't have time for you to tinker with the—"

The engine started. "If you guys could hop into the boat rather than stand around chattering," said Tilly brightly, "we can all get to breakfast."

They did what they were told. Soon they were speeding back toward the other side of the lake, and then on their way to breakfast. Tilly sat with Risera and Xoha and the rest of the gang.

"You're not going to believe this," said Xoha to the others. "Tilly just fixed the motor on our boat."

"No way," said Erisel.

"Tilly, you have some amazing hidden talents," said Semett.

Tilly, who was feeling rather cross about the whole business because, actually, nobody had as yet *thanked* her for getting them all back in time for breakfast, put down her slice of toast. "You know," she said, "all those cocktail parties and fancy dinners are all very well, but who'll be the first to complain if the lights and the food slots aren't working? Nobody can be"—she did air quotes—"'*diplomatic*' under those circumstances."

There was a silence. Her friends, Tilly realized, were all goggling at her.

"Okay," said Erisel, at last. "Well, I guess she told us."

They carried on with breakfast, but without conversation. Tilly looked at her friends, who seemed to be sharing glances with one another. *Have I said something wrong?* She looked around and saw, at the far end of the table, two of the teachers. One of them caught her eye, winked, and began to laugh quietly to herself. The rest of the gang finished up and made their way off to class, leaving Tilly alone. The teacher who had winked at her came past. "Tilly," she said, "never change. You're a hoot."

Tilly picked up her tray and carried it to the dispenser. She felt herself starting to flush. *I'm not sure*, she thought, *that I want to be a hoot . . .*

3

Five weeks into the semester, the school stopped for a short midterm holiday. By this time, they were all in need of a break. The nonstop whirl of classes, activities, and study, as well as the hothouse atmosphere that comes with any small, sealed-off community, made for an exhausting way of life. Students and teachers alike were glad to put down tools for a few days and take a rest. For most of the students, this meant simply a holiday from lessons for a while; for others, families came to visit for a few days. Siobhan, of course, didn't have the time to visit, Iain was out of contact, and Adèle and Quinn were away too, vacationing with old friends on Risa. Adèle had offered to cancel, but Tilly was insistent. "You've been stuck with me for a year," she said cheerfully. "It's about time you guys got to be on your own."

But as the holiday drew closer, Tilly was regretting her selflessness. Friends from both the rowing and engineering clubs began to talk excitedly about the arrival of their own families, and she began to think, as she often did, how nice it would be to have a regular family: Mom, Dad, maybe a baby brother or something, four of them, in a nice house somewhere. She shook herself. She'd had enough sociology classes by now to know that families came in all kinds of different forms. Andorians had all those parents, didn't they?

And what about Maltrisians, where the mother laid the egg, the father hatched it, and two uncles brought it up? How many human families did she know, really, who were a little foursome? Hardly any.

She put on a brave face and kept herself busy. The teachers were sensitive to the fact that some students had families who couldn't make the trip, so there were plenty of activities: interactive displays and exhibitions from the various societies and clubs for the visitors, demonstrations from the sports teams, even a short revue one afternoon, produced by some of the seniors. Tilly threw herself into creating a poster display for the engineering club, explaining the work that the members were doing, and the Arixxian rowers held a short regatta, not so much races as a display of colors and a good lively racket from the drummers. Altogether, there was a festival feel around the school for the week, and it made a good break from what was otherwise a fairly relentless routine. Still, Tilly couldn't help feeling sad that nobody was making the trip to see her. Dad had asked her to send him some footage of the races, and copies of her posters. But it wasn't the same.

Risera turned out to be sensitive to her feelings. Both of her parents were visiting, her father having arranged to stop over on Talaris IV en route back to Arixus from his posting out on Ktaris. One evening, the night before the break started in earnest, Risera was back in their room for once. She looked up from her desk and said, "Tilly, would you like to come out with me and my parents while they're here? They usually take me out one evening for dinner in the capital, and a show . . . We thought . . . Well, I know your family can't make it this time. And my parents are dying to meet you. I've told them all about you."

They want to meet me? thought Tilly suspiciously. *Or do they want to meet my mother's daughter?* She flushed slightly at such an ungrateful response to what was surely simply a friendly offer. "That's really kind of you, Sera. Really kind of your parents too," she said, and smiled. "Yes, I've been sad that Mom, Dad, Granna, and Quinn can't come. I'd love to meet your parents. They always sound so nice when you talk about them. I'd love to come along—thank you."

Risera smiled, and nodded, and went back to her work. Tilly felt happier than she had felt in ages. Things had been weird with Sera recently. Maybe it was just what happened after weeks of being busy. Maybe all they needed was a rest, and this would be the start of getting close again.

Even though Siobhan wasn't visiting, she still managed to impose her presence on the holiday. The midterm holiday also meant midterm results of a series of tests, and a report with teacher comments. Siobhan, having received the report, inevitably asked for a parent-teacher conference with Tilly's year-group teacher, Ms. Keith.

It was no different from any other parent-teacher conference that Tilly had sat in over the years, which meant that it was pretty excruciating. Tilly sat fidgeting and fiddling with a loose curl. Her mother was five minutes late for the call, apologizing for the delay in a perfectly polite manner, but not offering any explanation. Well, everyone knew she was a busy woman with plenty to fill her day, didn't they? Everyone knew who she was. *Why do you always have to find time for this, Mom? Why can't you leave it to Granna, or, better still—leave me alone!*

As often happened in meetings with Mom, Siobhan seemed to be reading from several sources of information all at once. There was some background noise too, the low chatter of a news feed, and part of her attention was on this. *"So I've had a look through these results, Ms. Keith,"* Siobhan said. *"I'm grateful to have received this information. I think we can see that there are some emerging issues."*

Tilly groaned to herself about the familiar term. But Keithy hadn't heard it before. She said, "I'm not sure what you mean—"

"I say 'emerging,'" said Siobhan, *"although those of us familiar with Sylvia's reports can see some continuing trends."*

"I think this is an extremely good report," said Ms. Keith firmly. "Tilly has only been here five weeks, after all. She's had to learn a new environment, make new friends, get used to new schedules—"

"Tilly?" said Siobhan. *"Huh. I don't like that, Sylvia. Let's stick with what we know."* She turned back to addressing Keith. *"I appreciate that this is a new environment for Sylvia. And I'm wondering whether or not the excitement of a new place and new opportunities means that she's spreading herself too thin."*

Ms. Keith gave a tight smile. Tilly, watching this conversation like a bystander with no vested interest, had to admit she was impressed with the way Ms. Keith wasn't letting Siobhan railroad her. *I wish I knew the trick*, she thought, before realizing that Ms. Keith most likely dealt with pushy parents all the time. *Lots of experience. Whereas I only have a sample of one . . .*

"I think with any student it's important to emphasize the successes," Ms. Keith said. "And they really are huge successes—the math and science scores are outstanding."

"Oh, they always are," said Siobhan. *"They always take care of themselves, and that's good. But look at this for debate . . . It's a real worry."*

"I don't think that score does Tilly justice," said Ms. Keith (and Tilly could have hugged her for sticking to her guns on the name). "Tilly's preparation—her research—for that assignment was outstanding. Probably the best in the year."

"But she didn't win the debate."

"It was close."

"*Close,*" said Siobhan, "*isn't winning.*"

Tilly and Ms. Keith exchanged a look. For the briefest moment, Tilly thought that Ms. Keith was thinking: *Is she for real?* Well, I'm afraid she is, Keithy. She's all too darn real. Welcome to Tilly-World. Population—me and my mom. It can get a bit intense here. You might want to make a dash for the border . . .

"Again," Ms. Keith said doggedly, "I'd like to emphasize how short a time Tilly has been here. She learned a whole new protocol for conducting debates. She had to come up to speed quickly with the personal preferences of her peers, something that other students have had years to learn. I think that she and her partner did remarkably well pushing the vote that close—"

"*But they didn't win.*"

Ms. Keith shifted in her seat. "Sometimes we learn as much from not winning."

She wouldn't know anything about that, thought Tilly glumly. *She's never lost in her life.*

"*Mm,*" said Siobhan, clearly not convinced. "*Okay, let's table that for the moment. What else is there? Language scores.*" She sighed. "*Not great, Sylvia. I'm starting to despair on that one, to be honest.*" An aide came briefly into view, passing a note to her, which she took and began to read. "*Excuse me for a moment, I've been waiting for this.*"

Ms. Keith moved smoothly into the gap. "Math and science scores are top of her year, comparable with the best of the grades being achieved by the seniors, and in some places higher. Some really fine work in economics, top three in political science and philosophy, top five in sociology and statistics. And I really want to commend Tilly's extracurricular activities. She's thrown herself into the life of the school—she's started an engineering club, she's part of a rowing team, and she stood in a couple of times at the last minute when one member of a string quartet was ill. And of course her research poster on astro-mycology has really been impressing the parents visiting this week—"

Tilly winced. She should have asked Keithy not to mention that. Siobhan frowned. *"Not that again!"* she said. *"Sylvia, I thought you'd be past that by now!"*

"Sorry, Mom. They're just so—"

"Whatever you see in them I'll never understand. Look, Ms. Keith, I think this is only reinforcing my original point. All this extracurricular activity is distracting from what's core. Some of Sylvia's scores just aren't up to scratch—"

"Not one of her scores is poor," said Ms. Keith, calmly and firmly. "Far from it."

Wow, thought Tilly, amazed at Keith's sangfroid. *How are you still standing?*

"But they are not high enough," Siobhan said. *"Sylvia, darling, I'm just trying to make sure you're not pulling your-self in too many directions. The whole point of coming here was to focus on what we need to get you into the diplomatic corps. But there's still these issues."* Siobhan shook her head. *"Per-haps some extra classes could be arranged?"*

Tilly felt slightly faint. *When, Mom? I have to sleep some-times!*

"For the health of the students we don't allow that," said Ms. Keith very firmly. "All our students, including Tilly, have enough on their schedules."

"All right. Then we need to free up space in the schedule. Sylvia, is there anything you could give up?"

Tilly, summoned to speak, hunched forward. "I've already given up the flute, Mom—"

"Yes, I'm sorry about that. Okay, you mentioned an engi-neering club. What's that all about?"

There was a pause. Ms. Keith nodded at Tilly and smiled. *Go on. It's great! Explain it.*

"Um, it's nothing big . . . Just four of us . . ."

"Four of you?" said Siobhan.

"We meet once a week in each other's rooms . . ."

"So it's a social club?"

"No, Mom! We talk about what we've been working on . . ."

"Mushrooms, you mean," said Siobhan.

Tilly flushed. "Not just that! We do some programming . . . One of us is working on a game . . ."

"A game." Siobhan was not happy. *"Okay, so this sounds like a social club. I think we can see here what I mean by slack."*

"It's research, Mom! It's all really interesting!"

Siobhan pounced. *"Research? So taking up study time?"*

"Well, not much, not really . . ."

"But some."

Tilly, cornered, sighed. "Maybe a little." She glanced at Ms. Keith, who had a pained expression on her face. *I'm sorry, Ms. Keith. Sorry I let you down . . .*

"All right, Sylvia," Siobhan said, *"I'm sure that this is all great fun, but we've talked before about how playtime needs to stop. You'll be seventeen soon, honey. Remember what we've said? About serious people?"*

Tiny voice. Tiniest of voices. "Sure, Mom. I remember."

"I know it must feel hard, sweetie, but these are such a crucial few years! What you do now shapes your future. Try not to feel bad. You're so lucky, darling! All these opportunities! I would have loved all this when I was your age!"

Yes, Mom, but I'm . . . I'm not you. I'm me . . .

"So," went on Siobhan, *"I think we agree that games club has to stop."*

It's not games, Tilly thought mulishly. *It's engineering.* But she said, "I guess."

"You don't sound so sure, Sylvia."

Tilly sighed. "No, Mom. I'm sure. You're right."

"Okay, we're agreed. Ms. Keith, I'm going to have to end this call—I'm late already for my eleven o'clock. Sylvia, I know you think I'm being hard, but in fact these are some really promising results. I think we're starting to get on track." She ended the call. The Federation logo spun around for a while on the display.

Ms. Keith reached over and turned it off. "Well," she said. "That was all very interesting."

"You know it wasn't a games club," Tilly said in a low voice.

Keith gave her a sad smile. "I know, Tilly," she said. "What are you going to do?"

"No more games, I guess," she said. "Just serious things, for serious people."

"Are you sure?" said Keith with a frown.

Tilly shrugged. What else could she do? Disobey Mom? Not likely. She was going to do what she always did—exactly as she was told.

After the meeting, Tilly went off to do a stint in the exhibition hall, where she stood by the poster display for the engineering club and explained to anyone who asked exactly how astromycology was pronounced and what it involved. After an hour, her duty done, she slipped back to her room. Risera wasn't there—presumably off in Semett's room or with the rest of the gang somewhere. Her parents weren't due to arrive until the morning. For once, Tilly was glad to be alone. She'd had a message the previous day that her father's ship, the *Dorothy Garrod*, was going to be briefly within range, and he was planning to try to speak to her in real time . . . Well, more or less; he wasn't quite sure how well it would work. Still, Tilly was excited. It was a few months now since they had been able to communicate via anything other than recorded messages, and she was longing to speak to him. Not just because it had been ages, but because . . . well, her father was her last line of defense. Okay, so he'd never intervened between her and her mother before, not when it came to decisions about her schooling, but Tilly was sure, absolutely and completely sure, that if she called on him, Iain Tilly would ride in, like a knight in shining armor, and put himself between her and the dragon of her mother. That's what dads were for, wasn't it? Knights in shining armor.

Tilly sat for a while at her desk. The time for the call came and went. Ten minutes . . . Twenty . . . After half an hour, Tilly opened a sociology essay and started tinkering with it. She was completely engrossed in theories of dysfunctional bureaucratic organizations when, seventy minutes late, her father's call came through.

The connection was awful, crackling and fizzing, but it was him, really him.

"Sills!" he said. *"I'm so sorry! I've been trying to get this damn call through for over an hour!"*

She closed her paper and smiled at him. "That's okay, Dad. You're here now." Well, more or less. She frowned. The picture was breaking up, the image of her father turning into big hazy blocks of color. "Hey, are you still there? Dad? *Dad*?"

"—quite hear you . . . Oh no! There you are! Yes, yes, I'm still here. It's so good to hear your voice, Sills!"

"It's great to hear you too, Daddy. Hey, I spoke to Mom today too . . ." Tilly trailed off.

"To Mom? How is she?"

"Oh, you know, the same as ever . . . We talked about my grades . . ."

". . . sorry, Sills, this is a terrible connection . . . So frustrating . . ."

"Daddy? Daddy?"

". . . just read your report. Fantastic work, Sills!"

Tilly beamed at him—or the big blocks that, if you squinted, looked very much like him. Look, that patch there was his red hair. Maybe.

"Thank you, Daddy! Hey, I've been having loads of fun with the engineering club . . ."

"The what?"

"The engineering club!"

". . . Oh yes, you said something about that in your last message! All sounds really interesting . . ."

"Mom wants me to drop it."

Silence. "Daddy?" Tilly felt a wave of panic. Had she said the wrong thing? She tried not to set her mother and father against each other, tried really hard, but this mattered so much. She felt like this was her last chance to do something that she still loved, that if this went, then there would be nothing left that was hers, and hers alone. She desperately wanted to carry on with the club, but she knew she couldn't stand against her mother alone. She needed backup. She needed a knight in shining armor.

". . . Drop what? Sorry, Sills, I can barely hear you . . ."

"Engineering club!"

Another long pause. Then: *". . . do what you want, Sills—"*

The channel cut out, suddenly.

"Daddy? Daddy?"

Nothing. Tilly sat back in her chair. She felt like crying. "Do what you want." What was that supposed to mean? Follow your heart? Or—you know, Sills, it's not that important in the great scheme of things? Whatever it was, it was hardly a ringing endorsement. Tilly sat at her desk for another thirty minutes, but, for whatever reason, her father didn't get the channel to work again. Maybe he'd only had a little time anyway, same as her mom. With a deep sigh, Tilly got up and went over to the bed. She lay down and stared at the ceiling. She'd wanted her father's blessing, a reason to go back to her mom and say, "Ah, yes, but there's *another* parent around here, *another* authority, and *he's* on *my* side . . ." But that? That hardly counted as his blessing, did it? "Do what you want."

Well, she knew what she wanted—more or less—but she didn't know how to get it. *It's always going to be like this, isn't it?* she thought frantically. *Whatever I want to do, it'll never be what Mom wants. And eventually, I'll start to forget what I wanted, and it'll be like I was never there at all.* Hot tears sprang into her eyes. She felt her breath shorten, and her chest contract, as if the air in the room was growing thin. She sobbed, just once, but then the door burst open and Risera and Xoha fell into the room, laughing over some joke or other.

"Tilly," cried Xoha, "we knew you'd be lurking around in here. Come on, the revue's just about to start, and the seniors are always super-snarky."

Tilly rubbed her eyes and put on her brightest smile. *Armor*, she thought as she followed her friends out of the room. *I'm wearing my armor.*

The next day Risera's parents arrived. They did the obligatory tour of the school, and then came and sat in the armchairs in their daughter's room, holding court as Risera's friends called by to say hello. They remembered each one well, not just by name, but remembered their circumstances and families, and it was clear that some of them had been visitors to their home during vacations, or even joined them on family holidays. Old jokes and stories were brought out, and there was a great deal of laughter. Risera's father—handsome and suave—could have charmed Klingons; her mother was petite and pretty, and very sweet. She also didn't miss a thing. Tilly had seen a lot of diplomatic pairings like this before, both working to support each other to make their careers a success. Risera's parents were the perfect diplomatic couple: her father personable and intelligent; her mother unthreatening and paying attention to everything that was happening, inviting confidences and intimacies. She had always found these pairings fascinating, and she had often wondered why her parents had never gotten their marriage to work in this way. But then, Dad had something about him of the absentminded professor, didn't he? He had a tendency always to be thinking about his latest line of study or pondering what a piece of evidence might mean. Dad had so many interesting things to say, but, if Tilly was being honest, his small talk was terrible. Meanwhile, Mom always wowed a room with her presence. She would walk in, and the center of gravity would shift toward her. People would gather around, wanting to be near her. But Dad must have known, when he'd married Mom, what he was signing up for. Mom had always made her ambition clear. So what had changed? Tilly thought she knew. *It was fine when it was just the two of them. But then there were three . . .*

Tilly sat rather shyly to one side. Watching the family together, she found herself envious of Risera. She could see now where her friend's confidence came from, and she wondered, rather sadly, what it would have been like to have parents like this—a team, working together, who knew the details of their daughter's life so well, and supported and nurtured her talents. Mom . . . To be fair, Mom had taken her to some amazing places, let her meet some amazing people . . . But Tilly always felt out of place in them, like she was about to say the wrong thing, or do the wrong thing. Glasses would get knocked over. Uncensored thoughts would pop out of her mouth. Tilly always had the feeling that she was disappointing someone, somewhere, somehow . . . And after the divorce Dad was always at arm's length, and then he had chosen to take the posting on the *Dorothy Garrod*, to go far, far away.

Midafternoon, Risera's parents left to go back to their hotel to get ready for the evening. There were huge hugs all around, even though the family would be together again in a couple of hours. When they'd gone, Risera fell back on her bed with a happy sigh.

"They're so great," Tilly said. "You must really miss them."

Risera rolled over onto her elbow. "They're not bad, I guess," she said with a laugh. "They have their moments."

Tilly gave a rueful smile. Like many happy people, Risera didn't realize what she had.

When it was time to get dressed up for the evening, Tilly opened her closet and pulled out some of what she thought of as her "mom-clothes": dresses chosen to make a splash at some diplomatic function. They were all designer. They were all custom made. And they were all, as far as Tilly was concerned, darned uncomfortable.

Risera, seeing the clothes laid out on the bed, came over and stared. "Wow, Tilly," she said. "Look at these *labels* . . ."

"I know . . ." Tilly said. "Hey, why don't you pick something out. It'll probably suit you more than it suits me."

Risera's eyes lit up. "Really?"

Tilly grinned. "Really."

With a happy sigh, Risera started looking through the heap of clothes. She settled on a bright-yellow cocktail dress with a slightly daring V-neckline. The waistband was beaded with tiny crystals, and the skirt flared out, ending just below the knee. She gasped in delight when she put it on, swirling the skirt around. She looked great: the yellow beautifully complemented her dark coloring. *Yellow*, thought Tilly ruefully. *With my hair. What was Mom thinking?* But the color had been superfashionable a season or two ago. Siobhan had gotten away with it, but Tilly couldn't. Tilly herself picked out something emerald green. That was more the right kind of thing. "Hey, Risera," she said. "You look *amazing*!"

They both, in fact, looked terrific, as their friends were eager to tell them when they went by. Tilly loaned Risera some jet beads that had been a present from Granna; Risera reciprocated by loaning Tilly a turquoise pendant on a silver chain. Risera put on high heels. Tilly opted for something lower. They both beamed at each other. Tilly thought she had never felt so happy. A pal, at last. Someone to dress up with; someone to giggle with. Someone to make some happy memories with.

They hurried, laughing, down the stairs and to the transporter. Ms. Keith saw them off, with strict instructions as to when they should return. "Have a good time, girls," she said. Then she smiled at them. "Look at you two! Don't you look fine?"

Risera's parents met them at the transporter near their hotel. An official flyer was waiting to whisk them off to the theater (a pretty good production of a new play by a local writer, all about the period before Talaris joined the Federation, with lots of glimpses into the old regime). Then they went off to dinner. Risera's parents had chosen a restaurant that had been receiving rave reviews for its Earth dishes. They'd picked it for her, Tilly realized, and felt really touched by this small kindness. She and Cesel, Risera's mother, chose the wine together. Then, poring over her menu, she heard a word close to her heart across the table.

"Are you talking about mushrooms?" Tilly said.

"You like mushrooms?" Ibas, Risera's father, said, looking up from his menu.

Tilly could have hugged him. She felt like she'd been waiting years for a question like that. "Gosh, I *love* mushrooms!"

"Well, great!" said Ibas. "I have to say they were one of my favorite discoveries when I first visited Earth. I studied there, you know."

"Well, you came to the right place," Tilly said. "There's some really interesting work going on—"

Ibas blinked slightly at that but he carried on regardless. "Oh, I'm not talking about anything fancy," he said. "Fried is best. Nothing like it."

Tilly looked at him in horror. "Oh, my goodness, no! No!"

He looked at her in bafflement. "What's wrong with fried?"

"No! Goodness!" said Tilly. "That would absolutely *destroy* the sample—"

Risera was by now in stitches. "Oh, this is priceless. Wait till I tell the gang about this. They're going to love this." She punched her father on his arm. "Dad, you idiot, she's not talking about breakfast. Tilly's hobby is mycology."

"Mycology?" said Ibas, his brow furrowing in confusion.

"Astromycology, to be precise," said Tilly.

"Oops, sorry, yes," said Risera. "I always forget the astro part."

"I haven't the faintest idea what that is," said Ibas.

"Space mushrooms," said Risera.

"Is that a *thing*?" said Ibas.

"Goodness," said Cesel. "Whatever will they think of next?"

"You'd better believe it's a thing," said Risera. She glanced at Tilly, who was starting to flush with embarrassment, and softened. "You know, guys, Tilly has a research poster up back at school. It's probably one of the best pieces of work anyone at the school has produced."

Tilly's blush turned from embarrassment into pride. "Is that *true*?"

Risera smiled at her. "Yes! I overheard Keithy talking about it with Stavath. And you know Keithy. She's not exactly what you could call *effusive*."

"No," agreed Tilly warmly. "Gosh. I don't know what to say."

Both Risera's parents were smiling at her. Cesel said, "Your mom must be so proud."

"Um," said Tilly doubtfully. "You know, if I'm being honest, I think she prefers her mushrooms fried too."

The whole family laughed. Tilly flushed again, but this time with pleasure. She often said things that made people laugh, but it wasn't often that she *intended* to make them laugh. It was a nice feeling. It made her feel part of the club. The dinner carried on cheerfully. Tilly didn't spill a drop of anything. Just before dessert she excused herself to use the bathroom. When she came back, she realized that the family was talking about her—and her mother.

"She's such a sweet kid . . . A little odd," said Ibas. "Mushrooms!" He laughed.

"It would be great for you to get an invitation," said Cesel.

Tilly coughed, and they all turned and gave her bright smiles. Risera said, "Hey, Tilly, it turns out we're going to be on Earth for most of the next vacation. Mom and Dad were saying it would be great for us all to meet up—"

"Sure," said Tilly, "though I have to be honest and say that if you were hoping to be introduced to Mom, you'd probably end up seeing more of Granna and Quinn. Still, they're fun and worth getting to know too."

There was a short, embarrassed silence, as if Tilly had somehow laid bare the transaction at the heart of the offer. She hurried to cover the gap. *Shoot, why does it always come out wrong?* "What I mean is, I'm usually at my grandmother's house in France for the holidays. It's pretty gorgeous there. Sunshine, wine, lazing around in the garden. Going to the market, coming home and cooking. Mom usually comes for a few days. Maybe we could do something then?"

"That would be great," said Ibas. Tilly nodded, although her heart sank a little. She was used to people showing more interest in her mom than in her. She'd hoped, though, that there was more to her friendship with Risera than simply a means for her parents to meet her mother. She clamped down hard on that thought. That wasn't fair to them. It wasn't fair to Risera, either, who had always been kind, if a little untidy and definitely *not* great on washing up . . . Tilly wondered whether it might be worthwhile drawing up a rotation, particularly if the rest of the gang were going to be spending more time in their room again . . . It had been nice to have them around again earlier that day, but, gosh, they did make a mess.

"So, Tilly," said Cesel. "What's your plan for the mock summit?"

Tilly blinked at her. "Excuse me?"

Risera patted her mother's arm. "I don't think that's come up yet."

Tilly looked at her in horror. "What have I *missed*?"

"Nothing, honestly—"

"A *mock summit*?"

"It's fun! Hard work though."

"It's a great idea," said Cesel. "Your year runs a mock UFP summit. You all pick a member planet, research their history and culture and so on, and then present to the school."

"National dress," said Ibas.

"You're kidding," said Tilly. "You're joking with me."

"He's not," said Risera with a laugh. "And—you're going to love this bit, Tilly—you have to make a speech in one of the official languages." She gave a sympathetic smile. "Sorry about that!"

"Oh my goodness," said Tilly, sitting back in her chair. "Oh my goodness. When? When do we have to do this?"

"End of term," said Risera. "It's our year's big project for the rest of the semester."

"Has everyone started *work*?" Tilly could feel her throat tightening. "There must be so much to do!" she wailed. "I didn't even know this was happening!"

Ibas and Cesel, surprised at the reaction, exchanged looks.

"Honestly, Tilly," said Risera, "it's all fine! Don't panic! Me and the others have chatted about it a few times, but most people don't really start thinking about it until after midterm break. The teachers don't bring it up because they don't want us fretting about it early."

Tilly took a deep breath. "Okay," she said. "So everything isn't lost?"

"Of course not!"

Tilly eyed her friend suspiciously. "You've been planning yours for ages, haven't you?"

Risera had the decency to blush. "But only because I knew it was coming. Honestly, Tilly, I thought you knew—"

Not when people start hanging out in other rooms, Tilly thought, a little bitterly. "Okay," she said. "Okay. I can do this."

Cesel patted her arm. "Tilly, sweetheart," she said. "You got the best mark on a science project that the school has ever seen. I think if you put your mind to it, you can probably do *anything*."

—

Siobhan, as was her custom, had not been idle since the conference with Tilly and her tutor, and the substance of that summit formed the chief topic of conversation with her mother on their weekly call. *"So she's taken on too much."*

Adèle didn't blink. "Oh yes?"

"Clubs, sports, you name it. Her marks are suffering."

Adèle, who had looked through the report in detail, and seen the glowing comments from almost every member of the staff, raised her eyebrows. "Are you sure about that, *chérie*?"

"She's never shown an interest in sports before," said Siobhan, and sighed. *"I don't know what's happened there. I was such a talented gymnast at school. You remember, don't you, Maman?"*

"I remember," said Adèle, with feeling. "My heart in my mouth, every time you went on that blessed beam. Sometimes I think that was why you chose to do it, but then, you have always liked pushing yourself to the extreme of your abilities."

"Iain, too—not what I'd call a great sportsman, not really, but we used to have some really good tennis matches, and of course he loves walking . . ." Siobhan, who was not the kind to be nostalgic, shook herself, and went on, briskly, *"Anyway, this interest in rowing is good news, and I don't want her to give it up. Rowing could be good for her. Good for strength, good for coordination . . . Maybe, just maybe, we can do something about that girl's posture—"* She stopped. Adèle was rocking backward and forward in laughter. *"What? What is it?"*

"Oh, *chérie*, I don't know what you're imagining, but this rowing that she's doing—it isn't the Boat Race!"

Siobhan's eyes narrowed. *"So what, exactly, are we talking about?"*

"It's an Arixxian sport—more a custom than a sport, if I'm being honest. Arixxian rowing. Go on," said Adèle, amused. "Look it up."

There was a short pause while Siobhan researched the topic. Adèle watched her expression shift from attention to bewilderment to astonishment to—inevitably—annoyance. *"Mother, what the hell is this all about?"*

"Yes, it is rather beautiful, isn't it? It's a very ancient tradition on Arixus, I understand. Tied to moon festivals and so on . . . I'm no anthropologist, Siobhan, get one of those bright interns you have on hand to research that for you."

Siobhan watched a short vid, her concentration intense. Adèle, hearing drums and pipes, covered her smile.

"Sure, it's beautiful," Siobhan said at last, *"but . . ."*

"Not what you were expecting, I should imagine," Adèle said. "I gather her roommate got her involved. She's from Arixus, you know."

Siobhan gave her mother a very dry look. *"Do you really think I don't know who Sylvia is sharing a room with? Risera Igova. Her father's rather interesting—he's done some very good work in his current posting on Ktaris. I wonder if he's going to be on Earth at some point in the near future? He might be a useful connection . . ."*

"The rowing, Siobhan," Adèle prompted patiently.

"Oh yes," said Siobhan. *"Well, it's very unusual, but it also looks like very hard work. She must be getting some first-rate exercise from it . . ."* Siobhan peered at her mother, who, once again, was laughing to herself. *"What now?"*

"Oh, Siobhan, can you really see our Sylvia pulling away at an oar? She's the *drummer*, *chérie*! There's practically no exercise involved!"

"The drummer." Siobhan ran her hand across her eyes. *"You know,* Maman, *sometimes I think Sylvia does these things on purpose."*

"Like you and the beam, eh?" Adèle muttered darkly, but her daughter did not hear.

"We agree on something, and she always finds a way around it."

"Don't be ridiculous, Siobhan, that's not the case at all. And I don't think that's a helpful way to think about it. So combative! So untrusting!"

"But—the drummer*!"* Siobhan shook her head. *"What's that doing for her, exactly?"*

"I think perhaps you should be less dismissive. There'll be more to it than you think. She'll be working with a team, giving instructions—"

"When did you become an expert on Arixxian rowing?"

"When Sylvia began taking an interest," Adèle said pointedly.

There was a short pause.

"You know, Maman, *I'm close to giving up on that girl."*

Adèle smiled. "Alas, Siobhan, one cannot simply give up on motherhood. That is not how it works. One can, however . . ." Adèle stopped.

Siobhan pounced. *"Can what?"*

"You can be less hands-on about the whole business."

"I've already sent her to boarding school!" Siobhan cried. *"She's almost two weeks away!"*

"But you still insist on directing so much about her life!" Adèle shot back. "Her choices of subject, her hobbies . . . You would, I think, timetable her every hour, if you were able."

"I can assure you, Maman, *that I really don't have the time to do that!"*

"You would, though, if you could. You would employ an assistant, if you could, to schedule that little girl's day from start to end—"

"Whereas you relied on nuns—"

"And yet, *chérie*," said Adèle, "you seem to *thrive . . .*"

"*Oh, for heaven's sake,*" muttered Siobhan. "*All right, I give up. She can go ahead and choose what she wants to do in her spare time. Drumming in a boat festooned with flags, or games club, it's up to her.*"

"*Engineering* club," said Adèle firmly. "It is a serious endeavor."

"*Engineering club, games club*—Maman, *I honestly couldn't tell you the difference.*"

"No," said Adèle gently. "I didn't think you could."

The call ended with an exchange of genuinely loving expressions of affection (enlivened with some mutual exasperation). After they were done, Adèle went out into the garden to find Quinn. "I have prevailed," she said, with considerable (albeit deserved) self-satisfaction.

Quinn, who was practicing his putting, looked up. "Ah," he said. "So the mushrooms are back on the menu?"

Adèle gave a rather wolfish smile. "Potentially. But, more importantly, she will be spending some time doing what she wants to do, and with some like-minded young people."

Quinn looked at his wife adoringly. "You're grand, Adèle," he said. "I'm glad you're on my side. And I'm sure that girl's glad you're on her side too."

That evening, Tilly was surprised to receive a short message from Granna. They usually spoke to each other once a week, at the weekend, catching up on all the gossip. Granna was the kind of person who stuck to her routines, so Tilly was surprised to hear from her now. She opened the message with some trepidation, fearing bad news.

"*Chérie,*" Adèle said. "*I have some good news.*"

Dad's coming home early, was Tilly's first thought, even though she knew that wasn't going to happen.

"I've spoken to your mother," Adèle said. *"I've explained to her about your engineering club, and how important it is to you to continue with it. She is still keen for you to cut back on your extracurricular activities in some way, but she is now of the opinion that she would be happy for you to keep up the club if you like. She suggests you might reconsider your commitments to your rowing team . . ."* Granna sighed. *"I know that would be a loss to you, Sylvia—ah,* pardon, *Tilly, oh, I shall never remember to get that right! But I think perhaps it would be a fair exchange?"*

Tilly put her head in her hands.

"Anyway, my darling," said Adèle, *"have a little think. The choice is yours—and how rarely does that happen! Now, I know that rowing is good fun, but I think it would be a shame not to have the chance to work on your real love. Do consider what you would like to do. Speak to your teachers about it, perhaps? They might have some good advice. Ms. Keith strikes me as a sensible woman with your best interests at heart. Talk to her, yes? Good night, darling girl!"*

Tilly turned off the screen. A fair exchange. No question, of course, of doing *both*, like she had been doing all this *time*, and doing pretty darn *well*, in point of fact . . . Sometimes, Tilly had the faintest suspicion that even if she did everything her mother wanted exactly as she wanted, if she somehow miraculously developed a talent for languages, perfect posture, sparkling conversation, even then it wouldn't be enough. Her mother would say, "Very good, darling, but I think we can see a few issues emerging here . . ."

The next morning, Ms. Keith caught up with Tilly as she made her way to class. "Tilly," she said. "I had a nice message from your grandmother last night. She says that the engineering club is back in the cards? Good news, eh?"

Tilly smiled brightly. "Oh, yes! Mom said I could choose between it and rowing."

"And?"

Tilly took a deep breath. "Well, I've decided I'm going to stick with the rowing."

Ms. Keith gave her an odd look. "The rowing?"

Tilly nodded. "Well, I thought about it, really thought about it, and it's like everyone keeps on saying—the engineering club isn't really core to my career. It's okay to be a generalist, and I think I'm good enough already as a generalist. Also, I was thinking about how doing rowing is really good for teamwork and leadership and all of that . . ." She gave a short, tight laugh. "You know, I'm the first to admit that people skills aren't always my forte, and so it's better to get some good experience there. I think it's a much better addition to my résumé than the engineering club." Plus it kept her in regular contact with Risera, and that was important . . . "And I don't want to let the team down, not when we've come this far."

There was a short pause. "Tilly," said Ms. Keith softly, "are you quite sure about this?"

"Oh yes, I'm sure. Definitely. Very sure." Tilly smiled brightly. "No contest really."

"Really?"

"Really," said Tilly. Yes, she was absolutely sure. When you thought about it, really, there wasn't a choice at all.

"Okay," said Keith. "Well, let's see how it goes. Off to class, then."

Tilly smiled, and nodded, and bounced off into her classroom. She went straight over to open a window. Goodness, but these rooms got really stuffy, didn't they? Sometimes you went in and you couldn't *breathe*.

4

With the second half of the term now under way, Tilly began to throw herself into preparations for the mock summit that was to be held at the end of the term. She had real ambitions for the event. At last, she thought, she had a chance to prove herself to her mother, to show how well she could do in something that her mother would understand. The task played to all her strengths: detailed research, putting together a presentation . . . Okay, so the speech was a big ask for her, but, over the years, Tilly had begun to get a sneaking impression that she wasn't, in fact, as bad at speaking other languages as people (by which she meant her mom) made out. The problem was that some of her other grades were so exceptional that expectations had gotten high . . . *Jeez*, she thought in frustration, *we can't be good at everything*. Take her own mom. Tilly knew for a fact that Mom relied on her immediate staff to explain, over and over, what Tilly thought were pretty straightforward statistical terms. Standard deviation, for goodness' sake! Her mother had to ask every time and ask why it was important! Seriously, though, you couldn't get more basic . . . And did anyone tell her mother that there were issues emerging? No, they didn't, or, if they did, they didn't get to tell her a second time.

So Tilly set to work on the project with her usual focus. The first major task was to find a member species that nobody else was covering—you didn't want to bore other people, and you didn't want to get into comparisons. The other students from her year were pretty good about this, sharing their basic ideas rather than concealing them—everyone wanted a chance to shine rather than to compete. The teachers warmly encouraged this mutual support; they also gave a list of suggestions of worlds to cover, striking them off when students picked them. Tilly, looking down the list, couldn't see anything that was right. Everything seemed so obvious. Surely, from eighty-two worlds, she could find something fresh. Something striking and original. She had been taught years ago that the best way to learn how to do a project was to look at prior examples, so she tracked down the best five projects from previous years and studied the holo-recordings and reports in depth. Her instincts were borne out: these students had all gone slightly further afield than usual. After that, Tilly surveyed every project from the last five years to determine which species had already been covered, and to see if there were any gaps. All this background research took her the best part of a fortnight. The presentation was at the end of week five. The half term was moving on rapidly.

Risera's project was already under way. She had gone with Ktaris, because she had so much information from her father, and because she had visited during her holidays a couple of times while he was out there. She admitted that it was an obvious choice for her, but she was hoping that her depth of knowledge would outweigh those considerations. And, of course, she was more than competent in the language.

"So," she said to Tilly one evening. "Are you going to let us in on the big secret? What's your choice?"

Tilly shrugged.

Risera frowned. "Haven't you chosen yet?"

Tilly shook her head. She wanted to get this *exactly* right. She wouldn't talk about it, either. She wasn't going to get panicked into making a bad choice.

By the start of week three, Tilly knew the names of more minor member species than anyone else in the school. She might well have been able to challenge her mother in a quickfire quiz. But she'd also made her choice: a fascinating but little-known member species called the Elisurians. Nobody had done their project on them before. There was a very good reason for that. What had attracted Tilly to the Elisurians was their unique method of communication: they spoke to each other via melodic quadratic equations. Tilly hugged herself in delight when she discovered this. *They're talking my language!* she thought. It was a huge relief to have found something so perfect, and she was glad she had held out and not settled for something else. Now that her choice was made, she put all her effort and energy into making it the best presentation that she possibly could.

At the back of her mind was the gnawing (and growing) worry that she might have been too picky, taken too long. But Tilly was more her mother's daughter than she realized. Faced with a challenge, she didn't give up. She dug in, and she worked out what needed to be done, and she made concrete plans to achieve it. First, she would get all the research done this week. Then, she would produce the costume next week. At the start of week five she would write the presentation, and by the end of the week she would be ready to rehearse it. Students were allowed to use a prompt or a script if they preferred, but Tilly intended to be word— or equation—perfect.

But excellence, as her mother had often told her, comes at a cost, and Tilly was about to discover, once again, that her mother was right. All this preparation for the summit had to happen alongside her usual classes. In order to keep up with the tight schedule she had set herself—as well as keep on top of classroom work and row with the team—Tilly spent every waking hour in her room, hunched over her desk. She knew she was missing her friends from engineering club—her one evening a week of daft, fun, and geeky conversations—and at the back of her mind she had a sad and guilty feeling that they were hurt that Tilly had so unceremoniously dropped them in preference for rowing with Risera and Xoha. If Tilly was honest, the boat crew was no substitute for her geeky friends; and, besides, as all her deadlines drew closer, Tilly became a tyrant in the boat: pushing the team to exert themselves more and more, blunt about ways that they could improve, and sparing with praise. Poor Risera bore the brunt of all this: not only did she get regular tongue-lashings in the boat with the rest of the crew, but she also found herself in trouble back in their room. Tilly, who had never shared a room before in her life, was starting to discover exactly how *annoying* someone else could be, all the time—clattering cups, sighing, snoring, and, for goodness' sake, do you *really* have to *breathe* so loud?!

Outside, the weather was turning from late autumn to early winter. The grounds around the school—had Tilly noticed them—were full of the most beautiful leaves, gently drifting to the ground, and the air was clean and crisp and fresh. But all Tilly saw was her desk, her notes, her schedule. One afternoon, she just couldn't concentrate, couldn't get comfortable . . . She was trying to memorize part of her speech, and a series of notes that explained how the Elisurians organized their careful, structured society. But she couldn't get the numbers to work . . . She just couldn't concentrate. She tried to force her attention on her work. She didn't have *time* for this; there was hardly enough time in the day as it was. And then she realized her throat felt funny, her chest felt tight, she just couldn't *breathe* . . .

It was terrifying, absolutely terrifying. Tilly found herself gasping for breath. She fell back in her chair and gulped in air. She remembered what she had read somewhere, that you needed to slow down your breathing, regularize it . . . She pictured herself in the boat, drumming slowly, watching the oars clip up and down at a steady pace. Her breathing started to slow down, but it was a good few minutes before she felt anywhere near okay.

"What just happened?" Tilly whispered to herself. She put her hand to her chest. Her heart was still beating away like crazy. "Am I *okay*?" She leaned back in her chair. Her notes were still there. This was *awful*. She wanted to crawl into bed, but she couldn't lose the time, she couldn't afford to lose the time. She felt her chest tighten . . . *Not again! Oh, no, please, not again!*

Tilly jumped up from her chair and looked frantically around. She hissed in frustration. The room was an absolute *dump*. Cups everywhere, plates . . . Okay, so everyone was working hard right now, there were all these wretched tests coming, not to mention these presentations, but, for heaven's sake, was Tilly the *only* one who ever did any washing up around here? And the books, and clothes, all over everywhere.

"So *selfish*," muttered Tilly. "She *knows* I have allergies. She *knows* this isn't good for me."

She stood in the middle of the room, her hands on her hips, glaring around. This couldn't carry on. But she was *damned* if she was going to tidy up Risera's mess! She'd done enough of that over the last couple of months, picking up cups and plates, washing them, putting them away neatly—and not just Risera, the others too! Sure, some of her own stuff was lying around right now, but nowhere *near* as much, and not *everywhere*, and not *every single day* . . . "The problem with some people," muttered Tilly as she whirled around the room, "is that they don't respect other people's *space* . . ."

The room quickly began to look completely different. Tilly sorted out everything that belonged to her from everything that belonged to Risera. She shook out her own clothes, sorting out the clean ones, which she put away in her closet, and getting the rest bagged up for the laundry. She took the books that were hers and organized them on her shelves (first by topic and then by author surname). She sorted out which cups and plates were the ones that she had used, and which were Risera's—many more were Risera's, she noted with a nod of her head, as if this confirmed something she had already guessed—and, ugh, was there something *growing* in that cup? "That," she said to herself, holding the offending cup at arm's length by the handle, "is *disgusting*. No wonder my allergies are back. No wonder I feel awful!" It had been the same during the divorce. Things had gotten so disorganized as both her parents had struggled to adjust to the new living arrangements and keep on top of their work, all the while caring for a bewildered little girl. Tilly's allergies had gotten *appalling*.

She gathered up her own dishes and went to the little kitchen to wash up. It felt good, filling the bowl with steaming hot water, scrubbing away at them until she was sure they were clean. When she got back to the room, she put her dishes away, and then nodded with satisfaction to see how tidy her own things were. But Tilly wasn't done yet. Now she had the rest of the tidying to tackle.

First she gathered up all of Risera's books and clothes, and she dumped them on the (unmade) bed. She heaped Risera's dirty dishes onto an armchair, pushed that up against Risera's bed, and stuck a note on it: PLEASE! WASH!

up! Then she stood by the door, folded her arms, and surveyed her work.

Tilly sighed with relief. Her side was fine now—better than fine. Tidy. Orderly. Clean. As for the other side . . . She shuddered. But it was okay. If she imagined a line down the room, she could pretend none of it was there. She stood in the middle of the room, where the line would be, looked over to her side, and took a deep breath. It came easily. "There," she said. "That's *much* better." She sat down at her desk and opened her notes again. Suddenly the notes and equations all made sense, and the problem that she had been worrying over disappeared. She smiled to herself. There. Much better. All she'd needed to do was make it possible to work in this space again . . . She soon lost herself in her studies.

She barely registered the door opening, and Risera coming back in.

"Er, Tilly," said Risera after a moment, her voice confused. "What's going on?"

Tilly looked up. "What do you mean?" Risera was standing by the door, looking around uncertainly.

"Have you . . ." Suddenly Risera rushed over to her desk. "You've not touched my notes, have you? They were all in order—"

Tilly looked at her in horror. "I wouldn't mess with anyone's notes!"

"But you've messed with everything else!"

"I've not 'messed.'" Tilly did the air quotes. "I've tidied—and, boy, let me tell you, it needed doing—"

"Tidied? Tilly, all my stuff . . . my bed . . . Was this really you? Did you dump all my stuff on my bed?"

"Look," said Tilly, "it was *everywhere*, okay? It was *completely* out of hand—"

"So you picked everything up and then you just . . . ? I

don't believe this." Risera, helplessly, started sorting through her belongings. "I can't believe you've done this. This skirt . . . I love this skirt, and look at it—it's really *creased*!"

"You can't have loved it that much," said Tilly, with some acid. "It was hanging on the back of a chair."

"It was flat! Now it's all screwed up! Tilly!"

"A chair," said Tilly pointedly, "is not a closet."

"These books . . . I had them in reading order . . ."

"Coulda fooled me! Big stack of them falling all over the place—"

Risera turned to face her. "Tilly, we *share* this room—"

Tilly folded her arms. "Actually, yes, I know that, and I've been meaning to say something for ages now. I have *allergies*, you know! All this stuff—there's dust, ugh, and have you *seen* the inside of that mug there? It's horrible! And those plates—vile! This is such a mess, Sera! I can't live with it! You *really* need to think more about other people!"

There was a pause. "Okay, Tilly," said Risera. Her voice was very calm and quiet. "I get it."

Tilly turned away to get back to her work (*I have a schedule, for goodness' sake!*), but it was hard to concentrate at first. Risera went around her side of the room, putting away her clothes, organizing her books, and moving her dirty dishes. When Risera pushed the armchair back toward the other side, Tilly tutted. Risera moved the armchair back again. She took her dishes out, and five minutes later brought them back clean. She put them away (Tilly bore the clattering with only a small sigh). When that was done, Risera picked up a couple of books and a pile of notes, and she went out of the room, closing the door quietly behind her, and without saying goodbye.

Tilly heaved a sigh of relief. *At last*, she thought, *peace and quiet*. She put her head down and worked steadily through the rest of the evening, even getting slightly ahead on the next day's work. The first bell went, but Risera didn't come back. She crept in after the second bell, when Tilly was already in bed with the light off, and she didn't whisper "good night."

There was no mention of it the next day on the lake, or indeed any time afterward. In fact, there really wasn't much of a chance to talk about anything, given how tight Tilly's schedule was. She rowed, she attended classes, she scurried through homework, and then she worked on her presentation until just before first bell. In fact, Tilly was so wrapped up in her work that she failed to notice how little she saw of Risera after that evening. Yes, they still saw each other every morning at rowing practice, but, under Tilly's leadership, everyone was so focused on practicing for the race that there wasn't time for chat. The rest of the time, Tilly was working, working, working.

"Is there something up between you and Risera?" said Erisel one morning at breakfast.

Tilly looked at her in surprise. "What makes you say that?"

Erisel glanced down the table. Risera was sitting at the other end of the group. "Nothing," she said. "She just seems to be in our room studying a lot these days."

Tilly looked at Risera. She was chatting away to Semett and looked perfectly happy. Tilly shrugged her shoulders. "She looks fine to me."

"Hmm," said Erisel.

"I wouldn't worry about it," said Tilly blithely. "You know how it is. People need to find the right space to work in, don't they? If your workspace isn't right, you don't really get anything done. I had to really tidy up the other day—I wasn't getting anything done. Once everything was tidy, I felt much better. Maybe Risera just needs a change of scene."

"Maybe," said Erisel, and she didn't push the issue any further.

But after that, Tilly did notice that Risera wasn't around much. She had to admit that it was something of a weight off her shoulders. Everything about the room was so peaceful now; she really felt like she was able to work, and, even more, to practice her speech, which was complex and needed careful work. But she did feel a little lonely. Sometimes, after both bells, when Tilly was right on the edge of sleep, she would hear the door to the room softly click open, and see, through the darkness, Risera tiptoeing over to her bed. She wondered what would happen if she sat up and tried to chat, ask how Risera was doing, how her project was coming along . . . But she squashed the idea firmly. No, there was no time to gossip late into the night. She needed her sleep to be able to work, you had to be very sure about that or else you got into bad sleep habits, and that would be a *disaster* this close to the end of term. The tests, the presentations, the whole term would be over soon. Then they could have the fun that they'd earned! Tilly made a mental note to remind Granna that they were hoping to see Risera's parents over the holiday.

The week before the presentations were due, when Tilly was working on her costume, her father was finally close enough for them to have a proper face-to-face real-time conversation, their first in ages. He listened all about her project, and said how impressed he was at her work, and what a hard language it was, and how amazingly she'd done. Then he said, *"You're not working too hard, are you?"*

She gave him a puzzled look. "What do you mean?"

"Just . . . it's important to have downtime, you know. You look tired."

"It's been a really busy few weeks, Dad. It'll be over soon. End of term! Then I'll be ready to *party*!" She gave him what she thought was a big smile.

"*Okay . . .*" Iain scratched his cheek. "*As long as you're not overdoing it, Sills. You need to make sure you're doing something other than work. It's good for your brain, more than anything else. It lets you rest, regroup. You tend to get stuck otherwise. Why do you think I go up and down all those hills?*"

Tilly laughed. "I knew there had to be a good reason. Otherwise it was just, you know, *masochism . . .*"

"*Leave your old man alone! But hobbies . . . How's the engineering club coming along? You haven't mentioned it for a while in your messages.*"

Tilly shrugged. "I don't know. I think they're still meeting." She was sure about that. In fact, she'd heard they'd managed to get a few new members. There were more than half a dozen regulars now, with a couple of other semiregulars, meeting once a week to shoot the breeze, share ideas, geek out together. Tilly felt sad, thinking about them meeting without her, but she tried to tell herself that it was great that her idea had taken off. That was the kind of thing she would be able to put on her résumé. Offhandedly, she said, "Oh, I dropped that."

Iain's eyebrows went up. "*Your club? You dropped it? Why, Sills?*"

"It was taking up too much time. I had to focus on this presentation, and then I didn't want to let everyone in the boat club down, and there just aren't enough hours in the day for everything." Her voice, she realized, was getting quite high pitched, so she stopped talking.

Dad was looking at her thoughtfully. "*Okay.*"

There was a pause. Tilly said, in a small voice, "What's the matter?"

"I'm just surprised you dropped your club, that's all. You sounded really happy with it. Did Mom ask you to drop it?"

"No, Daddy! She said I could choose!"

"Really?" He gave her a sharp look.

"Yes, really!"

"Okay," he said. *"Well, you're old enough to make your own decisions."*

But you think it was the wrong one, Tilly thought miserably. They talked on for a little while, about this and that, where the *Dorothy Garrod* was going next, how his latest article was coming along. It was nice just to be able to chat, but, even so, after the call ended, Tilly lay on the bed for a while, hugging her pillow. The worst thing, she thought, was that she agreed with him. She thought she'd made the wrong decision too. She really missed her little club, and her friends there, and try as she might, she knew that sometimes she didn't quite fit in with Risera and her gang. Their priorities were so different. *They're serious people,* Tilly thought. *The kind of person Mom wants me to be . . .*

She groaned. *Oh, I never get it right!* she thought. *And someone is always disappointed.* That this time it was her father only made things worse. She was used to her mother being disappointed and, while it always hurt and always would hurt, she had lots of practice in pretending that she didn't mind. But not with Daddy. Daddy was supposed to be on her side. Daddy was supposed to be her pal. Tilly buried her head in her pillow. Not long now. Everything would be over soon. She'd have her amazing marks. And then the holiday would be here.

She was right about that. The day of the mock summit was rapidly approaching, and the students barely had time to take a breath. The week before the summit was filled with end-of-semester tests, morning and afternoon, and, as a result, Tilly found herself working late into the night to complete her speech and put the final touches to her costume. The night before the event, well past midnight, she sat at her desk threading beads onto the headdress, when she heard Risera, on the other side of the room, stir in her bed and sigh.

"Please, Tilly," she said. "*Please*—put the light out!"

"I'm sorry, Risera, you're going to have to bear with me. I still have so much to do . . ."

"It looks *great*," said Risera. "It looks *more* than great. Honestly, Tilly, you've done so much work. Nobody else in the whole form has done anywhere near as much. Xoha's borrowed a costume, you know. Half the *class* has borrowed a costume!"

A feeling of panic rose up in Tilly's chest, a tight feeling. "Yes, but I've had hardly any time compared to the rest of you! You know what, if *anyone* had thought to *mention* this whole stupid summit to me at *some point* before midterm, I might not be left sewing beads onto a hat the night before a presentation because, let me tell you, Sera, this is *not* the best way to go into a major presentation—"

She was cut off by a muffled howl from Risera. "Oh, I give up! Do what you want!" Risera turned her back, pulled the covers over her head, and left Tilly to get on with things. Tilly tutted. Honestly, who in their right mind had ever thought that *room sharing* was a good idea? Thank goodness she hadn't been here when they'd been in dormitories. It would have driven her *mad*. Having to put up with one person's foibles was bad enough, never mind half a dozen other people. Eventually, Tilly was satisfied with her work and she went to bed, falling asleep the moment her head hit the pillow. In the morning, despite her nerves, she felt oddly fresh. Risera looked tired, though, and she went off to breakfast without her. That was okay. Tilly wanted to sit by herself for a while and read through her notes.

The mock summit took up the whole morning. Each of the twenty students in Tilly's year had a ten-minute slot, and woe betide anyone who overran. That was a ten-mark deduction right there. It was all part of the test, of course, not just whether their presentation skills were up to scratch, but whether they could follow the brief they had been given. Ten minutes, in a different language, introducing the main points about the species that they had chosen. Tilly wasn't worried about timing, to be honest. She had timed and timed herself over and over. The trick was to write the piece as a full script, and then rehearse the script so often that you had it memorized, and you sounded as if you were delivering it unscripted. A lesson learned from watching her mom prepare her speeches, and for once Tilly was glad of the training.

"Anyone who tells you they give their speeches off the cuff is a liar, Sylvia," her mom would say. "Or else they're giving some really terrible speeches. It's about preparation. Even the jokes. It's all about the preparation."

Tilly had taken this lesson to heart. The only thing that she was worried about was that she hadn't had a chance to rehearse wearing the complete costume. The hat just hadn't been ready in time. Looking at it now, she wondered whether it would have been better to choose a cut-down version. She'd found patterns for one, and she was pretty sure that it counted as full dress, but, being her mother's daughter, she had opted to "do things properly." And it was a pretty impressive piece of work, if she said so herself, though cumbersome and not easy to lug from her room to the hall. The rest of the costume had been easy by comparison: a loose-fitting orange robe rather like a caftan. What the Elisurians lacked in couture, they certainly made up for in millinery.

Tilly was late getting to the stage. She knew being late made it more difficult for her, but the audience—the rest of the school—took a short break halfway through the proceedings and came back refreshed and ready for the second session. Tilly was on third after the break. Risera had already done her speech—beautifully, of course—and was chatting to one side with the rest of the gang. Tilly tried to give Risera a thumbs-up, but found it impossible to catch her eye. Then one of the others from the engineering club came over. "Good luck, Tilly," he said, shaking her hand. "I'm sure you're going to be brilliant."

The speaker before Tilly was now halfway through their presentation. Tilly, standing in the wings of the stage, opened her hat box and lifted out her creation.

"Wow," said someone behind her. "Tilly, that's . . . *big*."

"It's completely accurate," said Tilly tartly. She lifted up the hat—gosh, but it was an awful lot heavier than she remembered—and she put it on her head. *Help*, she thought. It really *was* heavier than she remembered. And bigger. She moved toward the full-length mirror. As she moved, the tassels, with their handcrafted beads, began to joggle around. A few of them started to get tangled. "*Shoot*," she muttered as she tried to sort them out. She had tied her hair back for the occasion, but, as ever, a ringlet or two had popped out, and now they were busy getting caught in the tassels. "*Shoot, shoot, shoot!*"

The previous speaker was finishing. Tilly, who had planned to do one last run-through in her head before going out, found herself going on before she had expected. Added to that, the darned hat still wasn't sitting quite right and was turning out to be something of a distraction. Tilly's heart began to race. *Okay*, she thought firmly, *pull yourself together. Focus!* She took a deep breath. One of the tassels bounced against the tip of her nose, making her sneeze.

There was a murmur around the auditorium. Ms. Keith, directing the proceedings, shot a stern look out, and the room fell quiet. She turned to Tilly and gave a smile.

"In your own time, Tilly."

Later, Tilly wasn't quite able to say exactly what happened next. She did wonder, sometimes, whether the material that she'd used to make the tassels might have been something that triggered her allergies. Maybe her nerves had made her dehydrate. Whatever it was, all she knew was that when she started to make her speech, her throat was suddenly very dry and itchy. And, of course, the problem was that she had to sing . . . Those beautiful quadratic equations, the clear and lucid language that she had chosen because she understood it so well . . . at the end of the day, the Elisurians communicated in *song* . . . And someone with a dry throat, plagued by a costume she hadn't quite had time to fit properly, was going to struggle with that . . .

Tilly started out, but she knew at once that she was slightly off-key. *Darn*, she thought, *that doesn't quite mean what I want it to mean* . . . She pressed on. She only had a limited amount of time! She didn't want to lose ten marks for nothing. But she couldn't quite get her voice back in tune . . . *Oh gosh*, she thought, *this sounds dreadful* . . .

Somewhere near one side of the auditorium, someone began to giggle. Tilly stumbled slightly over her lines. Ms. Keith stared out around the room with laser-beam eyes.

But the damage was done. The giggling, down among the juniors, was off now, and spreading like wildfire. Soon enough, the whole room was trying to stifle laughter. Every shift of Tilly's head sent the tassels and the beads joggling, starting someone off again. Tilly, pushing on desperately, saw from the corner of her eye that even one or two of the teachers, sitting near the front, were struggling to keep themselves under control. She gritted her teeth, and got through the speech, and then stumbled offstage. There was rapturous applause behind her; a couple of the braver students managed a few whistles. In the wings, Tilly took off the hated hat, threw it to one side, and ran out of the auditorium. The school buildings were silent, but she didn't want to risk seeing anyone. She ran down to the lake, to the boathouse, where she sat in her team's boat, and she wept.

Tilly stayed outside until well after supper. She didn't feel in the least bit hungry, only sick. Most of all, she didn't want to see anyone. Nobody was sent to find her, which she assumed was intentional: the security at the school was such that any student could be located within seconds, so it could only be that people knew exactly where she was, but they wanted to leave her alone. *Or else they don't want to laugh when they see me*, she thought miserably. At last, though, the sun began to set, and the temperature started to drop. She couldn't stay outside any longer. She slipped back into the main buildings. She wanted some company now, some consolation. She thought that if she could just chat to someone about what had happened, she would start to feel a little better about things, maybe even begin to see the funny side . . . And then she would think about how flat she had sounded, and how people had laughed, and her heart would sink in her chest again. Right now, what Tilly wanted was a friend.

She opened the door to her room carefully, hoping to find Risera there. She didn't really want to go and find her with the others. She couldn't quite face the whole gang, not yet. She was ready to see someone, but not lots of people, all at once. And Risera was always so sensitive to her, so kind about how she was feeling . . . The room was dark. Tilly put on the lights and looked around. Risera wasn't there . . .

No, Tilly realized, it was more than that. None of her belongings were there either. Everything that had been on Risera's side of the room was gone. All her books, her notes, all her little personal bits and pieces—ornaments, pictures of her family, mementos of places visited, silly gifts from friends . . . The bedclothes on the bed were folded back, and Risera's own bright covers and cushions were gone. With a sinking heart, Tilly went over to open Risera's closet. Yes, all her clothes were gone too. Tilly checked her own closet. There was the yellow dress, washed and neatly pressed. One side of the room, Risera's room, had been packed up, emptied, and left bare. Left empty. Tilly's own belongings, all where she had left them, were clustered around her side of the room, and now looked somewhat lost and forlorn. The only sign left of Risera that Tilly could see was on a mug, standing on the shared table, washed up and perfectly clean. On it Risera had scribbled a note: *Thanks for the loan.*

The following morning, Tilly woke up to find that the whole ghastly previous day hadn't been a dream. She'd still made a complete fool of herself, and Risera was still gone. Risera hadn't crept back during the night and unpacked, and she wasn't there for Tilly to hustle out of the door down to the lake. Tilly pulled on her exercise clothes slowly, wondering if she could skip practice, pretend she was ill . . . She didn't really want to see anyone. She wanted to hide away until the end of the semester, and then crawl home to Granna and Quinn. But the race day was coming, and Tilly, who for all her faults was also loyal and brave, wasn't going to let down the team.

When she got to the lake, everyone was ready for her, and watching her carefully. "Okay," she said. "Let's get to work."

And work they did. She put the whole team through their paces, and they finished their practice with one of their best times yet. "Great work!" Tilly called out as they pulled back to shore. She had to stop for a few minutes to talk to one of the team about their stroke, but she was conscious of Risera, heading off back toward the main buildings. When she was done with her teammate, Tilly chased after Risera.

"Hey," she said, catching up to her.

Risera turned and gave Tilly a polite but distant smile. "Hey," she said.

"Great time this morning," Tilly said.

"Yes," said Risera.

They walked on, in silence. As they entered the building, Tilly burst out, "What's going on, Sera? All your stuff— gone!"

Risera stopped. Other students were passing by, on their way to breakfast, looking at them curiously. Tilly was something of a celebrity now.

"Look, Tilly," said Risera, keeping her voice low, "I don't want a scene."

"I really needed to talk to you last night! It was all so awful. I really needed to talk to someone. Talk to *you*!"

"I'm sorry you were alone last night," Risera said. "Look, Tilly, this is done. I don't want to talk about it—"

"Well, darn it, but *I* want to talk about it! You can't just move out like that!"

"Yes, I can," said Risera firmly.

"But what about *me*?"

"Look, Tilly," Risera said, her voice low but fierce. "You wanted the room, and you've got the room. Aren't you happy now?"

That stung. In fact, that *really* hurt. "Well, at least I don't have to listen to you snoring now!" she shot back.

She regretted it immediately. Risera shook her head and walked off, leaving Tilly behind.

Tilly realized that Ms. Keith was standing nearby. "A word, please, Tilly," she said, gesturing to her to follow. They found a quiet corner, away from the rush of students heading to and from the breakfast room. Ms. Keith looked at her steadily. "Bad day yesterday, wasn't it?"

Tilly, unable to speak, simply nodded.

"I know it feels awful," said Keithy, "but now you have to try to put it all behind you. Focus on the positive."

"*What* positive?" said Tilly in a choking voice.

"The work you did for your presentation—the research, the preparation—it was outstanding."

"But it all went *wrong*!" Tilly wailed.

"Yes, it did, didn't it?" said Ms. Keith solidly. "It was really bad luck. Not what you deserved at all."

"It was just *bad* . . ."

Ms. Keith shook her head. "No, it wasn't, and I won't have you telling yourself that. You were maybe too ambitious—but even then, you got more done in a few weeks than most students get done in their whole time here. Failure, mistakes, things not going to plan—that's what we learn from, Tilly."

But Tilly wasn't really in the mood for a sermon, or a teachable moment. She said, "Yes, Ms. Keith . . . Of course, Ms. Keith . . ." And then she ran back to her room to count down the days until the holiday.

There was only one more ordeal to get through: the school's meet day. The races started on the lake first thing. There was a festival mood down by the lake, but Tilly wasn't feeling it. Besides, this was serious business. This was her last chance to shine. She gathered her team around her and gave them her best pep talk. "We're great," she said. "We've worked so hard, and so well, and we deserve to win this. We're going to win it. Pull together, listen for the beat, and let's go and win."

They all hugged one another, and then got into the boat. The red and yellow banners fluttered gaily. They lined up alongside the other crews, and Tilly picked up the sticks. All of her crew were looking at her. She realized that they trusted her, believed in her. Even Risera looked at her with confidence. Then the whistle blew, and they were off.

She remembered very little of the race afterward, and she played it over and over again in her head for days. She knew, most of all, that she could not have asked anything more from her crew. They were on their very best form, stroking together the best they had ever done, responsive to her instructions, right on the beat. Still, it wasn't long before the seniors team, the purples-and-greens, began to inch ahead. Tilly gritted her teeth. *I'm not having this*, she thought. *I'm not losing everything!*

Her team responded to her new ferocity. They dug deep, deeper than ever before, and began to give chase. The fire was in them now. They wanted to show what they were made of. On and on they pushed, and they gained ground. The question now was—had they done enough to overtake? Ever so slightly, Tilly started to push the pace. Her crew went for it, went all for it . . . But it wasn't quite enough. The purples-and-greens were over the line, but only a nose ahead of Tilly's team.

The seniors were ecstatic, but, if anything, Tilly's team overtook them for sheer delight. Nobody had thought they would perform so well—nobody had been expecting a medal, never mind so close to the gold, not with senior teams out there. One by one, Tilly's crew came up to hug and kiss her, and hug and kiss one another, and hug and kiss their supporters, and then hug and kiss any passing person. Even Risera came over to give Tilly a hug. "See," she said. "I knew you'd be great at this, Tilly. I knew you'd be great."

But Tilly couldn't feel the same delight. Sure, it was their best time of the year, but it was . . . *second*. Who remembers second?

Risera was already heading off to see Semett, who had gotten through to the finals of the eight hundred meters, to see her race and to tell her the good news about her own success. Tilly thought for a moment about asking whether she could tag along, but she didn't want to be refused, so she let Risera go. The rest of the team were already heading off too, going to cheer on friends who now had their own races. Tilly wandered around for a while, watching the races and the competitions. She stayed to receive her silver medal with the team, and then she went back inside. It was very quiet, and she had nothing to do. With all the tests done, and the presentation over, Tilly was beginning to wonder how she was going to fill her time.

That evening, Tilly sat by herself in her half-empty room. She kept running the race over in her mind, wondering whether there was a moment when she could have pushed harder, or worked out the other team's tactics sooner, or been a little smarter on the beat . . . but she couldn't see anything. The simple fact was—they were second best. And that wasn't good enough. Not good enough for Tilly, and certainly not good enough for Mom. Miserably, Tilly thought about what her end-of-term grades would look like. She had been so sure that she would get the top mark for the summit. No chance of that. And sure, too, that there would be a storybook ending for the race, an amazing victory for the juniors, racing against their seniors. But no. Second place. So what?

The room was getting dark, but Tilly didn't put on a light. She listened to happy voices outside, other students coming back from supper, still enjoying the stories of the day. At least some people had their storybook ending. But not Tilly. In fact, now that she thought about it, there hadn't been a storybook ending for her whole term here, had there? When she'd arrived, and met Risera, she'd been so happy and excited. A ready-made friend, a roommate, someone to share jokes and happiness and sadness with. A pal, at last. And now, sitting alone, Tilly was realizing that she'd blown it. She'd been her usual self—bossy, and rigid, and insensitive, and she'd pushed Risera away. There'd been no more mention about Risera and her family coming to France, and Tilly had heard on the grapevine that they would be spending most of their time on Earth in and around Mexico City. She knew that other people had invitations to visit throughout the holiday—and she had nothing. It would be just her, and Granna, and Quinn, the same as ever . . . Tilly wasn't sure she could face the holiday, never mind another term, starting over again, trying to make friends . . . The simple truth was: she didn't fit in here.

So what are you going to do about it, Tilly?

What can I do? I'm stuck, aren't I?

And that thought nearly made her despair.

But Tilly had a core of resilience, deep within her. Tilly could never quite be quashed. Something about her always bounced back. Suddenly, she sat up. "That's it," she said to the walls. "I've *had* it."

And in the peace and quiet of her now sole-occupancy room, Tilly hatched a plan.

Part Two
Winter

5

The end of term at the academy on Talaris IV was a very relaxed time. Formal classes were over, and all the major tests, presentations, and sports events were out of the way too. Students suddenly found that they had a great deal of free time on their hands, and, better than that, the day had become more or less unstructured. Of course, most of this was spent preparing for their journeys home, packing up clothes, clearing up rooms that had become chaotic during the weeks before end of term, but there was some time as well to hang out with friends, chat and gossip, share plans for the holiday, or maybe just to find a quiet corner and read. A handful of students left almost immediately, particularly those with long journeys back home, but most of the student body had at least a day or two to kick back and relax and enjoy being with each other without the pressure of work.

The teachers enjoyed this period too. It was good to see the pressure on their students relieved after so much stress and anxiety, and, of course, they were all looking forward to their own time away. They were still very much on duty, aware as ever that among their charges were students with very high-profile parents. Security around the academy didn't slacken for even a second. Students were still obliged to turn up for their attendance twice a day, and entrance and exit to the grounds was as strictly policed as ever. Still, if anybody *was* going to attempt to take one of the students, this would surely be the ideal time, with people leaving every day, and formal activities at their minimum, and a general air of everything winding down for the holiday. Change was in the wind. People were coming and going.

Despite all this relative chaos, nothing got past Ms. Keith, who was the first to realize that Tilly was no longer among them. She was hampered somewhat by the slow-moving mornings, with students slipping into breakfast late, and making their way to their first attendance at a leisurely pace, and without a particular sense of urgency. When Keith's class finally managed to assemble itself in her room, she counted off fifteen of them, eyeing them with her usual mixture of fondness and exasperation, and started ticking off names against her list. Four had already gone home from her class of twenty, so she no longer had to worry about them. But that meant that someone was missing. She counted the room again—yes, fifteen—and ticked the names off again, more slowly. She cross-referenced the names of the students who had gone home against the office records of those who had been signed out officially by parents or designated guardians. Then she went through the whole process for a third time. When she was done, she was in no doubt that she had a student missing, and no doubt which one.

Around the room, the other students were talking and laughing, and hadn't even noticed that Keithy hadn't yet started talking to them. This was all just a formality, really, and soon she would send them off to enjoy the day. They would have been shocked to know that Ms. Keith—unflappable, omniscient, and occasionally crushingly sarcastic Ms. Keith—was in fact starting to get worried. Quickly, Keith checked on Tilly's whereabouts via her tracking device. She breathed a sigh of relief. Her missing student was, apparently, down at the lake. But that was itself a puzzle, since Risera, who was on the same team, was sitting right here, next to Semett.

"Risera," Keith said, "did you have training this morning?"

Risera shook her head. "No, Ms. Keith. We haven't been down to the lake since the meet."

"Champions!" someone called from the back of the room. "Almost-champions!"

There was general laughter and good humor around the whole room. Risera clasped her hands over her head. More cheers. Ms. Keith gave a rather forced smile. "Okay," she said, "all done. Go and be happy somewhere else."

She pondered holding Risera back for a moment on her way out, to ask whether she had seen Tilly that morning, but rapidly dismissed the idea. There had obviously been a rift there (top of the list for Keith's agenda for the following term was to steer Tilly back to her friends at the engineering club and to find the girl a more compatible roommate). But more than that, Keith didn't want a whisper of her alarm to get anywhere near the students. Chances were Tilly was sitting somewhere by herself, feeling bad about the previous day, and Keith would have a little chat with her, offer some tea and sympathy, while also reminding her gently and firmly that attendance was compulsory for very good reasons.

The students poured out of the room to enjoy their holiday. Once the room was empty, Keith closed the door and sent a message to Stavath. *Sylvia Tilly has missed attendance*, she said. *I'm going to look for her down by the lake. Could you please send somebody to check her room?* Keith nodded. Yes, probably someone would put their head around Tilly's door, and find her in bed with the covers over her head, feeling miserable. Nonetheless, she hurried out of the school and down toward the lake. There were one or two students down there, students who were of competitive standard in their sports and had special permission to be out on the water all morning. A quick chat with a few of these established that none of them had seen Tilly. Keith checked the tracking data again. This now said that Tilly was in her classroom waiting for attendance. Convenient. And deeply worrying. She sent another message to Stavath. *I think we have a problem. I think Tilly has gone.*

Ten minutes later, Keith, Stavath, a couple of other teachers, and the academy's security officer were gathered in the head's office. Tilly was not in her room, security had confirmed, and the other teachers also confirmed that none of Tilly's immediate group had seen her that morning. Stavath immediately reported the absence to the local police. The teachers were off to corral students back inside—without alarming them—and the security officer went off to start assembling footage and information for the police when they arrived. There was a tricky balance here: they didn't want to scare the students, but they had to take the threat of kidnap seriously, particularly given Tilly's mother.

"We also need to contact her mother and grandmother," said Stavath.

"I'll do that," said Keith with a sigh. It wasn't that she was eager to speak to Tilly's mother, far from it, but she knew that she could handle her. Stavath nodded permission (that would leave her free to deal with the police), and Keith hurried off to her office to put in the call. The thought of a kidnapping was simply too much to bear, but Tilly was probably one of their most high-profile students. It was the staff's constant nightmare that one of the students would be taken. *Oh Tilly,* Keith thought fearfully, *wherever you are—I hope you're okay.*

Several hours earlier . . .

It wasn't easy, Tilly thought, to travel anonymously with hair like hers. Stupid curls. Stupid bright red curls. That night in her room, when she had planned out this adventure, she had seriously thought about cutting off the lot. She even sat before the mirror with a pair of scissors, but something had stopped her. As much as they frustrated her, got in her way, they seemed . . . *core* somehow. If they went, something important about Tilly would have gone. It was funny to put it this way, but she felt that she would have been *tamed*.

There was a practical reason not to cut it off too: she had by that point already prepared her fake ID, and the curls were all over the picture on that. A different hairstyle would draw attention to her. All the same, *pretty* distinctive, and Tilly was in no doubt that as soon as people were aware she had gone, they would be looking *everywhere* . . . "Missing girl! Bright red curls!" Hard to miss. But you had to make the best of things. She tied up her hair, found a cap, and tucked her curls under that. So far, nobody had said anything.

Altogether, Tilly had been surprised at how straightforward her escape had been so far. She had hacked her tracking device so that she couldn't be found, creating an alias identity that not only placed her safely within the school grounds, but was even able to move around from place to place on a preplanned itinerary. It was actually a very neat piece of programming, and under other circumstances with a project like this, she would have shown it to her teachers and negotiated extra credit. This project—not so much. The proof of its success would be exactly how far she would get before someone stopped her. Her goal was . . .

The truth was, Tilly hadn't really given much thought as to her goal in all this. Once she had made the decision to leave, to get away from all the mistakes and the unhappiness and the sense of being trapped, she had set about the whole business with her usual intense focus. Hack tracking device—check. Create fake ID—check. Choose a ship to take her offworld—check. Disguise—check. Then get on with it. Later—not much later, in fact—Tilly would come to understand that it didn't matter how well you carried out a task if the basic premise was extremely flawed. But right now—well, she was sailing on her success.

With her tracker cheerfully reporting her false whereabouts, Tilly had found it relatively easy to slip out of the school grounds. Her exit, under darkness, set off no alarms. As far as all the security devices were concerned, she was tucked up safely in bed sleeping. Instead, she was biking under cover of darkness down the long road that led to the spaceport.

At the spaceport, there was a short wait until the ship she had chosen was ready for passengers to board. This brief period of hanging around the spaceport was the part that Tilly was most worried about. Sooner or later, when she didn't appear for breakfast, or for class attendance, someone would go and check on her. Maybe they'd assume she was still in bed, sick, perhaps, down with a cold, or being lazy on what was, in effect, a holiday. But they wouldn't find her in her room. They'd check the tracker, which would show her down by the lake. She'd picked that as the farthest plausible point that she might be away from the main buildings, so there would be a little time wasted while someone went down there to look for her. Her hope was that she could keep them running around the school for a while, as long as it took for her to board the ship and get offworld. She needed a window of time before they realized she was gone and the alerts went out. Someone like Tilly, with her mother . . . Kidnap was a real threat. If Tilly thought about how much anxiety her absence would cause, she did not figure it into her plans. Perhaps, at the back of her mind, she thought: *This will show them how much I matter.*

At the spaceport, she got herself a cheap coffee and sat in a quiet corner. Her plan was to look like a surly teenager. A surly teenager, traveling to meet her father. Yeah, she's a Federation citizen. No, it's not a Federation world. Is that an *issue*? Why are you *hassling* me? That was the sum of Tilly's plan and, in fact, it was a pretty good one. Nobody at the spaceport at Talaris IV wanted to be troubled with a surly teenager, sulking under the brim of an oversized cap. Nobody, absolutely *nobody*, wanted to talk to a surly teenager for longer than they had to.

At last, boarding was called for her ship. The *Constance Markievicz* was a cargo ship that had been doing a standard route around three dozen or so small worlds, some within the Federation, some just outside. Mostly it carried goods and supplies, but there were always a few spaces available for passengers so that the ship could earn a little more. The next planet along from Talaris IV was Oyseen. This was where Tilly intended to get off. She'd heard her dad mention the planet once, from one of his trips, and that seemed to be as good a reason as any. Also, she didn't want to risk staying in one location, or on board one ship, for too long. Best to keep moving. Oyseen was a busy, nonallied world, and Tilly figured she could lose herself there pretty quickly. And that, above all else, was what Tilly wanted. She wanted to lose herself, shake herself off, because the truth was she didn't like the person that she was all that much, and she didn't like where she had ended up, and she couldn't face any of what was coming next. She couldn't face another conversation with her mother about her failings. She couldn't face not hearing from her dad for weeks at a time. She couldn't face Granna and Quinn being kind anymore. And most of all, she couldn't go back to school. She had failed there, completely failed, at all her ambitions, and most of all, her chance for friendship. It was time to start over.

The line shuffled forward. Tilly clutched her bag in one hand and her fake ID in the other. When she got to the front of the line, the official there checked her ID, rather peremptorily, and waved her through. No questions. Nothing. Tilly hadn't expected that. She walked past the barrier and along the corridor that led to the docking bay. As she hurried along, she felt light, as if the weight of years were being lifted. This was all proving so easy! She should have done this *years* ago.

Adèle Quinn started the morning as she always did, with coffee and croissants, some fresh fruit, and a daily news digest, which she plowed through with grim concentration and scant regard for her blood pressure. "One has a moral obligation to be well informed," she liked to say. "Besides, I like to know what my daughter will be doing next." Across the table from her, Quinn was polishing off eggs and bacon with equally scant regard for his cholesterol levels. "If I've got the gene, I've got the gene," he liked to say. "In the meantime—nobody's getting their paws on my breakfast."

It was a quiet time, with little in the way of conversation, but with plenty in the way of companionship. Tilly had fit nicely into these breakfasts, being happy to chat and read and sit peacefully (although Adèle had to admit that it had been pleasant in recent months not to have to hurry her out to school each morning). Soon Tilly would be home for the holiday, and that in itself would be a great pleasure. Everyone would be able to relax and enjoy one another's company. Adèle had not been sure about this school, when Siobhan first suggested it, but, yes, she would admit that being without responsibility even for such a sensible girl had been pleasant. As long as Tilly was happy, that was the main thing. Adèle wasn't yet convinced about that. Tilly, in their last few conversations, had been bright and peppy, but Adèle had not failed to notice that certain names had fallen out of her conversation. Risera, that nice girl with the beautiful accent whom she had met on the first day. Xoha, who had been another regular character. Tilly, Adèle thought, seemed not to mention them as much as she had done earlier in the year. Adèle was surprised, too, that Tilly had not asked whether a friend could visit over the vacation. She'd signaled, without explicitly saying, that the house in France was open to anyone whom Tilly would like to invite. But Tilly had always sidestepped the offer. Adèle picked up her cup. Perhaps these were all minor issues. Perhaps Tilly had simply been too busy with tests and all the rest for socializing. Perhaps a visit from a friend would be brought up now that she had more time on her hands, and they could look forward to some cheerful company over the holiday.

Adèle's quiet morning was, however, about to be disturbed. As she sipped her coffee, the comms channel chimed gently. As a rule, Adèle didn't take calls before ten o'clock, so at first she ignored it. But the chime persisted.

"I'll get that if you like," said Quinn obligingly. Disturbing her morning routine could put Adèle in a mood for the rest of the day, and nobody benefited from that, Quinn least of all.

"No, no, finish your poison," Adèle said. She stood up and went over to the desk. When she read the message, she almost fell to the floor with the shock. *Oh, dearest heaven*, she thought. *Our worst nightmare . . . Everything we have always feared might happen to one of my dearest girls. Happening now.* Slowly, she went back to the breakfast table, where she sat down heavily.

Quinn took one look at her face, and immediately

jumped up and came over to her. "Adèle, love," he said. "Who was that? What's the matter?"

"It was the school," she said. "Sylvia's gone."

"Gone?"

"She's not at the school. They can't find her . . ." Adèle looked up at him, tears in her eyes. "Quinn, they don't know whether or not she's been taken . . ."

Quinn swore fiercely under his breath. "All right, love," he said. "You stay there. I'll get us passage booked out to Talaris." He went over to the comm. "What's the school doing? Has anyone managed to reach Siobhan yet?"

"The school is trying to reach her," Adèle said. "They said that the local police have already contacted her security team . . ." There was Siobhan's safety to think of too, of course, and Tilly's stepsister. If one daughter had been taken, the other might also be at risk.

"All right," Quinn said, busy organizing the journey. "Iain. Someone needs to contact Iain." He glanced at his wife. "I'll do that next."

"Bless you, Gabriel Quinn," said Adèle. "I don't know what I'd do without you."

He came back over to kiss her gently on the head. "Go and pack," he said. "We'll find our girl, I know we will."

Less than half an hour later they were on their way to the spaceport. Nobody had yet been able to reach Siobhan, who had been in closed session since early that morning, but Tilly's sister was safe and secure, although, by all accounts, she was also fairly distressed and very frightened for her stepsister. Her father was on his way to be with her. Adèle gratefully struck that worry off her list. Quinn, too, had been trying every five minutes to reach Siobhan. He'd also sent a message to the *Dorothy Garrod* to ask Iain to contact them as soon as the ship was in range. The school had been sending them regular updates, although there wasn't much to tell them other than that the local police were throwing resources at the problem and that the Federation's own security people were helping. A small team was already on its way out to Talaris. A threat to one of the Security Council—if this was what it was—was a threat to Federation security itself.

"*Merde*," muttered Quinn. "What a mess."

Adèle took his hand. "I suppose," she said, "we always thought this might happen. It's good to know how quickly everyone has responded . . ."

"I suppose," said Quinn.

The comm inside the groundcar chimed. The Federation logo appeared on screen.

"Oh dear," murmured Adèle, steeling herself for what was coming.

"Be brave, my love," said Quinn, taking her hand.

Siobhan appeared on screen. Her face was pale and frightened, and her eyes brimmed with tears. "Maman . . ." she said, and began to cry.

"Oh, Siobhan, my darling," said Adèle, her heart going out to her girl, and filling with the desire to make everything better for her. "We'll find her, *chérie*. I promise we'll find her."

The *Con Markievicz*, as Tilly quickly realized, was very different from anything she had ever traveled on before. Tilly was the child of a high-ranking Federation official and, as a result, had from a very early age been used to comfortable and spacious quarters—to suites, rather than rooms. A bedroom for her, a bedroom for her mother, one for her stepsister, if she was with them, and a communal space. Maybe even a separate little office for Mom. Even on the smallest ships, or at the smallest embassy premises, there had always been a certain amount of luxury. And now Tilly was learning how the other half lived.

The ship was elderly, and a little rough around the edges. It was also functional and undecorated. Federation ships weren't exactly rococo, but there was always that understated comfort. A few cushions here and there. Plenty of fresh flowers or plants—oh yes, plenty of that. But there was something else too, a fundamental difference that was bringing home to Tilly what space travel was all about. Federation ships cocooned you from the void. You could, if you wanted, spend your whole journey ignoring the fact that you were traveling between stars and star systems. All the edges were smoothed away. But with this ship? Tilly knew she wouldn't forget that she was on board something that had been built to lumber through space. Something constructed, assembled, and scrupulously maintained. For another kind of person, this might have been deeply unnerving. But Tilly, walking along the corridor in search of her cabin, found the cargo ship's interior oddly soothing. She realized that she liked being able to see the workings of things. Tilly liked to see how things functioned. It made her think that if anything *did* go wrong, she'd be in a position to fix it. Okay, so the ship didn't *smell* so great—a combination of fuel, old thermids, some unusual food smells, and not to mention good old-fashioned multispecies sweat—but the funny thing was that none of this was triggering her allergies. Another big difference, and a pleasant one at that. Tilly had lost count of the number of times she'd arrived with her mother in some palatial cabin or suite of rooms and had to go around moving the vases of flowers as her eyes streamed and her nose itched. No chance of that here! Nobody got an asthma attack from good old-fashioned sweat and lubricant.

At last Tilly found her cabin, tucked away down a small corridor just off a small rec and mess area. The cabin was

a tiny berth that was, she realized, intended to accommo-
date four people. There were two stacks of two beds, one
on each side of the room, and not much space in between.
You couldn't have all four people in the room and not have
two of them on their beds, and even two people standing at
once would be a tight squeeze. The individual berths had
heavy covers so that once you were in bed, you could seal
yourself in for some privacy.

Tilly looked around nervously. One of the berths was
already occupied, but the heavy cover was sealed up, and
she couldn't see her traveling companion. The other three
berths were empty. Tilly checked which one was hers—on
the other side, fortunately, and at the bottom. She sat down
on the bed. It wasn't too bad. Not for a couple of days,
which was how long she would be in here before the ship
arrived at Oyseen. Okay, the room was small, and the walls
were grubbier than Tilly would have liked, but you couldn't
have everything, and the bedclothes were perfectly clean.
She gave the bed a little bounce. It creaked.

Across the tiny room, her traveling companion stirred
in their berth. Tilly held her breath, waiting for whoever to
emerge, not looking forward to having to make conversation, which would involve telling lies. To her relief, whoever
turned over in the bed, and then settled down again. After a
moment or two came snoring.

Tilly rolled her eyes. Snoring! She couldn't believe it!
She stood up, in the middle of the room, her arms akimbo,
glaring at the occupied cabin. Should she give them a
nudge? Honestly, she just couldn't catch a break! She'd
come all this way, literally *hacked* her way out of school,
only to be stuck with yet another noisy roommate! She
glared at the cover of the berth, willing them to *shut up* . . .
Eventually, she sighed and gave up. It probably wasn't a
good idea to disturb them. You didn't know how people

would react, and she wasn't keen on drawing attention to herself. With a huff, she restricted herself to moving her berth-mate's bag and clothes closer to their side. She put her own bag on the bunk above her own berth and pulled the heavy cover over, sealing herself away.

She sighed and lay back. The bed was slightly harder than she liked, and there was only one pillow. She struggled to relax. Her mind was racing, going over all she had done that day, all the rules she had broken, all the crimes she had committed. Tilly knew she was still running on adrenaline, and that she ought to try to sleep, but at the same time part of her couldn't rest because she was sure this was as far as she was going to get. She was sure that someone would arrive before the ship even had a chance to leave, drag her back to school for the telling-off of a lifetime. She lay awake, waiting for the knock at the door.

And then she realized she had dozed off. What had woken her again was the gentle shuddering of engines powering up, and then the ship moved off. *I've done it!* she thought in delight. *I've gotten away!* She closed her eyes. Even then, knowing that she really had escaped Talaris, it took Tilly a while to get to sleep. The snoring from the other side of the room stopped at last, but then Tilly began to hear a drip in the ventilation. On and on it went, *drip, drip, drip* . . . Eventually, she did fall asleep, but she dreamed of drums, and of coming in last in an important race, weighed down by a huge hat with tassels.

By the time the *Con Markievicz* left the Talaris system, the various security teams assigned to Tilly's case were starting to get a clearer idea of what had happened that night. They were beginning to come to the conclusion that what they were dealing with was not a kidnapping, but a runaway. The first clue had been the complete lack of any evidence that a transporter had been used to spirit Tilly away. While this didn't preclude the use of some new kind of shielding, it did turn the investigation toward looking at how someone might leave the grounds in a more traditional manner. This closer-grained examination of the grounds revealed, of all things, the missing bicycle, and this in turn prompted yet another review of all the security footage not just from the school grounds but from farther afield. Up to a distance of half a kilometer, the footage showed nothing of interest. But when the range was extended? Suddenly, a figure on a bicycle popped up as if from nowhere, a dark shape pedaling along at great speed, clearly keen to get away. Someone, it seemed, had tampered with the sensors, to show old footage on a loop for a little while, perhaps to allow a getaway.

"Could Tilly do that?" said Stavath, quietly, to Keith.

"I wouldn't put it past her if she decided to," said Keith. She was tentatively starting to feel relieved, although at the same time she was getting ready to give Tilly the dressing-down of a lifetime. Behind the relief and the fury, there was another worry: that the longer Tilly remained on the loose (since that was what it seemed was going on), the more of a chance there was that she might run into some trouble she might not be able to handle. More chance that her identity might be inadvertently revealed to someone who might realize her worth and take a chance at capitalizing on it. While Tilly remained on Talaris, all would be well. But what if she decided to go offworld? What if she left Federation space? Keith knew that this, at least, was not something she had to deal with. Their chief worry was to make sure that the students still at the school, who were now aware that something odd was happening, didn't become alarmed. Parents, and others, were arriving to take students home for the holidays, and the staff were swamped meeting each one in turn, explaining that it seemed that a student had left without permission, and trying to alleviate fears and worries about security at the school. Had Tilly thought about any of this? Keith wondered. Had she considered how many people might be affected? She suspected not. Tilly, set on a goal, became narrowly, and this time catastrophically, focused.

A couple of technically savvy people from the local police were assigned to work out exactly how Tilly had managed to leave the grounds without raising any alarms, and how she'd hacked the security sensors. In the meantime, attention shifted toward trying to work out where she might be heading. A team from Federation Security had arrived now, experienced officers who moved quickly to identify destinations that Tilly might have reached in the time available. Officers were activated in the major towns around Talaris, in case Tilly had taken local ships out. And, of course, with the spaceport nearby, there was always the possibility that Tilly was trying to head farther afield. A quick scan of the spaceport revealed that she was not there, but meanwhile officers had identified three ships on which she might have traveled. Two of these were heading back into Federation space, and it was therefore relatively easy to place officers at the relevant spaceports to wait for the arrival of these ships and see who disembarked. The other ship was heading out to Oyseen, which, being a non-Federation world, meant that some negotiation with local officials was necessary, but, since it was always sensible to keep on good terms with a big and powerful neighbor, this was easily achieved. But when the *Con Markievicz* arrived at Oyseen, nobody matching Tilly's description disembarked.

Other leads were drying up. Tilly hadn't arrived at the two Federation worlds either, and these ships, Federation registered, had quickly checked their manifests for anyone matching Tilly's description, and come up with nothing. There were no sightings in any of the major travel hubs around Talaris. The Federation team went back to the officials on Oyseen and asked them to check again on the passengers who had left the *Con Markievicz*. There was some delay when a local official took slight offense at the implication that they hadn't done their job properly, by which time the ship had departed without anyone being able to check who was still on board. They'd sent a message straightaway to the ship, but it didn't seem to have gotten through, and it was briefly out of contact.

It was heading toward the third day since Tilly had left the school. Everyone involved in tracking her was now certain that this was a runaway rather than a kidnapping, particularly once the technical teams were able to show how they thought she had gotten past the security systems. The best guess was that she had boarded the *Con Markievicz*, but after that, uncertainty set in—had she left the ship on Oyseen and been missed? Or had she carried on, heading farther out of Federation space, and Federation protection?

Meanwhile, Adèle and Quinn were drawing closer to Talaris. Stavath and her staff consoled troubled students and tried to calculate the damage done to their school's reputation. Siobhan, stuck on Earth, unable to take action, found herself each night in a state of sleepless terror about her younger child, imagining horrors. And the captain of the *Dorothy Garrod* received a message for one of her hitherto least-conspicuous lieutenants and had the unhappy task of calling him into her office for a quiet word.

Tilly woke feeling hungry and wondering where she could get breakfast. She imagined there would be some food slots somewhere. Hadn't she passed through a little mess room while she was looking for her cabin? It would be easy enough to find. She stretched out first, luxuriating in what she thought of as her first morning of freedom. She smiled to herself. Things weren't so bad. She decided she would explore the ship and find out something about it, before it arrived at Oyseen and she disembarked, ready for the next stage of her adventure. *You're doing okay, Tilly*, she said to herself. *In fact, you're doing just fine. You can do it. You can make it*.

She listened for movement but heard nothing. Certainly there was no snoring! She opened the cover on her berth slightly, just enough to be able to peep out and look around the room. There was nobody there. Good! She could get up and dressed in private. She maneuvered herself out of the berth and into the narrow space between the bunks. Then she frowned. That was odd. The other berth was opened up, and her companion, whoever it was, had taken their bag and clothes. The bed had been cleared, the covers folded, and the pillow placed on top. Huh. Why would someone do that?

"That's a personal best for driving away a roommate," Tilly said somewhat bitterly. Well, never mind. It would be much better to have the cabin to herself for the next couple of days. No chance of being drawn into tricky conversations, of having to keep track of the story she was telling. She could just lie low, get on with her journey, and plan what she was going to do once she arrived on Oyseen . . . Tilly stretched again and reached up to the top berth for her bag.

It wasn't there.

"Huh," said Tilly. She stood on her tiptoes, to make sure, but the bag definitely wasn't there. Puzzled, she looked around the room. She thought, guiltily, about how she had moved her companion's bag and clothes last night. Maybe this was their revenge. But where would they put it? There was absolutely no space in here. No closets, no cupboards, just four berths. Four *empty* berths. Her bag wasn't on any of them. Tilly felt the first sick wave of panic.

"Okay," she said. "Check everywhere first."

She did that, and she did it again, and she did it a third time, for luck. That took her no more than a few minutes, because the cabin was so darned small. You could stand in the middle and see the whole space, and when she did that, it was clear that her bag was nowhere to be seen. Her bag, which contained her ID, her spare money, her clothes and possessions—it was definitely gone.

Tilly sat down on her berth with a bump. "I *really* don't have luck with roommates," she said, putting her head into her hands. She felt panic rise up in her chest and she stopped herself firmly. "Okay," she said. "Constructive thoughts. What can you do about this?"

Not much, was her rapid conclusion. She couldn't identify the other person, of course—she hadn't seen them. Only heard them, and she doubted she could identify someone by their snores. But maybe there was some record of them, some way that she could find out who this was, who had been assigned to share this cabin with her. Hanging on the wall was a small comms and data slate. Tilly lifted it off its stand, switched it on, and sat down on the bed again. She found the ship's manifest. She checked the passenger list and found that she was the only person booked into the berth. Her heart sank. The obviousness of the scam was becoming clear to her. Board a ship. Check for single-occupancy cabins. Conceal yourself in one of the berths there. Wait until the other passenger is fast asleep. And then help yourself to anything left around by a stupid, trusting, and *cosseted* teenager who really should have known better but thus far in her life had only traveled on supersafe Federation ships that catered to her every whim . . . Yep, Tilly thought. She had been well and truly screwed, and frankly she deserved it.

She bit her lip and wondered what to do next. That bag had contained everything . . . Without her ID, she would not be able to disembark quietly at Oyseen as she had planned. There'd be questions, and investigations, and Tilly didn't flatter herself that the fake ID she had knocked together would hold up to proper scrutiny. And trying to get fake ID was the quickest way to reveal her real identity. And then . . . ? Suddenly, some of the enormity of what she had done struck Tilly. She checked the chronometer on the slate. More than twenty hours had passed since she had left the school. Her disappearance must surely have been noticed by now. Breakfast would be over and first attendance would have been taken. Ms. Keith would go on the warpath, and *nothing* got past Ms. Keith. There would be a massive security alert, possibly even fears that she had been kidnapped . . . Tilly knew the drill. There'd be a media blackout, but everything would be moving behind the scenes. Mother would know. Granna and Quinn would know. Perhaps even Daddy would know . . . What could they be thinking?

As she sat alone in her cabin, her thoughts turning to her family, Tilly's nerve seriously wavered. This, she thought, was getting much more complicated than she had planned. The idea had been to take control, take charge of her own life for once, get away from all the stress and the pressure and the unhappiness and try to be alone. But now? Everything was spiraling out of control. *What should I do?* she thought, her fingers twisting around anxiously. *What's the best thing to do?* She knew, in her heart, what the responsible thing was. People would be terrified that she was in trouble. What Tilly ought to do was approach the crew of the ship, explain who she was and what was going on, and ask them for help. Ask them to send a message back to Talaris to let them know where she was and that she was safe, and then to send a message ahead to the Federation consulate on Oyseen and ask someone to meet her there when the ship arrived. That was the best thing to do, the sensible thing to do.

But . . . she knew she wasn't going to do it. She couldn't. Not because she couldn't face the uproar, and the arguments, and the telling-off that would happen (which, in her heart, she knew was more than deserved). She wasn't going to ask for help because she wasn't prepared to admit that she had failed. She couldn't bear to think of having to tell this story. Having to tell everyone how she had boarded a freighter and had her bag stolen within, well, *minutes*. She knew what would happen next. Once the shock was over, once everyone had had their say and told her exactly what they thought of her, the whole story would become a family joke. Silly Sylvia, ran away from home and had to call her mom the very next day to get help. She would become a laughingstock. Even Granna, even Quinn—once they had gotten over their upset—would find the funny side of the story.

Tilly hugged herself. "I'm not having it," she whispered to herself. "I'm not going back just for people to laugh at me. I'm going to find a way through this, and I'm going to come home on my terms—or not at all."

And that was that—decision made.

In many ways, it was the path of least resistance. All she had to do was stay put. So she did. She stayed in the cabin. She hacked into the manifest and marked her cabin as out of commission. She lay on her berth with the data slate and found some word games and played them ferociously, competitively. She tracked the ship's route obsessively, counting down the hours until its arrival at Oyseen. The whole time the ship was docked, she hid inside her berth, the door of the cabin locked and the lights down. She lay there with only the light from the slate for company. And she listened to the drip from the ventilation system.

Drip, drip, drip . . . Drip, drip, drip.

6

The *Con Markievicz* had traveled the same route around three dozen worlds across two dozen systems for the best part of thirty years, and Salla Mannin had been the ship's engineer for almost that entire time. Month after month, planet after planet, a year-long journey that took her in and out of Federation space, always coming back to where she had started. Captains had come and gone, but Salla remained, queen of her own little country, safe in the knowledge that nobody knew the ship as well as she did. She watched the worlds she traveled to change, and sometimes change back again, and then the ship would move on, to yet another world that seemed both familiar and strange. She never got too close, she never felt the urge to settle. This way of life suited her. Salla had never been the kind to long for adventure. Her homeworld, Leyta, well outside of Federation space, had been troubled by strife for more than a century, almost long enough that the reasons for the trouble were beginning to be forgotten—although new grudges formed easily, and demanded immediate reprisal. Ordinary people, like Salla, struggled to survive there. Sometimes the war passed you by for a while—three years, five—and you were lulled into thinking that some kind of life could be led there. But always it returned, like a virus that lay dormant and couldn't be destroyed. You built a little home, from the fragments of the last one, but it never lasted. At sixteen, Salla left Leyta, never to return. All she had wanted, all those years ago, when she left her homeworld, was a place to live in peace, somewhere she could go and create a way of life with a peaceful rhythm. War, drama, conflict—she wanted no more of these things. She wanted to be quiet. She wanted to live steadily.

When she first left Leyta, she had traveled around a lot, hopping from world to world, learning her trade from whoever would teach her, and then plying it with more and more success. As she gained a reputation for skill and excellence, she began to build up reserves and create a network of fellow journeymen. Others with skills like hers, perhaps with different specialties, traveling and looking for work. Many of them were refugees, like her, from Leyta, or from other worlds with similar troubles. A confederacy of exiles. With that special understanding, never spoken about, they did not compete, but instead kept one another in the loop. Mutual support. They let one another know when they heard of ships in need of people with specific skills. They passed on job opportunities and openings. They shared expertise and tips, keeping one another abreast of new developments. Given their backgrounds, few of them had had much formal schooling, and so they supplied one another with that too. It wasn't a bad way of life, not at first, and better than what she'd left behind, but after five or six years of shifting from ship to ship, Salla knew that her traveling days were coming to an end. She was weary of moving around, learning new ships and their ways, learning new people (always the harder task). She wanted something different.

Her network obliged. One of her cronies let her know about an opening that had come up suddenly on a new cargo ship that was partway on a new route. The engineer they'd hired had suddenly taken sick and was retiring back to his homeworld. Salla was on the spot, showed her skills by fixing a temperamental secondary navigation system, and was hired within minutes. And there she'd been ever since, doing the run around these systems, as crews came and went, and she and the ship grew older together. These days, Salla knew this ship's aches and pains as well as her own. She knew what could be fixed, and she knew what had to be borne. She wasn't sentimental about the ship: being sentimental had no place in a job as practical as hers. So she didn't give the ship nicknames, or pretend it was a child or a lover or a friend, but there was nothing in the universe that Salla knew as well as the *Con*. She knew the ship's clanks and groans; she knew what she sounded like when things were well, and what she sounded like when things were off. She knew which bits of bulkhead to hit, and how hard, and the quick fixes that came from long experience.

Altogether, Salla was more than happy with her lot. Every so often there had been some fraught times, when *Con* had fallen into the hands of idiots, some of which had nearly sent Salla on her way. But she'd outlasted them all. And the good news was that the current captain was all right, as captains went. Maris had been running the show for three years now—no, nearly four! How the time flew. Competent and good-humored, Maris worked with her team rather than against it, and that was surely something to be thankful for. Salla might wish that Maris was a little less parsimonious, but at the same time she understood that buying a ship and a route like this meant taking on a lot of debt, and the captain didn't want to throw money around when the whole point was to be making a little money. Still, you got what you paid for with these aging boats, and sometimes you had to spend more now than you would like to avoid spending later. Salla didn't push her case too often, but when she did, she was implacable. On the whole, the engineer and the captain understood each other pretty well, and they got along just fine. Only every so often would the captain look at Salla, and sigh, and say, "You do know who's the boss around here?"

Salla would smile and nod. She surely did.

But not everything could last forever. *Con* had maybe another decade in her, but Salla didn't think she'd be around to see the ship's last days. She didn't want to; she'd earned that much sentimentality. Salla knew that her days aboard ship were entering the final stages. She was starting to find that she was tired a lot these days. She couldn't put in the hours like she used to. She wasn't quite getting around to everything that she would like to get done. Small things were left unfixed. *Con* deserved better; no, she would need something better, if she was going to last as long as she could. Salla wasn't afraid of retiring. She and a pal, another engineer she'd worked with back in the early days when they were both starting out, had bought a little place together in a small town in a quiet province on Talaris. They had a few more years building up the nest egg, and then, Salla would say, they'd be hanging up their spanners for good. In the meantime, Salla was content to move around the ship that had been her home for so long now, and to spend her days walking from one end of the *Con* to another, doing her rounds, making her repairs, adding items to her list. She knew that sometimes she frustrated Maris, who was young, and just starting out, and perhaps might have preferred someone with a little more zip. But Salla knew her worth—and she knew that Maris knew it too.

So Salla was pretty clear that something was up. What she didn't know yet was what. She didn't mention it at the crew meetings that they held every morning, because she already knew the rest of the crew thought she was—well, maybe a little *eccentric*? They all looked so young, these days, these captains and 2ICs, and they all looked in a hurry, and they weren't always patient with a slow-moving, aging engineer who hadn't, as far as they knew, been farther than the walls of this ship. It was funny, sometimes, to think back on the experiences of her youth, Salla thought. These young people might think a little differently, if they knew about the Long War that she had left behind, the broken buildings and ruined families, the sadness and the despair. They might have enjoyed her tales about the worlds she'd seen, the ships she'd traveled on. Or they might not have believed a word of it. Either way, it didn't matter. But Salla knew her ship, and she knew that something was not right, and when she found out what it was, she would get whatever help she needed—or, better, fix it without mentioning the problem to anyone.

For one thing, there had been some odd activity around the data banks. She thought at first that maybe it was one of the kids who had come on board this time on Talaris, messing around too much. A few careful questions and a handful of sweets put an end to that theory, and also stopped them from trying to hack the food slots. She also had the strangest feeling that the ship's manifest wasn't looking right. That took a little time to work through, cross-checking names and boarding points and so on. But no—everyone who was supposed to be on board was there; everyone who had left at Oyseen or who was coming on at Zymne wasn't. She even went so far as doing a head count during her rounds, ticking off everyone one by one, and the numbers came out just fine. Still, she couldn't shake the feeling that something was going on. Something wasn't right, and she couldn't put her finger on what. *Maybe it's me*, Salla thought. *Maybe I'm done. It was sooner than I expected. But maybe it's time to say goodbye,* Con . . . But she knew her instincts were still sound, even if her pace was slower these days. She knew she'd get to the bottom of this eventually.

She was right to trust her instincts. Two days out of Oyseen, something happened that really got Salla worrying. Something about the ship changed. Nothing major, not in the great scheme of things, not something that would affect anyone, or would even be noticed by anyone other than an engineer with thirty years' experience on a small ship. No, it wasn't *what* changed that troubled Salla. It was the fact that *something* had changed—without her intervention, and without her permission. She didn't know how, and she didn't know why, and that was insupportable. That was something that needed to be stopped.

Quietly, unobtrusively, and unknown to anyone but herself, Salla Mannin went on the warpath.

Perhaps if the several dozen people who had been most directly inconvenienced by Tilly's adventure had been able to see how miserable she was stuck in a cabin with a dripping ventilation system, they might have felt slightly avenged. A more efficient way of tormenting poor Tilly than confining her to a small room with a persistent noise tapping away in the background could not have been designed. And stuck she was. During the day cycle, she didn't dare step outside of the cabin, for fear of being discovered, and all the time the ventilation system kept on dripping. It stopped her sleeping and, when she did sleep, she heard a constant *drip, drip, drip*, which became muddled up with someone knocking on the door, someone opening up the cabin to find her and drag her off to face her mother.

The problem was that Tilly really didn't have anything other to do than listen to the wretched drip. The data slate offered a limited amount of reading material (she was beating the word games pretty solidly by this point), and, besides, she was worried that too much interaction with it would lead to someone checking out all the activity from these supposedly empty quarters. She tried to sleep, but between the drip and her anxiety about being discovered, she could only manage an hour or so here and there. So there was no escape through sleep. And then she was getting hungry, very hungry, and there was nothing to eat, because all the food slots were outside. All told, Tilly spent a very miserable day, lying on the bed, cursing her luck, and wishing that somehow the drip would stop. A lot of people would have taken some satisfaction from knowing this.

When the ship's night cycle finally kicked in, Tilly lay for another hour, trying to be patient. At last she could bear it no longer. She *had* to find something to eat. She took a deep breath, opened the cabin door, and poked her head out. Nobody around. Everything was quiet; everything was dark. Softly, she slipped out of the cabin and down the corridor, where she found a food slot in a small communal area. The slot made some pretty awful noises (*Jeez*, she thought, *this ship! What a bag of bolts! Is there anyone around here taking care of things?*) but she did manage to assemble a decent enough meal, and all without disturbing anyone's sleep. She sped back to her cabin, where she ate her supplies ravenously. That helped her mood immensely: she felt a little better after, as if her adventure had won a new lease on life, or, at least, she could carry on for a while longer. But there was still nothing to do. She could hardly run out and clear up her dishes, so she dumped them on the berth opposite. Then she stuck her head under her pillow and tried to sleep through the drip-drip-drumming. It was worse, much worse, than anyone snoring. Tilly stared up into the darkness. *Why can't I catch a break?*

That was her chief thought throughout most of the following day, which was the most miserable so far. She spent the day hunched up on the bed, her arms wrapped around a pillow, thinking about how awful this adventure was turning out to be, and how much trouble she would be in if she got caught. But eventually, Tilly's natural optimism, her enviable ability not to be squashed but to bounce back, began to assert itself. She simply wasn't the kind of person who would sit around brooding about how badly life was treating them. She liked to be up and doing—which was part of what made her very like her mother (and was, of course, also what had gotten her into this mess in the first place). Still, she thought, you have to make the best of things. And the way to do that was to do something—anything!—about your situation.

So, midafternoon, bored beyond reason and hungrier than she had been in her entire life, Tilly rolled off the bed, stood in the middle of the tiny cabin, raised her fist, and said, "Okay, drip. I've been patient, but you've pushed me too far. But now Sylvia Tilly is *coming* for you."

Anyone watching over the next ten or fifteen minutes would have been treated to the sight of Tilly wandering around the tiny space, her ear pressed against the wall, trying to find the precise location of the drip. When she found it, she gave a little cry of triumph, and set to. She still had a knife from her supper, and she used this as a makeshift tool, attacking the panel and taking it off the wall. Then she dug about inside. She quickly worked out where and what the problem was. It really couldn't have been more trivial. A fitting had loosened.

Tilly stared at this in amazement. *Goodness, is that all? I can have this fixed in no time!* Then she frowned, pursed her lips, and shook her head. Someone should have done this ages ago.

"What kind of a show are they running here?" she said

to herself. "Whoever's in charge of maintenance, this really isn't any good. Don't you know there are *regulations* about noise levels in residential spaces, and that includes ships' quarters? I mean, I *know* this isn't a Federation ship, but it stops at Federation worlds, and my goodness, you'd better believe that you're as subject to those regulations as everyone else . . ." Tilly was discovering that talking out loud to yourself lessened the feeling of loneliness. She sealed up the panel again, for safety's sake. "Slapdash," she tutted, shaking her head. "Well, it's not good enough. I'm not putting up with it any longer!"

Tilly was, perhaps, not being fair to Salla, who, with a staff of one (herself), was constantly battling with a to-do list longer than the ship itself. Tilly, more familiar with smooth-functioning Federation vessels, was also not particularly well informed about how other people had to cobble together solutions from what was available, quickly and within budget, and all without risking life in the hostile environment of space. Tilly had found the problem; now she wanted to implement her solution. Preferably before the drip drove her completely out of her mind.

Once again she didn't dare go out of her quarters until the night cycle was beginning. But her success with finding the drip made her bolder in her foray. This time she ventured farther into the ship, down another corridor leading from the tiny mess room, until she found what she wanted: a maintenance kit on the wall. She took this—and some supper—back to her room. She decided to wait until the morning to fix the drip: it was something to look forward to, something to fill the following day. But it didn't disturb her sleep that night. She lay back in the darkness and gave a grim smile.

"Drip," she said, "your days are numbered. Sylvia Tilly is on your case."

When she woke up, partway through the day cycle, she got straight down to work. She quickly tightened the fitting, and then there were some other minor pieces of repair that caught her eye, so she set to work on those. As she tinkered away, Tilly felt her breath come more freely and her shoulders relax. There was something so incredibly *soothing* about routine work like this; something very special about working with your hands. So much of what they did at school was so, well, *cerebral*. She didn't mean that she struggled—far from that—but their studies often tended to the conceptual. Languages, strategy, tactics, political theories. That was all very well, but Tilly was of the opinion that there wasn't enough working with your hands, there wasn't enough working out problems through your body. And that meant that you got disconnected from the world. Something like this—it reminded you that you *were* connected, to something bigger than yourself. This was why she loved astromycology, of course. Everything was connected there. You weren't displaced, you weren't alone.

Funny how little she had thought about school in the past couple of days. Everything had seemed so important there—the rowing, the clubs, the situation with Risera—and now that she had stepped away from it, it was as if her sense of proportion was coming back. It wasn't a good idea, she decided, to put people into such a small, closed environment. Sure, it made them focused and accomplished—chiefly because they had nothing else to do other than the tasks set for them. Didn't prisoners start to adopt the mores of the jailers? She'd read something about that in one of her psychology classes. Well, Tilly had broken out of jail now, and she didn't care anymore about stupid mock summits and sports days and club posters. She had better things to do with her time. Starfleet, that was another one. All those people holed up on their ships, following regulations and obeying commands, and without any outside influences to tell them how weird it all was. No wonder Dad had gone off. When you thought about the whole thing, Starfleet was practically some kind of *cult*.

There was nothing left to be fixed. Tilly sealed up the panel and stood in the middle of the room, her hands on her hips, and listened.

Nothing. Peace and quiet at last. Blissful.

"I did it," Tilly said softly to the silent room, and a smile crept across her lips. "I did it." She clenched her fist and punched the air: the queen of infinite space.

Salla stood in the little cabin and looked around. She had been sure she would find somebody here. But the room was empty, just as it should be. There had been a solo passenger in this cabin from Talaris, some kid heading to Oyseen, and who had presumably gotten off there. All four berths were neatly made, waiting for their next occupants, just as they should be. There was no sign of any possessions: no bags, no clothes, none of the little bits and pieces that people inevitably accumulated and that they liked to leave around in even the most temporary accommodation, to give themselves a sense of being at home.

And yet . . . And yet . . .

Slowly, Salla heaved herself across to the wall. She flipped open her kit, dug around for a spanner, and whipped the panel off the wall. Anyone watching Salla work was always slightly startled to see the big, almost sleepy woman shift into action. When the panel was off, Salla took a look inside. After a moment or two, she nodded with approval. Whoever had fixed this had done a very nice job. Tidy work. Nothing left out of place. Fixed up a couple of other things too, things that Salla wouldn't have had a chance to get around to for ages, if ever. Salla didn't give compliments lightly, but she was fair. She knew she couldn't have done a better job herself.

And yet . . . And yet . . .

Salla put the panel back up and screwed it back in place. The problem was—you couldn't just have someone wandering around the ship fixing things, could you? She didn't feel this way out of a sense of territoriality: Salla wasn't really so inclined, no matter the impression she gave to successive captains, that this was, in some indefinable way, her ship rather than theirs. That was all just propaganda, really, part of making sure that she got the resources she needed, when she needed them, and without taking any shit in the meantime. The *Con* wasn't Salla's ship. No, Salla's concerns were, typically, more about the practicalities. Because it was all very well taking it upon yourself to fix a faulty ventilation system (and the lords of Leyta knew, if they *were* using this cabin at all, that drip must have been driving them crazy), but you never knew what else was going on. Ships were complex systems. They needed someone with an overarching view. Perhaps that drip hadn't been fixed because fixing it would set something else off, something more critical to sustaining life in this little vessel. So, no, it wasn't that Salla minded that someone else had done something for her—she could do with a second these days. What she minded was that, no matter how good the work was, the fixer didn't have a real idea of what maintaining a ship involved. And that? *That* Salla could not allow.

She pondered for a while whether this was the moment she should go to see Maris with her suspicions. But, again, she knew she didn't have anything to tell her. So a drip wasn't there that used to be there? Maris would laugh. These things fixed themselves sometimes, didn't they? Well, yes, Salla would admit that, but drips didn't open up panels and have a little tidy around while they were busy fixing themselves. Still, Salla could picture the conversation. Maris would nod and listen, politely, but there would be the merest hint of impatience about her, a slight curve to the lip, and she would say, "Oh, well, that sounds very worrying, but are you *sure*, Salla?" And when Salla had gone, Maris would turn to her 2IC, and say, "Don't you think Salla is looking tired? I think she might be starting to lose her touch. Do you think we should start looking for someone else?" And before Salla knew it, she would be packed off to the house on Talaris, and the problem with that was she hadn't quite yet gotten as much in her savings as she would like.

Besides, Salla thought, tapping her tool against the palm of her hand, what did she know, really? She knew that someone had been using a lot of data, and it seemed to be centered around this part of the ship. She knew that someone had fixed a dripping ventilation system in this cabin. And she knew that the last occupant of this cabin had gotten on at Talaris and had, presumably, got off at Oyseen. That was all she knew. Maris wouldn't be interested. No. What Salla needed was evidence. Good, hard evidence. But of what? Salla sat down heavily on the nearest bunk, to think what that might be.

Tilly's success with the drip emboldened her. The next morning, she decided to go out earlier, during the day cycle, and wander around the ship, seeing what was out there. She had checked the manifest and decided that with sixty-odd passengers, it was probably busy enough for her to be able to blend into the crowd. The passengers were a diverse bunch, traveling from Federation and non-Federation worlds alike. She sat in a little public area, where two corridors met, where there were a few couches and chairs dotted around so people could sit and chat or do the same as Tilly and simply sit and watch. Everything was so *interesting*. Sure, Tilly was used to Federation diplomatic functions, and they were nothing if not diverse. But some of these people—she had never seen these species before, never heard of them (and Tilly had recently made very close study of all the minor member species of the United Federation of Planets). Some of these—nope, she didn't have a clue. And the conversations—bartering, quarreling, off-color jokes, things you would never hear at a soiree, where all anyone ever seemed to do was ask polite questions about each other, and talk about the ambassador's amazing clothes, and remark about the unusual weather we were having right now . . . *Urgh*. Tilly shuddered at the thought. She would never put herself through that again, not if she could help it. The most interesting thing was turning off her universal translator, to see how much she could follow. Not much, and of the languages of the unfamiliar species nothing at all, beyond what she could guess from gesture and context. But every so often, she caught bits and pieces of a language she had studied, and she smiled to herself and thought: *There. I knew I wasn't as bad at languages as everyone made out. I knew I'd be able to get by.*

The nicest thing about being there was just to sit and do nothing. No early alarm to send her off to a rowing practice. No bell to tell you it was time for breakfast. No attendance, reminding you that security was rigid and everyone was anxious about what might happen if you were out of sight for two minutes. No classes, no tests, no papers, and absolutely no presentations. And, best of all, no relatives talking all the time about your grades and your *emerging issues*. For a moment, Tilly felt light-headed. And then she realized that this feeling was . . .

happiness. She hugged herself. *So this is what it feels like! They should bottle this! It feels great!* All she needed was a holiday. Here, on this grubby little cargo ship, out in the middle of nowhere, surrounded by ordinary people. All by herself, free to do what she wanted when she wanted, without a relentless school timetable or the stress of parental interaction.

After a couple of hours, she realized that she felt hungry, so she went in search of a food slot. She found a small public dining area, pretty busy around this time, and there was quite a line: two of the five slots were out of order. As she joined the back of one line, Tilly tutted. More slapdash maintenance. Feeling braver by the second, and seeing what the previous person had chosen, she chose the same for herself. It turned out to be a spicy dish, made from some kind of pulse, with a hot sauce that made her lips tingle and her eyes water before she had even taken a bite. It was never something Tilly would have chosen for herself. More than that, it was the kind of thing she usually couldn't bear someone else ordering, if she was eating out with them. Her allergies went *crazy* over this kind of thing. She eyed it suspiciously, piled up on her tray. Then she remembered her new motto: *Try.* She stuck in her fork, gathered up a pile, and shoved it in her mouth.

It was freakin' delicious. "Gosh," said Tilly.

The woman who had been in the line in front of her, and who was now sitting next to her, smiled. "Have you never had it before?"

"No," mumbled Tilly through a second heaped forkful.

"Okay, well, take your time! Even with this mass-produced stuff, the flavors are really delicate. Let them unfold in your mouth. And here—have a sip of this in between each mouthful." She pushed over a glass of a milky liquid. Tilly eyed it uncertainly, but, seeing the woman's encouraging nod, and not wanting to offend, she took a little sip. The woman was right. The heat of the spices was diminished by the drink, but the delicious flavors were enhanced. *Umami*, she thought hungrily. *I want more of you in my life* . . . She polished off the rest in short order, sighing happily at the feeling of being replete after her hungry day. The best thing, though? She had eaten something that she would have avoided at home, and it had been great. Better still? She had spotted something to keep her busy later, through the long, boring night.

When the night cycle started, Tilly gave it an hour, then she picked up her maintenance kit and went back to the dining area. The door was closed, but not locked, and she was able to slip inside. She found the light directly over the food slots and turned that on rather than the main lights. She needed illumination to be able to work, but she didn't want to send up a flare. She put her kit down on the nearest table, opened it up, and pulled out a spanner. Then she opened the flap on the first of the broken food slots and stared in horror at the brown sludge within.

"Oh, my stars," she said. "That is *revolting*. That is *literally* the most horrible thing I have ever seen. Seriously, the standards on this ship! It's amazing they're allowed anywhere *near* Federation space!"

She dove right in and soon found the blockage. When that was clear, she ran a cleaning and sterilization cycle on the machine. The next food slot wasn't quite as bad, but she still needed to screw up her nerve (and hold her nose) before she dug her hands into the goo. She worked briskly and without any fuss. Soon the other food slot was going through a sterilization cycle too. Tilly went off to wash her hands. When she came back, the slots were ready for use again. "Well," she said, "the proof is in the pudding." She giggled. "Literally, in this case." She ordered dessert:

chocolate mousse. It tasted great. Better than that—it tasted of success. What could ever top this? Delicious, chocolate-flavored success. Tilly thought she had never felt as happy in her life. Humming quietly to herself, Tilly packed up her case, left the dining room, and went back to her cabin. She slipped inside, switched on the light, and turned . . .

To see a woman, sitting on the bed, waiting for her.

The woman was very striking. Her skin had a purplish tint, and her hair, long and pulled back off her head into a ponytail, was a kind of pale green color that Tilly knew instinctively hadn't come out of a bottle. The woman's eyes were jet black. No whites, no irises, just all black. Tilly gulped. This was all really very unnerving. And then the woman stood up.

She was big—taller than Tilly, and thickset, broad. She looked like she could pick up very heavy things and throw them a very long way. She looked like she could pick up Tilly and throw *her* a very long way. Worse than that, she looked not only as if she might like doing it, but that it was something at the forefront of her mind. It wasn't always easy to read the body language of other species, particularly ones you hadn't encountered before, but Tilly was ready to call this one. This woman was absolutely furious.

"So," the woman said, in a deep, slow, sonorous voice. "Here's the secret stowaway fixer."

Tilly looked down at the maintenance kit that she was still clutching in her hands. She licked her lips, which still tasted of chocolate. There was no point in denying it. There was no point in denying anything, really. "Okay," she said. "I can explain—"

"You certainly can," said the woman. "And you certainly will. But you can explain it all to the captain." She lumbered over, put her hand firmly on Tilly's shoulder, and shoved her out of the room. "For your sake, I hope she's feeling a lot friendlier than I am. But I wouldn't count on it."

"Really?" said Tilly faintly. "But I fixed her food slots—!"

"Really," said her captor. "Because we're about to wake her up."

7

Captain Reah Maris had been asleep for about two and a half hours, and was therefore deep into her sleep cycle, making this by far the most disruptive and unpleasant time to be woken, when Salla hammered on the door to her cabin. Now awake she was—eyes heavy and tired, mood grouchy, patience low—watching the unlikely spectacle of her chief engineer manhandling a teenage girl into the room. A teenage girl with a lot of red curls.

Maris sighed and pinched the bridge of her nose between her fingertips. The previous captain, handing over the *Con*, had told her that Salla was indispensable, that the ship wouldn't run without her, but that she could "sometimes go a bit funny." This had turned out to be a completely accurate appraisal. Salla was worth her weight in latinum, she kept the *Con* running on next to nothing, but every so often she would be at the center of some very odd situations. The last one, involving a Zymnean merchant and a shipment of onions, had been . . . What? Ten months ago? A year? Maris supposed they were due for another. Still, couldn't it have waited until the morning?

Wearily, Maris sat down behind her desk. The teenage girl was now standing, arms folded, with a rather mulish expression on her face. Marvelous. Maris had a younger brother and remembered from his adolescence what the sulks looked like when she saw them. Salla, meanwhile, had her hand clamped on the girl's shoulder, and was glowering at her back. She looked *furious*. She looked like she might breathe *fire*.

Maris took a deep breath. "Salla," she said. "Why exactly am I awake right now and not asleep? What the hell is going on?"

"This," said Salla, her eyes ablaze, pointing at the girl. "This is what's going on. This . . . *creature* has been messing around with our ship!"

It wasn't Salla's ship, of course. It wasn't really its captain's either, not for at least another half dozen payments, but Maris didn't particularly want to argue that point right now. "How about we all calm down and sort this out?" Maris said. "Salla, let go of her! She's only a kid!"

Salla pushed the girl over to the nearest chair, and then planted herself in the next chair over with a thump.

"All right," said the captain. "What's this about messing around with the ship?"

"I knew this was going on," said Salla bullishly. "The ventilator somehow sorted itself out—"

"Ventilator?" said Maris.

"In one of the cabins near the cargo bay. Didn't I mention it?"

"No," said Maris, wondering what else about the ship hadn't been mentioned. She made a mental note to run a full diagnostics check in the morning—without Salla's help.

"Well, I couldn't think of a way it could have done that all by itself. So it meant that someone had fixed it. I didn't know anyone aboard who could fix it. No one should be messing around with the ship. So I did a little bit of investigating, and I found this girl!"

What the hell was all this?

"Okay, Salla, let's take this from the top."

Slowly, Maris began to piece the story together. And maybe it was because it was so late, or maybe it was because she was coming to the end of her patience with Salla, or maybe it was the fact that *some dumb kid* had been messing around with her ship, but once she had the whole story, Maris absolutely blew her top. Years of payments had gone into this ship, years of hard work. Maris was so close to owning it outright, so close to finally having a chance of a decent way of life that didn't involve schlepping around to some of the dullest and dirtiest worlds that a person could have the misfortune ever to visit, and then along comes some *dumb kid*.

"You've been *messing around* with my ship?" Maris yelled. "What sort of idiot are you? Do you have any idea how dangerous that could be?"

The kid, unbelievably, was trying to interrupt her. She held up her hand. "Excuse me, but actually, I think you'll find—"

Maris recognized that kind of accent at once. Some rich kid from the Federation, slumming it out here in the sticks, and—had she mentioned this?—*messing around with her goddamned ship*. "You stupid little idiot!" Maris yelled. "I should throw you off right now! Seriously, come on, we're going to the airlock *right now*." She stood up and pointed toward the door. The kid was staring at her as if she didn't believe her.

"You think I wouldn't do that?" said Maris.

"Er, no," said the kid. "Because wouldn't that be, like, *murder*?"

"You want to bank on someone coming out here to investigate?" Maris said. "As if they'd even know you were on board. You're a stowaway!"

The kid's eyes narrowed. "Er, I think it would be a really *bad* idea—"

"I bet you do," said Maris. "Anyway, who *are* you, exactly? Who's looking after you?"

There was a pause, then the kid said, "You know, I don't think that's important information right now."

Maris felt her jaw drop. "You don't think— Hang on a minute, kid, who's in charge around here?"

"Actually," said the kid, "I'd quite like to make a complaint. Because I was traveling quite peacefully, you know, and then someone *stole* my bag, and *stole* my ID, and, to be honest, I'm not *hugely* impressed by all this. I mean"—she folded her arms—"what kind of a ship are you *running* here, exactly?"

Salla, watching this exchange unfold, was starting to calm down considerably. Deep, deep inside, she felt the first stirring of laughter. And it seemed the girl hadn't finished yet. "And then there I was, stuck in that cabin, and do you *realize* how annoying that drip was? Honestly, were you intending to make someone *pay* for that berth? Because I'd be asking for my money back—"

Yes, Salla thought, this kid had some nerve. And Salla—for many reasons—had a soft spot for mouthy teenage girls trying to make their way in the world. Particularly ones who were good at fixing things. That drip had been on Salla's list for nearly four months, and she had never gotten the chance to fix it.

The girl still hadn't finished. "And then the food slots!" She made a face. "Oh my goodness! Those things were awful! You should have seen some of the sludge coming out of them! I'm a big fan of mold, in the right circumstances, but there were things in there that no eyes should see—*you know*? That thing was a health risk! You could get your passenger license taken away for that! Anyway, you're welcome."

There was a long silence. Maris stared at the girl. "Are you for real?"

The girl gave her own forearm a slight pinch. "Uh, well, I *guess* . . ."

"You're out of here," said Maris. "Seriously—I'm happy to take my chances and throw you out right now—"

"Oh, I don't think that's a good idea! That would get you into terrible trouble—I mean, *really?* You think I'd take a threat like that *seriously?* How about this as an offer instead? You let me stay on board for a while, and I don't make a complaint *right now* to the Federation about the state of your food hygiene, and the fact that a passenger can't simply go to sleep in her berth without having her *ID stolen* . . . Honestly, I think you could be caught up in red tape for *months* . . ."

Salla couldn't stop herself. She burst out laughing, a big, deep laugh that shook her chair. "Oh my, this is *wonderful!* I didn't think this was going to turn out to be fun. Well, that's life for you. Tell you what, Maris—we'll do a deal. Let her stay on to the next planet, and I'll keep her away from you. She can help me with maintenance."

"I'm failing," said Maris through gritted teeth, "to see what I get out of this arrangement."

"Really?" said Salla.

"Really. And right now I'm having the kind of start to my day that will only be made better by making someone else's life a real misery—"

Salla leaned forward in her chair. She put two big purplish hands down flat upon the captain's desk and gave Maris a big smile. "Here's what you get out of it," she said. "You get me."

"I've already got you, Salla—"

"Not if I quit."

Again, that silence. "You wouldn't—"

"I might."

Maris pinched the bridge of her nose. "You'd quit over some stupid kid?"

"Actually," said the girl, "I consistently get some of the best grades in my year—"

"Sweetheart," said Salla amiably, "shut your mouth and keep it shut."

"Jeez," the girl muttered, hunkering down in her chair. "So *rude . . .*"

"Yes," said Salla. "I'd quit over some stupid kid."

Another pause. Maris stared at Salla through narrowed eyes. Salla smiled lazily back. Maris was clearly trying to work out if this was a bluff. Salla had made no secret about squirreling savings away. But Maris had no idea how much, and whether it was enough for her to be able to leave the *Con* on a whim. What Salla did know was that leaving now would sink Maris. She wouldn't find a good engineer for months, maybe as much as a year.

Maris got there in the end. She sighed, and capitulated. "Not past Zymne. Do I make myself clear? And she's to touch nothing—*nothing*—without your oversight. Am I clear, Salla?"

"Dead clear."

"All right, then." Maris glared at the girl. "And as for you—you can thank your lucky stars that Salla's taken a shine to you, and that I won't find a better engineer in ten systems."

Salla preened, and then jerked her head at the girl. "Come on, kiddo. Let's show you the ropes."

"Wow," said the girl as they headed for the door. "The power of the engineer. I *knew* I dropped the wrong club."

Tilly let Salla push her out of the captain's cabin. They stood in the corridor outside, Salla looking thoughtfully at her, Tilly looking back at Salla with trepidation. Tilly felt slightly shaky. It was just starting to hit her how much trouble she had been in, and how much she owed Salla for providing her with an out. That could have gone a lot worse. There had been an airlock mentioned. Tilly had no idea whether Maris would have done it, but the threat had seemed very real; she had been starting to worry that the only way out was to deploy Mom's name. And that would be it—game over. Tilly had no idea why Salla had come down on her side, but she was profoundly grateful.

"Okay," said Salla. "You can thank me now."

"Well . . . thank you," said Tilly.

"You're welcome."

"Will that cause you problems with the captain?"

Salla shrugged. "We'll see. Doubt it. But I think she'll be keeping a more considered eye out for my replacement. She won't find anyone."

"One last question," said Tilly. "Er—*why?*"

Salla sighed. Whatever fire and frenzy that had propelled her to the captain's office had now dissipated. She now looked like a very calm, very quiet woman toward the end of her middle years. "You know, I never have enough time in the day to get to everything. Partly it's because I'm getting a little old, you know?"

Tilly looked at her blankly. This was getting heavy.

"No," said Salla, "I guess you don't. Anyway, I don't work anywhere near as fast as I'd like these days, don't quite keep up with things as much as I'd like. And, if I'm being honest, there's never been enough of me to get everything done. There's things on my list that have been there for ages. They've got as much mold on them as some of the food slots." She gave Tilly a sharp grin that showed her silvery teeth. Tilly smiled nervously back. "So having another pair of hands around, even for a little while, would be good. Hope so, anyway. You did some nice work, you know. Absolutely stupid and irresponsible, but still some nice work."

Tilly flushed. She appreciated the praise, in between the scolding, because she knew the latter was probably deserved, and she knew the former came from someone who knew what they were talking about. "Thanks."

"Shall we see what else you can do? See what we can get done? It's only three days to Zymne, but I think we can make a difference." She gave that sharp silvered smile again. "Think of it as an apprenticeship."

Tilly's heart soared. Learning on the job, she thought. Proper, practical experience, and taught by someone who really knew what they were doing. "I would absolutely love that!"

"Thought you might," said Salla. She stuck out her hand, to shake on the deal, and Tilly clasped hands with her. Salla's hand was rough and firm, strong and warm. Friendly. She beamed at her. Tilly gave a shy smile back.

"All right," Salla said, heading off down the corridor, "follow me."

Tilly trotted behind. "Where are we going?"

"First? Cup of tea. Never do anything without a cup of tea first. After that? Well, we'll fire up that list of mine and see what takes our fancy."

The tea proved to be a slightly odd brew that Salla made fresh each morning in a samovar, and then carried around with her all day in a vacuum flask. What started out as a quite pleasantly fragranced tisane turned into something considerably more robust by the end of the day. Tilly did wonder once or twice whether there was something alcoholic in it, but decided discretion was the better part of valor. Perhaps it had an effect on Salla's biology, but not on hers. Yes, probably best to believe that, and never ever mention this to Mom and Dad. With the tea ready, Salla, as promised, flipped open her to-do list. "Right," she said. "Let's get started."

And so Tilly started following Salla on her rounds. The pace was as stately as Salla had promised, but Tilly still marveled at how much the woman got done. Slowly and steadily, throughout the course of the day, she lumbered her way from one end of the ship to the other, and back again, and back again. Thorough and methodical. "The trick," Salla told Tilly, on the earliest of these passes, "is to have a good routine. Make sure that everything is running smoothly. Don't skip past something because you're sure it's fine. You've got to keep an eye out for anything that's changing. Don't be caught unawares. Know your ship as well as you know the back of your hand."

To the outside eye, this must have been an odd sight, the woman in her fifties, bulky and solid, heaving herself slowly but surely around her small domain, and the teenage girl, nervous but attentive, eager to learn but worried that she might inadvertently put a spanner in the works somewhere along the way. But Tilly didn't. Quite the opposite, in fact. She wasn't as hands-on as she thought she was going to be, but she didn't mind. She was busy listening, listening hard, because she knew that Salla had plenty to teach her. And when she did get to try something out, there were no problems. It had always been like this, Tilly thought. For some reason, tools came naturally to her. Nothing like champagne glasses, which seemed to topple at Tilly's touch; or high heels, which seemed to buckle beneath her; or lipstick, which always went off at an odd angle. Somehow the tools that Salla showed her, explained to her, and then let her handle seemed to be a perfect fit for Tilly's hand. She seemed to get on with them perfectly well.

And the work—this routine maintenance of an ancient, run-down ship—was fascinating. Tilly had known intellectually that she was interested but hadn't really realized how much. As they knelt over an open hatch, waving hand lights around and peering in, pulling faces at the pretty nasty smell that wafted up, Tilly found herself wondering vaguely what her school friends were doing right now. What was Risera doing? Xoha, and Erisel, and Semett? Most of them would be on their holidays. Visiting chic planets and chic cities. Dining, gossiping, socializing. Maybe some crazy sports. They were big on sports, her schoolmates. And most of all, they would be networking, relentlessly networking. Making connections that would stand them—and their careers—in good stead. Tilly shuddered at the thought. She was up to her elbows in lubricant, and she wouldn't have swapped places with them for all the world. Ghastly, that way of life was. Ghastly. But this? This was incredible. This was the *life*.

I'm not going back to any of that, she told herself firmly. *I'd rather spend my life pottering up and down this ship with Salla, fixing things, doing something useful.* She did feel a little pang of guilt at that thought. She knew, in her heart, exactly how important her mother's work was, but she knew too that she wasn't cut out for it. She was starting to understand better with every hour she spent in Salla's company that there were things she was capable of doing. But it was scary. *I'm sorry, Mom. I'm just not . . . not what you wanted me to be. I'm something else.*

Is that okay?

Tilly tried to imagine saying this to Mom, but her imagination couldn't get the conversation to work. She was sure she knew how it would go—she would open her mouth to explain what she wanted, what she needed, but the words would dry up, and her mother would move smoothly into the gap and explain what it was that Tilly *really* wanted. That was how it always went. Then Tilly shuddered. The next conversation with Mom was going to be the hardest ever. What was Mom going to say? *I am in so much trouble* . . .

"You okay?" said Salla softly.

"What?" said Tilly.

"You look like someone waiting to hear bad news."

"I'm okay."

"Hmm," said Salla. She eyed Tilly thoughtfully. So far she hadn't, thank goodness, pressed Tilly directly about why she was here, but Tilly knew she was fishing for information. Of course she was! Where had this Federation kid come from? Why was she here? Where was she going? It must be very puzzling. And Tilly wasn't sure how many secrets she could keep from Salla. The engineer was good at burrowing away at something until she worked out what was going on.

The direct questions came toward the end of their first day together. "So," said Salla, leaning back comfortably in one of the chairs in the mess, "now we've gotten to know each other a little better, why don't you tell me who you *really* are and how you *really* got here?"

Tilly blinked. "I told you. Traveling to meet my dad. My ID got stolen—" They had stopped, yet again, for tea. Salla's brew was now strong and brown and tarring the inside of the mouth. Filthy stuff, but Tilly didn't want to refuse the hospitality. She took a tentative sip, and swirled the liquid around in her mouth, hoping to dissipate some of the taste. She shrugged noncommittally rather than answer Salla's question.

Salla shook her head and laughed. "Okay, you're going to play hard to get. So I'll try guessing. You got on at Talaris, yeah?" she said. She was dropping a sweetener into her mug. Three, four, five, six . . . Tilly found this whole ritual fascinating. It was as if Salla's whole ambition for her tea was to turn the darn stuff solid . . .

"What makes you say that?" Tilly said carefully.

Salla gave her a rather wolfish smile. "Well, that's when your cabin was occupied, by someone who was meant to get off at Oyseen. Then after Oyseen my to-do list started shrinking, all of its own accord. But I wonder what was on Talaris that was so bad? It's nice there. Posh."

"I guess," said Tilly, unwilling to commit to even knowing the place. She deflected the question with other information, in the hope that this would satisfy Salla. "You're right about one thing, though," she said. "I *was* going to get off at Oyseen. I wasn't planning on stowing away, you know. That wasn't part of the plan."

"Oyseen?"

"My dad's there." Tilly saw Salla's face and knew her old story wasn't going to wash. "It just looked like a good place to get off."

Salla nodded. "Yeah, it's not so bad. So why didn't you?"

"My bag got stolen. My ID was in it." Tilly looked at Salla thoughtfully, and then risked explaining some of the circumstances. "I fell asleep and when I woke up it was gone."

"Sheesh," said Salla. "Rookie error. You really are green, aren't you?"

"I know," Tilly said mournfully. "Hey, any chance of getting it back, do you think?"

Salla gave a sad smile and shook her head. "That'll be long gone," she said. "Okay, so your bag got stolen."

"Yeah, so then I was kind of stuck . . ."

"But why not get off at Oyseen anyway?" Salla said. "Folks there would've helped you—nice girl like you, the authorities would be jumping to help."

That was close to the mark. There would, of course, be people looking for her everywhere . . . Tilly didn't answer.

Instead she took a swig of the tea. She gulped it down as quickly as possible. Small sips next time, she thought. Or would it only prolong the agony?

"Huh," said Salla. "Not gonna answer that one?" Her brow crinkled in thought. "Hmm, I wonder why?"

Tilly stared into her tea.

"Well, the obvious reason would be that you've done something bad, maybe criminal, and you don't want to be arrested or something." Salla gave a quiet laugh. "But that doesn't seem to quite fit for you!"

Tilly frowned. "Thanks, I guess!"

"So something else, I reckon. What could it be . . ." Salla mused on this for a while. "How about this? Maybe the problem wasn't that the authorities would help you, but that they would've helped too much?" She looked at Tilly sharply over the rim of her mug. "Is that closer?"

Tilly drained the last of her tea, like a pro. She even smacked her lips.

"Another cup?" said Salla dryly.

"You know what? I'm think I'm good for tea," said Tilly. "How about we get back to work? I don't mind working a while longer. There was a clanking noise along level five that I wasn't too happy about."

Over the next two days, they settled into a nice routine. Salla would come by first thing—early, *really* early, even for someone who had been the drummer on an Arixxian rowing team—and tap gently on Tilly's door until she rolled groaning out of bed. So this was working for a living? Schoolkids didn't know how good they had it. They would have a snack standing by one of the food slots (with some of the ever-flowing tea), chat about what was on the agenda for the day, and then get on with their rounds. As the day wore on, and they did their little, crucial jobs that kept the ship in motion and everyone on board alive, Salla would continue with her guessing game.

"So. Talaris," Salla mused. "What do I know about Talaris? Quite a bit, as it happens, as I'm planning to retire there. Like I said, it's posh. Nice climate, you see, one reason I fancy ending up there. People love a temperate planet with some sunshine and beaches . . . I always get off there if I can. I like the quieter places, off the beaten track. Some of the bigger cities—well, I felt like I was making the whole place fifty times grubbier! No, I don't like that kind of place. But some people do. They like that kind of place, don't they? Safe, friendly, bland. What about you, Tilly? Did you like living there?"

"I never said I lived there," Tilly replied. Her concentration was almost entirely on a piece of ODN wire that was not doing what she wanted. "I only ever said I got on there—"

She clapped her hand over her mouth. Too late! *Damn. Damn damn damn!*

Salla gave her silvery, wolfish smile. Tilly flushed furiously. She had realized far too late Salla's trap. Tilly had never in fact confirmed that she'd gotten on board at Talaris. Salla had guessed—sure, on the basis of some pretty good grounds. But now Tilly had stupidly confirmed that her guess was good.

"Okay," said Salla. "So that's one piece of information to add to my picture."

"You could just let me be," said Tilly, a little petulantly. "Isn't it enough that I'm here?"

"Sure, and it's nice having you here, but I don't like a mystery. Can't afford them, in my line of work. Something mysterious? Next thing you know, there's alarms and flashing lights and emergency routines . . ." Salla shook her head. "No, I like figuring things out. And you are a puzzle that I am going to enjoy solving."

"Or you could just *enjoy* having me around for a little while?" They had gotten more playful with each other as the hours went by. "You know, *teach* me, talk to me, maybe tell me a few stories about your rich and varied life?"

Salla snorted. "Where's the fun in that?" she said. "Pass me that spanner."

They worked on for a while. But Tilly wasn't going to let this one pass. "Go on," she said. "You tell me how *you* got here."

Salla sighed. "Oh, it's not a very interesting story."

"I'd like to hear it."

Salla gave her a sharp look. "I'm not sure you would."

"Yes, I would. Really, Salla."

There was a pause as Salla finished tightening a bolt. Then she put the spanner down, heaved herself up, and started walking along. Tilly hurried after her, carrying the toolbox. "Have you heard of a planet called Leyta?" Salla said at last.

Tilly shook her head. "No." All those worlds she'd studied and visited, and when it *really* mattered, she didn't know. "Should I have heard of it?"

"No reason," said Salla. "It's small. Not very important. And the reason it's never become very important is that it just can't seem to get the hang of peace."

Tilly frowned. "I don't understand."

"There's been a war on Leyta for over a century now," said Salla. "It's been going on so long that they call it the Long War." She glanced at Tilly. "Hey, don't blame me, I didn't name it."

A war for a century. Tilly, the child of peace and plenty, tried to imagine what that might be like. "That must be terrible."

"Well, when you're born to something, you tend to assume that's just what things are like. But, in this case—yes, you're right. It's terrible. The problem is that you can't sustain anything. You try to farm—someone burns the crops. You try to build—someone blows it up. You try to make a family—someone recruits your parents and kills your kids."

Tilly gasped.

"I'm sorry," said Salla. "That was a bit much, eh?"

"No, no . . . I just . . . I didn't realize . . . I mean . . . I *knew*, but I didn't *understand* . . ."

Salla nodded her head. "So, like most people from my world, I decided to take my chances elsewhere. You'll meet a lot of us around, in this part of the quadrant. Quite the emigrant community. Your lot—the Federation—we keep thinking they might come in, but you've got these grand ideas about nonintervention."

She shot Tilly a sharp look. On the tip of Tilly's tongue were all the standard defenses that she had learned from her mother, but she stopped herself in time.

"In your favor," said Salla, "you're kind to refugees."

Tilly thought hard. "But growing up like that, Salla. That must have been awful . . ."

"Of course it was. On the plus side"—Salla held up her spanner—"I'm very good at fixing things."

"How old were you," said Tilly, "when you left?"

"Sixteen," said Salla.

"Sixteen," said Tilly softly. "That's how old I am."

Salla smiled. Tilly flushed. Another piece of information, given away. Salla patted her on the shoulder. "Well, there's my story."

"I'm sorry, Salla."

Salla stopped in her tracks and turned to look at her. "Why are you sorry, my pet?"

"It's . . . it's a sad story."

Salla patted her on the cheek. "That's kind of you, but I don't feel sad. I've had a good life. I've had a lot of fun. And for most of it, I've been safe and warm and happy. Those are not bad things to have in life, you know." She was looking at Tilly very steadily. "Don't underestimate them."

That night, trying to get to sleep, Tilly couldn't stop thinking about all Salla had said. Tilly had always known how privileged a life she led as a Federation citizen. Both her parents, and her mother in particular, had always been careful to make sure she understood this. This, Tilly knew, was part of what drove her mother to work so hard. Striving to bring people together. Trying to keep the Federation safe. To bring other worlds to the point where they were able to join its great, diverse community. Tilly had never doubted the value of her mother's work; she just didn't think she was good enough to do it—no, that wasn't fair, she thought, her brow wrinkling, she wasn't cut out to do that. But maybe there was something else she could do? Maybe there were other ways of contributing?

But most of all, Tilly couldn't stop thinking about Salla—lovely, kind, clever Salla—aged sixteen, the same age that Tilly was now, leaving home and family behind, for good. She would never go home, that much had been clear. Home just didn't exist for her, other than what she made for herself.

Tilly rolled over on her pillow. *And I just walked away, without a backward thought. And all the time I know that I just have to say my name to the right person, and everything will be fine again right away. I don't think I really knew how lucky I've been. How lucky I am.*

But she wouldn't take back her decision to leave, because if she'd stayed, she would never have met Salla, and never heard her story. The other kids at school—they were off into these diplomatic careers. But what had they seen of the front line, Tilly thought. What did they know about the kind of life that Salla had led? It was not that Tilly would wish danger or fear for them, of course not, but it seemed now to Tilly that something was lacking from their lives. *I have to keep on*, she thought to herself, rather grimly. *I have to see more—understand more. I can't ever go back.*

Altogether, they only had three days in each other's company, but Tilly would always remember this as one of the happiest times of her life. Zymne was drawing closer, and that meant her time aboard the ship was coming to an end. The captain wouldn't let her stay.

"My, but I'm going to miss you," said Salla, sitting back on her haunches and looking fondly at the girl cross-legged before her. "I've got more work done over the last few days than I've managed in months."

Tilly grinned. Her hair was dragged back, she was wearing a filthy pair of overalls, and she had lube all over her hands and face. Her mother, if she had seen her, would have passed out. But Tilly wasn't really thinking about her mother right now. "I'm glad I've helped."

"I'm not kidding," Salla said. "I'd keep you on, if it was my call."

They looked regretfully at each other.

"Is there any chance . . ." Tilly started to ask wistfully. She would happily stay on board a while longer. She knew there was so much more that Salla could teach her. They had barely scratched the surface. "I mean, I don't take up much space, do I? And I'm already earning my keep. Imagine what I'd be like with a few more months under your tutelage. And, even better, maybe when you decided to retire, Captain Maris would have a fully trained engineer all ready to take up your job—"

But Salla was shaking her head. "I'm sorry, kiddo, it's not going to happen."

"Please? Please can't I stay?"

"It's not up to me," Salla said.

"Can't we talk to the captain?"

"I don't think you're her favorite person."

Tilly sighed. No, she supposed not.

"Besides, that cabin of yours is about to become cargo space. There's only so much one ship can carry and there's only so far I can push my luck with Maris. If I went to speak to her, the likely outcome would be that we'd *both* be kicked off at Zymne. And I don't fancy that much. Orders. Zymne is where you have to get off."

Tilly nodded. She knew Salla was telling her the truth, and she didn't feel like she was being pushed away, either. With her mother, Tilly had always felt like she was taking up time, that she was a bother, a problem to be solved. Even with Granna, sometimes, Tilly felt like she was intruding. Granna hadn't expected to spend much of her later years looking after yet another teenage girl. Not that Granna would ever say that, or even think it, but, still, Tilly knew . . . And as for her dad . . . Well, he'd made it really clear the past year how much he wanted to be near her. But she didn't get that feeling from the engineer. Salla liked having her around, and it wasn't just that Tilly was useful. It was that she was good company. Salla was comfortable with her. She *liked* Tilly, and that was a nice feeling. Tilly had always found it so hard to make and keep friends.

Perhaps I haven't been meeting the right people, she thought, and she nearly snorted out loud with laughter at that, thinking of what her mother would do if she ever saw Salla. There was no world, no *universe,* in which Salla would fall within Mom's definition of "the right people." Mom would be *furious*. Tilly smiled. It was funny how she was starting to think of her mother's fury more as something to laugh at than to fear. Of course, her mother was a very long way away right now. She might feel different about that if they were face-to-face.

Salla was watching her, a thoughtful expression on her face. She said, "What do you know about Zymne?"

"Not much," Tilly admitted. "Just what I found in the ship's databanks."

"You didn't really do much planning for this trip, did you?" Salla sighed. "Okay, well, Zymne is nothing like Talaris. And it's nothing like Earth."

There was a pause.

"What makes you mention Earth?"

Salla laughed. "You're learning. You really are learning."

"So how is Zymne different?"

"It's tougher," said Salla. Again, she looked at Tilly, seemed to be taking her measure, to see if she was equal to some task. "I think you'll be okay."

When the ship docked, and it was time to say goodbye, Salla walked Tilly down to the hatch. Maris was hovering around, ostensibly overseeing the arrival of the cargo, but also, presumably, to make sure Tilly really did get off this time.

"Well," said Salla. "I guess this is goodbye . . . And I never did work out who you were and where you'd come from."

Tilly winked.

"Hey," said Salla, "if you ever need a reference, get in touch."

"I might just take you up on that," said Tilly. "Where will you be?"

Salla waved a hand. "Here, of course." Unexpectedly, she pulled Tilly into a rough hug. Tilly wrapped her arms around the older woman, nuzzled her head against her shoulder, breathed in Salla's warm scent of soap and lubricant.

"Thank you," she said. "Thank you for looking out for me."

"You did a great job, kiddo," said Salla. "Good luck."

They released each other, and Tilly headed toward the hatch. Just before she left the ship for good, she looked back and saw Salla still watching. Tilly waved her hand in farewell, and then turned to face the world ahead. She took a deep breath. A new world. A new set of problems . . . *No, not problems,* Tilly thought. *Challenges. I can do this.*

I can do *this.*

Salla watched her go. "Poor kid," she said. She wouldn't choose to get off at Zymne: it was a tough old colony world that didn't have the time or resources to take care of strangers. She was going to face some real difficulties there. But Salla had some faith that she was up to the task.

Beside her, Maris, who had heard, snorted. "Poor kid? She was lucky not to get spaced!"

"Ah, cut her some slack!" said Salla.

"Slack? Some grubby kid, messing around with who knows what—"

"A kid who ran rings around you and who knows more about engines than you will ever do! This ship is working a lot better thanks to her. She's got promise. And you got all that work out of her more or less for free."

"She ate enough," said Maris.

Salla shrugged. "I guess." She lumbered down the corridor.

"Hey," said Maris, following, "did you ever work out what she was doing here?"

Salla smiled. "No," she said, and went back to her daily rounds.

It wasn't true. Salla had worked out early on exactly who Tilly was. She knew she'd gotten on at Talaris, and she knew what a wealthy Federation kid looked like. She'd guessed runaway almost immediately, and she also knew there were some nice schools on Talaris. After that, all she'd had to do was dig around, take a little look where she shouldn't, pry into security feeds and that kind of thing. Nothing *too* illegal. So she soon knew that everyone was in an uproar about a student missing from a very select academy on Talaris, and she wasn't surprised when she learned exactly who the kid's mother was.

And then the message had come through from the Federation authorities, just after they left Oyseen. A teenage girl, Sylvia Tilly, red hair, age sixteen . . . The picture clinched it. They wanted the people on the *Con* to conduct a ship-wide search to see if she was there. Salla had received the message, and she hadn't passed it on. Reading up on the kid's background, she thought she had a good idea why Tilly had run away. She bet there was a lot of pressure on her. She bet she just wanted some space. Why not let her have the space she needed? Salla had been old enough at sixteen to make decisions about her life—more than old enough. This kid surely was too—if they'd just let her get on with it.

She'd debated with herself, while Tilly had been on board, whether to let her know. She'd debated too whether or not she ought to alert the authorities. There was a real panic, after all. But in the end, she'd decided to mind her own business, and let Tilly's adventure run its course. Probably not the wisest thing to do, but the kid had been working so hard, had thrown herself into the tasks that Salla set her, had been ready to take on some really dirty work (Salla had enjoyed pushing those up the schedule). It wasn't hard to read between the lines. Unhappy at home, unhappy at school, taking a little time out to find herself. And, after a few really stupid mistakes, like getting her bag stolen, she'd gotten her act together. Salla nodded. That kid needed to see something of the real world, needed to prove to herself that she could make it out here. And that was why, in the end, she'd decided not to interfere. Because she saw a glimpse of something in Tilly, and she thought it deserved the chance to flourish.

As for the message? She supposed she'd have to sort that out with Maris later. Salla knew she had a reputation for eccentricity. Maybe she'd say she had just forgotten this one had come through. Or, better, maybe she might have a little tinker with the records, make it look like it had been delayed in arriving . . . She didn't want Maris to get any flak from the authorities for not responding to their request for assistance. They still had to travel around these systems, after all, and it was best to stay on the right side of the Federation. They were so big, so important, so well resourced. You never knew when they might come in handy. They'd find the girl eventually. In the meantime, she could get on with making her own way.

The ship pulled away from Zymne. "Good luck, Sylvia Tilly," Salla said. "I wonder how far you'll get?" She raised a mug of tea in her honor. "Hope you reach for the stars." And then Salla went slowly and steadily back to work.

8

Zymne did not make a good first impression. Everything about the place seemed to be gray: the sky, the buildings, the faces of the officials who were looking at Tilly with outright suspicion. The *Con*, shabby but comfortable, and Salla, much the same, already seemed to be a very long way away and a very long time ago. Nobody else had gotten off here, although a few had gotten on, so Tilly stuck out immediately, attracting the attention of the people tasked to monitor arrivals. She was taken to a small, dirty office, and left there, with nothing to do but stare out of the window over a muddy yard. It was raining, and there was an odd tang to the air, bitter and greasy. Tilly was starting to think there were good reasons that people didn't get off on Zymne.

She was by herself for about an hour or so. She tried the door, but it had been locked, and, besides, she didn't want to get off to a bad start. But there was nothing to do. They'd left her a cup of water, which she sipped, slowly, not sure how long she was going to have to make it last. The water tasted flat, as if it had gone through too many filtering cycles. No, Zymne was not a great place, all told. Was there anything here for her? Tilly wondered. Perhaps she should move on as soon as possible.

Eventually, the door opened, and a young woman wearing some kind of official badge came in. Tilly, not sure what was best to do, jumped to her feet, but the woman, who had a pinched and tired expression, gestured to her to sit down. "I'm sorry we've kept you waiting," she said. "We're short-staffed."

"That's okay," said Tilly. "I don't want to be any trouble."

The woman gave her a rueful smile. "I'm afraid you're that already, Miss, er . . ."

"Ms. Trace," Tilly said, pulling a pseudonym out of the top of her head.

"Trace," repeated the woman. She didn't look as if she entirely believed the name, but she entered it into the documents she was carrying. "All right, then," she said. "I should probably explain your situation to you."

"Am I in trouble?" Tilly said.

"No, but you're not out of trouble, if you get my drift," the official said.

"I'm not sure I do . . ."

"Let me explain your situation, then. And explain our position."

Tilly nodded and listened closely.

"The problem is that you've arrived out of nowhere without any ID or any visible means of support. And— while we're not hostile to new arrivals, by any means, we can't support people who can't contribute." The woman nodded out the window. "Look out there. You can see what kind of place this is. There's not much here—frankly I'm amazed you decided to get off your ship here."

"I was sort of . . . *pushed*," Tilly said. "I mean, I don't want to sound ungrateful, I know I'm causing you a head-ache and you're being very nice about it, but I would have preferred to stay on the ship a little longer."

The woman tilted her head in acknowledgment. "Fair enough. But you're here now. And the simple fact is that we can't support you, not if you have nothing to add. If you want to stay, you have to prove that you have something to contribute. People who can contribute are very welcome here." The woman gave that dry smile again. "As I say— we're short-staffed. And not just here. All over."

"When you say contribute," Tilly said slowly, "what do you mean? You don't want me to help with your workload, do you?"

"No, although maybe if you stuck around a while you might end up with the job." The official cast an appraising eye over her. "You're pretty young, aren't you? Which means you probably don't have much in the way of experience or technical skills. I could find you farm labor easily enough, we're always short of people out in the sticks, but, speaking frankly, Ms. Trace, that isn't much fun and you might find that you'd rather move on to somewhere else." She started looking through her notes. "There's a ship heading back to Oyseen tomorrow, but you'd have to make yourself useful in the meantime."

"Farm labor?" said Tilly.

"If you think that's all you can do." She put her notes down. "Look, Ms. Trace, this is the long and short of it. We're living on the margins here. We can't carry you. If you've got something to offer us—then we're interested. You've got a day, twenty-seven hours, before that ship heads off to Oyseen. We can give you a bed for the night, something to eat, and that's it. If you can't prove your worth, then I'm afraid that means you're on the next ship out."

Tilly, processing all this quickly, tried to think what was best. She didn't want to head all the way back to Oyseen, not least because surely people had worked out by now that she had gone that way. Going back toward Talaris was likely to be the best way to get caught. But that was the only option: she very much doubted, looking at the woman's firm expression, that she could persuade them to wait a day or two and put her on a different ship. So that meant trying to stay here on Zymne for a while, at least, if she could meet the entry requirements. Tilly frowned. Was this even a world she wanted to stay on? She glanced out the window. The rain was persistent, the kind of rain that would get into your bones, leaving you feeling permanently cold. And farm labor wasn't going to be indoors, was it? To Tilly's credit, she didn't for one second at this point think of using her mother's name to get her out of this. Instead: "Technical skills," Tilly said. "You mentioned technical skills."

The woman looked at her in interest. "That something you've got?"

"I paid my way on the *Constance Markievicz* by helping out their engineer," Tilly said quietly, but with a fair amount of pride. "I'm pretty good at fixing things." She drew a deep breath. "So—do you have anything round here that needs fixing?"

The woman smiled at her. "Oh yes," she said. "There's a lot of that about."

"Okay," Tilly said. "Then why don't I take a look at some of it?"

The woman made a few notes, then nodded and stood up. "All right, Ms. Trace. I'll sort out a bed for you, and I'll get some work projects organized for you. Remember what I said, though—twenty-seven hours, that's all you've got. If it doesn't work out—back to Oyseen." She headed toward the door. "I'll send someone to take you to your room, when it's ready. And one request," she said. "Please don't try to run away."

"Into that?" Tilly jerked her head toward the window, and the miserable rain lashing down outside. "Not a chance."

She waited another hour or so, trying to be patient and remembering that they were short of people, and eventually another official turned up. He was a middle-aged man, not much taller than Tilly, and had the same tired look that the young woman had. Tilly had to admit that this was pretty off-putting: Was that what living on this world did to people? Did they all just end up exhausted? Still, when he walked into the room and saw Tilly, he gave her a big smile and said, "Well, what do we have here?"

"Hi," she said, giving him a little wave. "I'm . . . Zoe Trace. I'm here to fix things."

"That's what I heard," he said. "All right, come with me."

She followed him out of the room and to the door of the building. He threw her a coat, too big and rather badly made, but with a hood. She pulled it on quickly and went out into the rain. Yep, this was the mean stuff, she thought as they dashed across a concrete yard; the kind of rain that wastes no time getting you wet and then dedicates itself to keeping you that way. You definitely didn't want to be out for long in this. The air, too, had that rather greasy tang to it, and Tilly saw black clouds on the horizon—smog. Her companion, she noticed, had covered his mouth and nose with his hand. Tilly did the same. Fortunately, they were going no farther than the next building, and her new friend hurried her inside and closed the door behind them.

This building was another rather bleak affair, with little in the way of comforts. Behind the entrance hall there was a long corridor, with doors on either side; glancing in, Tilly saw little bedrooms. These were mostly empty; one or two had inhabitants, lying on their beds, waiting for passage to Oyseen, Tilly guessed. She frowned. She wasn't going to get sent away, she decided.

Her guide came to a halt by an open door, and ushered Tilly inside. She looked around, her heart sinking. A narrow bed, a sink, one rather harsh light source up in the ceiling, and a big wooden bench piled high with all kinds of old tech. "Welcome to Zymne," said her guide wryly. "There's a tool kit in there somewhere. I'd get busy, if I were you."

Tilly looked in dismay at the chaos on the table, then drew a deep breath. "Okay," she said.

"That's the spirit." Her guard went out and began to head off down the corridor.

"You're not locking me in?" Tilly called after him.

He popped his head back around the door. "Lock you in? You're not a prisoner! You're welcome to leave at any point. But, er . . ." He laughed. "That rain doesn't half soak through, you know. Speaking for myself, I wouldn't like to have to spend the night in it." He looked around the room. "It's not much, but it's warm and dry. No, you'll stay here. It'll be supper soon. In the meantime . . ." He gestured at the table. "I heard you were an engineer of some sort."

"Apprentice," she said.

"Well, sunshine, time to prove your worth."

He left her to it. Tilly, looking at the pile of stuff on the workbench, sighed, and felt her shoulders slump. But then something caught her eye. "Is that a *drill*?" She went over to pick it up, turning it around in her hands, trying to see what it was exactly, and what had gone wrong. And that was it. She dug out a tool kit and got to work.

That day turned out to be her best yet. She got through everything on the table within the first few hours and had to go looking for something else to do. Her guide, whose name, he had told her, was Orlotz, had taken rather a shine to her. He would come past every hour or so to check on her. Mostly she was so engrossed that she didn't chat for long, but when he turned up with supper, she took a break and asked him about himself. He was from upcountry, and had come here, to the main spaceport, in search of work.

"I've got a girl, about your age," he said wistfully. "Had to leave her back home with her mother when I came up here. Someone has to keep the farm going. But I do miss her . . ."

"I hope you speak to her as often as you can," said Tilly sternly. "It's not right for fathers to be out of touch too long. Their daughters *really* miss them, you know?"

"We speak every night," he said with a smile. "I'm going for a chat as soon as I get off shift."

Tilly looked down at her hands. She realized that she had tears in her eyes. She felt a stab of pure envy toward this girl, who must have nearly nothing, and lived in the back of beyond on a harsh world out in the middle of nowhere, but whose daddy managed to speak to her every single evening. Tilly, blinking back her tears, thought, *I'd give up all the big houses and exclusive schools and fancy dresses and nice shoes and just about everything, if Dad was able to do that. I'd just like to see him. Talk to him. Be with him . . .*

She coughed. "Well," she said. "You're right to do that. You'll be making her happy, doing that. Gosh, listen to me *rattling* on!"

He left her to it, and Tilly threw herself back into her task with renewed vigor. An hour or so after this, Orlotz put his head around the door. "Hey," he said. "It's getting late. You should get some sleep. You're running out of things to do anyway. I've put out a call for more projects, and we'll have some more stuff for you to do in the morning."

Tilly sighed and sat back in her chair. She balled her fists and rubbed them into her eyes. She did, suddenly, feel very tired. "Okay," she said doubtfully. "I guess I could stop for a while."

"You're going to have to," Orlotz said prosaically. "It's lights out in fifteen minutes, all across the city. We can't keep the power on all night, you know."

Not long after, the harsh lights on the ceiling of her room and in the corridor outside went out, and the whole building was plunged into darkness. Tilly lay on her bed, too tired to sleep, and thought about her options. She was pretty sure that she was doing well, maybe enough to keep her here. But did she want to stay? This was a hard world, with bad weather and poor air, and tired people who had to work hard just to keep themselves going, and without much pleasure in their lives. Supper had been pretty basic. Tilly suspected that you'd always feel slightly hungry here. But at the same time, everyone had been kind—or not actively unkind. She thought about other things they could have done when she'd arrived without anything but the clothes she was wearing: locked her up, frightened her, threatened her. Instead, they'd made clear what the situation was, and given her every chance to prove herself. *I could make a difference here*, she thought. *I'm young, and fit, and I have skills that they need. I could do something worthwhile here*. And that, Tilly thought as she drifted off to sleep, felt good.

The next day, Tilly excelled herself. A whole pile of equipment had come in from a factory down the road, the workers desperate for someone to look at it. Orlotz, bringing her a rather slight breakfast, raised his eyebrows at her pace.

"Slow down, sunshine!" he said. "This stuff isn't going anywhere—and I don't think you are, either!"

Midmorning, the young woman who had talked to her the previous day came past. She too was amazed to see how much Tilly had done. "You know," she said dryly, "you could probably take the rest of the day off. I think you've done enough."

"That's okay," said Tilly. "Those guys need these 3-D printers back as soon as possible, don't they? And I like fixing things—so, win-win, all round, really."

The young woman sat down on the bed and watched Tilly work for a while. "Zoe," she said eventually, and Tilly, who had almost forgotten this was her alias, took a moment to reply.

"Yep?"

"Why do you want to stay here?"

Tilly frowned. "What do you mean?"

"I mean—you're from the Federation, aren't you?"

"Is it that obvious?" Tilly said.

The young woman nodded. "So why . . ." She gestured around helplessly. "Why *here* of all places? This is hardly Risa."

Tilly stopped work. "Why? Because you've all been nice to me," she said simply. "And because you asked me to help, and it turned out I could."

The woman, listening, nodded. "Well," she said, "I think that if I could travel freely around Federation space, I might not stay here. But you know your own business." She stood up slowly. "You don't have to do any more today if you don't want."

"No, I'll get this done . . ." Tilly said.

"What I mean is, you're welcome to stay."

Tilly flushed with pleasure. "So what happens next?"

"What happens next is that I find you a work assignment, and somewhere to live. I've got some ideas of the first, and there's a boardinghouse just down the road from here that should be able to fit you in. I know the people who run it. They're . . ." She gave her wry smile again. "They're nice."

"That's great!" said Tilly. "Thank you!"

"Don't thank me till you find out what your job is," the woman said, and left.

She was back within the hour with a pile of documents. "Here's your work permit and assignment," she said, passing these to Tilly. "Here's your ration book—that covers food and clothes, plus water and power. And here's a map of the city. I've marked the boardinghouse—they're expecting you—and you start work tomorrow *here*." She pointed on the map. "And here's a credit chip," she said, handing one over.

Tilly frowned. "I wasn't expecting this."

"No, it's not usual. But you've done so much that you've earned something." She gave that tired smile. "We're not slave drivers, Zoe," she said. "We don't have much. Anyway, you've earned something, and it should help you get started."

Tilly looked down at the small but precious pile of things she'd been given. "Thank you," she said. "I really mean that. Thank you so much."

The woman looked pained. "I've given you hardly anything," she said.

"You don't know how much you've given me," Tilly said.

Suddenly, the young woman stuck out her hand. "I'm Natalia," she said. "Why don't we meet up one evening? Have a bite to eat? It might be nice for you to have a friend in town, while you're getting started."

Tilly beamed at her. She stuck out her own hand, and they clasped and shook. "I'd love that," she said. *A pal*, she thought. *I've made a pal.*

They smiled at each other, and then Tilly headed on her

way. She had a short walk into the city, and she wanted to get as far as she could while there was a break in the rain. She was halfway across the compound when Natalia came out of her office and called her back. "Zoe! Wait! Come back a minute."

Tilly walked back. "Is something the matter?"

Natalia was looking at her with a very odd expression. "I don't know," she said. "But there's someone here to see you."

Tilly frowned. She followed Natalia back inside, and into a small office.

There, like something from a different lifetime, stood Granna. All Tilly's hopes and dreams for a new life came crashing down.

"Tilly," Adèle said reproachfully, "how could you do this to us?"

Behind her, Tilly heard Natalia say, in a puzzled voice, "'*Tilly*'? Is *that* your name?"

"Oh my," said Tilly faintly. Her grandmother, here, on Zymne. And there was Quinn, too, standing a little behind Granna, a hand on his wife's shoulder, looking considerably sterner than she had ever seen him before. "Oh gosh. Granna, I didn't expect . . ."

Tilly drew in a short, tight breath. All of a sudden it felt as if the net was closing in around her again. "How did you *find* me?" To herself, she thought angrily: *More importantly, why did you find me?*

Granna and Quinn exchanged an exasperated look. "Tilly," said Adèle, "if someone like you disappears, it's a major incident. The security implications . . ."

Slowly, Tilly became aware of the two figures standing at the far side of the room, busy reporting back to the superiors that they had her. Federation Security. Of course. She'd forgotten what it was like to have them around all the time. Again, she had that feeling of the net closing in on her. She was suddenly aware of Natalia, standing just to her side, an odd expression on her face as she looked between the security officers and Tilly. One of the officers stepped forward to speak to Natalia. "Thank you for all your help," she said. "We can take it from here."

Natalia's eyes widened. "There'll be some paperwork to complete so we can officially release Ms. Tilly into your care," she said rather stiffly. "I'll get that arranged straightaway." She walked toward the door. On her way through, she looked back and gave Tilly her wry smile. "Federation Security Council, hey? I guess we won't be having that bite to eat after all."

She left. Tilly felt awful, like she'd betrayed her new friend in some way. She put her hands to her head and turned back to face the others. She gave a deep sigh. She had known, of course, that there would be a search under way, and that they wouldn't give up until they had found her. She had disappeared into thin air, after all. *Perhaps I should have done something to stop that,* she thought glumly. *Left a note: Don't come after me, I'm fine.* But they wouldn't have listened, would they? They never listened. *All I wanted was some space to do my own thing for a while,* she thought bitterly. *But no—it's always, always about Mom.* Still, she thought that she might have been able to have a little more time.

Suddenly, Tilly realized that Adèle was crying. Not much, not so as you would notice, but there were definitely tears in her eyes . . . "Granna," she said, stepping forward, reaching out hesitantly to touch her arm, "are you okay?"

Quinn, ever the gallant, bent down to pass his wife a handkerchief, which she used to dab delicately at her eyes.

"Don't worry, Adèle, love," he said softly. "Look, she's fine, isn't she? She's grand. Everything has turned out fine."

Granna, nodding, wiped her eyes dry and tucked the handkerchief away. Suddenly, Tilly was overwhelmed with shame, and a full realization of what her disappearance must have meant to everyone. Mom wasn't the only one involved, was she?

"Oh Granna!" she cried. She folded Adèle in a huge hug. "I'm sorry! I'm so, so sorry!"

"I know, darling," said her grandmother. "Oh, but, Tilly—why? Why did you do such a foolish, thoughtless thing?"

Unexpectedly, Quinn had something to say. "I think we all know why, don't we?" He gave Tilly a sharp look. "Fed up, weren't you, kiddo? Always someone telling you what you should be doing, what you shouldn't be doing, how you should be doing better?"

Tilly, who by now had her head burrowed into her granna's arm, looked up and nodded. "I . . . I just couldn't keep on. Granna, Quinn—I didn't mean to frighten any-one! I was fine, the whole time, I was *fine*." Okay, so there'd been a few hairy moments, but there was no need to go into all that right now. "I just needed . . . I needed some space to *breathe*."

Granna was stroking her hair. "But Tilly, you're still a *child*. We *have* to look after you."

"Not a child, love," said Quinn softly. "But not quite a grown-up either, eh, Tilly?"

It was funny how quickly everything changed, Tilly was to think later. Only fifteen minutes earlier, she had been walking out onto a completely alien world, with a place to live and a new job starting in the morning. And now . . . It was like she was a schoolgirl again—a teenager who needed someone to look after her. Part of her, a treacherous part,

Tilly thought, was overwhelmingly glad to have them here. Everything had been so scary—losing her bag, being threatened by Maris, ending up in this strange, bleak place. All of a sudden, her worries had gone. She was safe, back in the bosom of her family. But at the same time, she had been doing just *fine*, hadn't she? She'd landed here on Zymne with absolutely nothing, and by the end of the day—one *single* day—she had found work, a place to live, and made a new friend. Someone who had liked her well enough on her own terms, not because of who her mother was. She thought about her classmates back at school and wondered how many of them would have done so well in the same circumstances. (She pushed away the thought that none of them would have run away in the first place.) All of these thoughts flashed through her mind when Quinn said she wasn't quite a grown-up. All she said was, "I was doing *okay*."

Granna and Quinn looked at each other. Granna sighed.

"You were okay for the moment," Quinn said firmly. "But what if your name had come out, eh? What if someone had worked out who you are? Someone who was willing to take advantage of you because of who your mother is?"

Mom, Mom—it always comes back to Mom . . .

"I think you've been lucky so far with the people you've met, Tilly," Quinn said gently. "But not everyone is like that."

It was certainly true that people had been good to her, Tilly thought, looking back over the past few days. Salla had been amazing—stood up for her with Maris, helped her as much as she could. And here on Zymne—Natalia, Orlotz—they had been completely fair. They had been kind. They had taken her on face value, taken her for who she was and what she could do. She doubted that Salla would have cared one jot who her mother was. Did that get the ventilation fixed? No. Tilly had done that, all by herself, because she was smart and hardworking, and that was why Salla had liked her. But at the same time Tilly knew in her heart that Quinn was right. Not everyone out here was a Salla, prepared to put themselves out for a kid on the run, or a Natalia, ready to be fair and give someone a chance. Tilly swallowed. She was starting to understand very clearly now that she had been lucky that Salla had found her before anyone less decent and more venal. She was starting to understand now that Zymne could have been a much colder, crueler place.

"It's hard, Tilly, I know," said Quinn softly. "And worse, it's not fair, is it? You didn't ask to be your mother's daughter. But you're stuck with it, and so now we have to work out a way to live with it."

Adèle gave her husband a sharp look. "What do you mean by that exactly, Quinn?"

Quinn sighed. "I mean . . . we can't keep on like this, can we?" Adèle, her eyes flashing, started to speak, but Quinn lifted his hand, palm up, to stop her for a moment. "Adèle, my love, this is your family, but I've kept my lips sealed for too long—and I know you've been doing the same. This poor kid—she's not happy. She's made that perfectly clear, wouldn't you say? This can't carry on."

Tilly was amazed to see that Granna was nodding. "I know," Adèle said softly. She looked at Tilly. "Very well. There's a great deal to discuss, isn't there? And first we need to speak to your mother—"

Tilly nearly burst into tears. "Mom's *here*?"

Both Granna and Quinn hurried to stop her panic. "No, no!" said Granna. "No, she's back on Earth."

"We wouldn't do that to you, kiddo," said Quinn, and he winked at her. "She couldn't get away."

Tilly sucked in a deep breath. For once, she was grateful for the sheer impossibility of her mother's schedule.

"No," said Granna. "I've asked the officials here to set up a link so that I can speak to her." She looked at her granddaughter. "They can't keep the link open long, so I think we can delay your talking to her until we have left Zymne and you have had a chance to rest, Tilly. No," she said grandly, "*I* shall speak to Siobhan."

"Oh, lord," said Quinn. "She's going into battle."

Tilly smiled. *I'm glad these two are here.* But at some point that conversation with Mom was going to have to happen. "Granna," said Tilly faintly. "Will you be there when we talk?"

Granna patted her hand. "Of course, my darling girl."

"We're on your side, Tilly," said Quinn. "And we do outnumber her, after all."

Adèle had found the authorities on Zymne extremely helpful. Adèle often found this in life. She swept into a room, and minor officials danced attendance on her, and did their best to fulfill her every need. This was nothing to do with her daughter, although that certainly did no harm. This was more to do with how Adèle imposed herself on any given situation. It was not that she made demands, or, indeed, had any intention of causing a scene or trouble. She simply acquired knights in shining armor.

"*Monsieur*," she said to the man at the desk, who had been goggling at her ever since she had transported down to the surface with Quinn and her security in tow, "I am extremely grateful for the courtesies you have shown us since our arrival. We must be disturbing the routine of your day in a most infuriating manner—"

"Oh, that's fine," Orlotz whispered, mouth dry. He was thinking that he was going to have some story to tell his wife and daughter that evening. Federation citizens didn't come by every day, and when they did, they were always so grand. "Er, whatever you need, ma'am."

"How kind of you. I am wondering whether the link back to Earth is now available?"

"Yes, it is, absolutely!"

Adèle gave him a smile that oozed glamour. "How extremely efficient of you! May I therefore make a request? I would like to speak to my daughter alone. But I would like her to be able to see my granddaughter. Is this possible?"

Orlotz jumped up, anxious to oblige. A way was indeed found, and very quickly. Adèle sat down in front of the link, straightened up her back, and arranged her features into her most austere expression. *Into battle*, she thought, and sighed. When had this relationship with Siobhan become so combative? Had it always been thus? The link took a little while to connect, to Orlotz's mortification, but at last, Siobhan appeared on the screen in front of her.

"Maman?" she said. *"Have you found her?"*

"Yes, my darling, I've found her."

Siobhan put her head in her hands. *"And she's all right? She's not been hurt."*

"She is, in fact, thriving," said Adèle.

Siobhan closed her eyes for a moment, and gave a deep, heartfelt sigh of relief.

Adèle moved smoothly into the gap. "She seems to have acquired a knack for making friends. Everyone here speaks very well of her. I gather she has been making herself extremely useful—"

Siobhan's eyes narrowed. *"Useful?"* She was starting to look angry. *"That girl! Has she explained her behavior yet?"*

Calmly, Adèle said, "I think the reasons for this little

escapade are quite plain to everyone who cares to think through the matter—"

"*I want her on the next ship and back here* right *away,*" said Siobhan. "*My goodness, that girl isn't going to know what's hit her! What a stupid, selfish,* childish *thing to do! Does she realize how much trouble she's caused? Does she* know *what kind of operation has been mobilized? And for what? If she'd wanted a holiday, she could have said—*"

"Siobhan, stop," said Adèle, raising her voice ever so slightly. "Stop talking for one second and listen."

There was a silence. "*Maman?*" said Siobhan uncertainly.

"Now," said Adèle, "I have also been making friends with some of the charming officials here on this world, and they have been most obliging. See what they have contrived for me."

"*Maman—*"

"Now," said Adèle. "This link is set up so that, if I turn it slightly so . . . There we are! You will be able to see Tilly for yourself and be satisfied that she is safe and well."

Orlotz had done her proud. Siobhan was now able to look at a screen showing a feed from the room where Tilly was sitting. She was chatting away to Orlotz and the security team.

"Look at her, Siobhan," said Adèle softly. "Look how straight she is sitting! Look at her shoulders. No hunching there. I haven't seen her like that in years! Look how she's talking to that nice man who has done so much to help me, and those charming young security people. Look how confident she is. Look how easily she's talking to them."

"*Maman, I'm not sure what the point is that you're trying to make—*"

"The point I am trying to make is that you have bullied that girl for years—"

"Bullied!" Siobhan was openmouthed, and very, very angry. Adèle did not let her gain momentum.

"Yes, bullied! And I've held my tongue, and let you make these mistakes, because she is your daughter and I didn't want to meddle . . . Well, that was my mistake, and a bad mistake, and look where it's got us!"

"Maman, bullied is completely out of line—"

"Maybe, but it's also true."

"I'm not going to argue with you about that, but whatever your opinion of my parenting style, Sylvia should know better*!"* Siobhan said hotly. *"She has had it drummed into her from year one that the life we lead brings with it certain responsibilities. Her sister has never pulled a stunt like this!"*

"Her sister had considerably more freedom. You were earlier in your career for more of her childhood. Poor Sylvia has always had these constraints."

"Poor Sylvia!" Siobhan snorted. *"That child has led a privileged life! You know, I thought we'd dodged the worst of the teenage years. I thought Sylvia had more sense. But—oh no! Sylvia has to go one better than everyone else—"*

"This is precisely what I mean, Siobhan," Adèle shot back. "Quick to judgment. Slow to understand. You demand compliance, but you do not reciprocate—"

"Okay, so here's the shuttle schedule. I'll send you the details, and I've booked passage for you and Quinn—"

"And, worst of all, Siobhan; you do *not* listen!"

Siobhan sat back in her seat, stunned by her mother's words.

"So listen to me now," Adèle said. "Tilly—yes, Tilly, you must learn to say this, and as quickly as possible!—Tilly is a *good* child. She has always been a most obedient child. But she *ran away*. And she did so because she is afraid of you."

"Afraid—?"

"Yes, afraid. For her to do something like this? Life must have become unbearable."

Siobhan sat and digested this. Adèle took the opportunity to press on.

"Siobhan, *chérie*," she said softly. "We have been lucky this time. Next time she might be taken for real. Next time we might not get her back."

Siobhan didn't reply at once. She sat with her hands steepled in front of her, the straight line of fingers pressed against her mouth. When she did at last speak, she sounded exasperated. *"So I am the monster in this."*

"You are the *mother* in this, *chérie*. Very different."

Siobhan ran her hand across her eyes. "Maman, *what am I supposed to do?*"

"You could start by asking Tilly what she wants."

"And what if she says she wants to stay out there—I can't leave her there!"

"No, no, of course not! Tilly understands that. The point is to have a conversation with her, Siobhan—"

"We talk all the time! Twice a week since she started at that school, more often when we can manage it!"

"No, you don't. *You* talk. No, that is not quite right. You *lecture*. Tilly is required to do nothing more than listen—"

"Maman, that is not fair!"

"Yes, it is fair. She told you not to send her to that school! And she was right! It was not the correct place for her! And when she tried to make a place for herself, found a small group of like-minded friends, you put a stop to it!"

"What? How did I do that?"

"Her engineering club!"

"Her what?"

"Siobhan!"

"Oh, that . . . I didn't stop that! That's completely unfair! I gave her a choice!"

"Oh, Siobhan, that is disingenuous of you! She knew what you wanted her to do! Of course she was going to drop the club! And she ended up lonely, and unhappy, and now we find ourselves here! My darling, we almost lost her!"

Siobhan fell quiet again. This time, when she spoke, she sounded chastened. *"Maman, I don't know what to do . . . I've tried, I really have. I just don't ever seem able to get it right."*

Adèle gave her daughter a rueful smile. "I know, *chérie*. Mothering—it's not the easiest task in the world."

"Huh," said Siobhan. *"Sometimes I think diplomacy is easier."*

"Quite. But rest easy, darling. I have called in the cavalry."

"The what?"

Adèle smiled. "Wait and see."

Tilly, sitting chatting to Orlotz and the security detail, was starting to wonder when exactly her mother was going to speak to her. Not that she was in any hurry to get started on that particular conversation, thank you very much. If Granna wanted to take all day talking to Mom, that was absolutely fine as far as Tilly was concerned. Maybe they could spin it out for the next *decade*.

The door opened. Tilly, expecting Granna, was surprised to see someone else ushered into the room. Someone wearing a Starfleet uniform. Someone with short, very red, very curly hair. Someone with a worried expression that made his boyish face look lined and tired.

"Ah, Iain," said Quinn cheerfully. "Always good to see you, son!"

Iain Tilly came over to his daughter and bent to plant a kiss on the top of her head. "Hi, Sills," he said. "What's this all about then? Bit drastic."

Tilly, over her initial shock, immediately went pink with fury. "Dad!" she said. "Honestly, how many times do I have to say this to people? It's not Sills, or Sylvia, or anything else! It's *Tilly*!"

"Well," said Iain Tilly. "That's told me off." He looked around the room, nodding his hello back to Quinn. Then, dryly, he said, "Is everyone ready to go yet? It's just that I've left a starship parked outside."

Part Three
Spring

9

Captain Yindi Holden of the *Dorothy Garrod* was on one of the treadmills in the gym, coming to the end of a 10k run. As she entered the last kilometer, she got a message informing her that her lieutenant was, with her permission, ready to come on board with his family. Holden glanced at her time. It was good. No way was she going to stop right now, not even for Iain Tilly, whom she liked a lot, and who didn't deserve the week he was having. Holden picked up her pace and all but sprinted to the end. *Good time!* she thought, leaning on the sides of the machine for a moment to get her breath back. *No way was I stopping in the middle of that.* The rest of the Family Tilly had caused enough disruption already. She grabbed a towel and wiped her hands and face, and then she threw the towel around her neck and bounded off to the transporter room, still in her sweats. Her T-shirt said: *Dotty*.

Her transporter chief, Sunita, was waiting for her. "Lieutenant Tilly's just requested to come on board again, Captain," she said with a smile. "I think he's starting to worry we might leave him there."

"Poor Iain," said Holden, with feeling. Iain Tilly was possibly the least troublesome person she had ever served with. He made no fuss about anything and just got quietly on with being one of the best xenoarchaeologists of his generation. Having to ask his captain to drag her ship across several systems in order to pick up his runaway daughter hadn't come particularly easily to him. Holden was trying to make this as easy as possible. The kid—well, she was a different matter. Holden wondered whether she had any idea exactly how much trouble she had caused for how many people. Distraught parents and grandparents. Security teams scrambled across several worlds. A starship pulled off mission to collect her. *Well, kiddo*, thought Holden, *you certainly know how to make a first impression*.

Iain had suffered enough. Holden gave the okay and Sunita operated the controls, and six figures came on board. Holden studied the little party with considerable but well-concealed amusement. Two security officers; she gave them a nod—she'd have a meeting with them later. Then came the main event. First to come over to speak to her was a very grand woman, beautifully dressed and turned out, surely the most impressive sight that poor bloody world had ever seen. She swept toward Holden and took her hand imperiously. Her grip was incredibly strong, which was okay, because Holden's was, too.

"Captain," said the woman, "*enchanté*."

"G'day," said Holden, with a grin. This would be Granny, then. The former mother-in-law. *Jeez, Iain*, she thought. *She's a force of nature. The holidays must have been grim*. But then she caught the older woman's eye, and she saw how sharp she was, how on the ball. *Okay*, she thought, *you're someone to have as a mate, aren't you? I bet you're a good mate. I certainly don't want you as my enemy*. She grinned at Adèle once again, and the older woman's eyes sparkled in response. *Yes, I think I'd like you as a mate*.

Next to come over was a handsome, somewhat raffish man slightly younger than the grandmother. This, presumably, was her husband, Quinn. Sheesh, what a complicated setup! Holden had a ton of brothers and sisters, and even more aunts and uncles and cousins, but her grandparents, at least, could be counted on the fingers of one hand. As the step-granddad passed, he gave Holden a wink. She knew from what Iain had told her that these two, and Quinn in particular, were more observers than participants in this particular soap opera. She winked back.

Next came the source of all the drama. A teenage girl, rather grubby and with a splotch of something on her left cheek. Holden peered curiously at that. Was it *grease*? What the hell had she been doing? She studied the girl with interest. Sylvia Tilly looked considerably less subdued than Holden might have in her situation. In fact, with her furrowed brow and her bottom lip jutting out, she was looking pretty mulish. She looked like someone who knew she was heading toward a major argument, and she was ready to get on with it. And someone who wasn't planning to give way. Holden smiled to herself. *Okay*, she thought, *we have a live one here.* As the girl went past, Holden gave her a wave. "G'day," she said. "Welcome aboard the *Dorothy Garrod.*"

The girl blinked. "Hi," she said uncertainly, and then her interest was clearly piqued. "Are you the *captain*?"

"Yup."

"Oh!" The girl looked her up and down, and her nose wrinkled at Holden's sweaty, disheveled appearance. "You're not what I was expecting from a Starfleet captain."

With some effort, Holden held in her laugh.

"Tilly . . ." said her father in warning tones.

The girl went scarlet. "Oh gosh, I meant your sweats . . . I thought everyone went around in uniform all the time . . . Plus, obviously, I was expecting to be *court-martialed* or something—"

"There's still time," said her father.

"Takes a while to set one up," said Quinn.

"Yeah," said Holden. "And I need to find my *special* black cap."

The kid blanched. Holden took pity. "I can't court-martial you," she said. "You're not Starfleet. Anyway," she said mischievously—because, after all, this had been some bloody big disruption—"that's a job for the parents."

The girl flushed again. "Ain't that the truth," she muttered miserably, and, despite all the trouble she'd caused, despite the spanner she'd thrown into the works of her ship's schedule, Holden's heart went out to her. Tilly's mother's reputation preceded her. *Cheer up, kiddo. We're all pulling for you.*

Last of all came Lieutenant Iain Tilly, his arms folded in front of him, a rather complicated expression on his face. Holden thought that she saw apprehension, exasperation, amusement, and no small amount of sheer relief. As he walked past her, he nodded at her sweats and said, "How was your time?"

She grinned. "Not bad." She nodded at his family. "All sorted now?"

He gave her a pained look. "Not even started." He lowered his voice. "I can't thank you enough for all your help over the last few days, Captain," he said. "I know this has put us back."

She gave him a lopsided smile. "No worries," she said. She meant it. They'd had to take the ship some way off course to get to Zymne and pick up Iain's runaway kid. It was a measure of her considerable regard for Iain that Holden had been willing to do this. What was the point of being a captain if you couldn't help out your crew? Besides, once they'd known that the kid was safe, and she'd realized that what was coming next was a big showdown, she had been absolutely gripped. She knew the rest of the crew were too. Iain's ex-wife was a well-known face, all over the news, a public figure, and you wouldn't be human if you weren't a tiny bit nosy about what was going on behind the scenes. Iain was completely discreet about her; he always spoke very warmly about her when he had to say anything. Which made this whole affair even more intriguing. She was tempted to send for *popcorn*. She glanced again at Iain's face. Nah, leave the poor man alone.

With the party now safely on board, Holden welcomed them all properly. "Good to have you all here," she said. "We've sorted out some comfortable quarters for you, and I hope you'll make the ship your home while you're on board." She turned to Iain. "Lieutenant, once they're settled, we can open a channel back to Earth. I think Tilly's mother is waiting to talk to you all?"

The girl groaned audibly. *Poor kid*, Holden thought again. Iain nodded, and ushered his small but impressively complicated family out of the room. Holden turned to Sunita, who had been standing quietly by the transporter, watching this whole business like a hawk.

Sunita raised her eyebrows and whistled. "Wow," she said, shaking her head. "To be a fly on the wall of *that* meeting."

They reached the quarters assigned to them, and Dad ushered them inside. Granna made polite noises about how nice it looked and how they would be comfortable here. "If it's okay," said Tilly quietly, and trying to sound contrite, "I think I'll have a lie down."

Her dad nodded and pointed her toward one of the bedrooms. Tilly lay on the bed, but she didn't try to sleep. She just wanted to put her thoughts in order. She thought about meeting Captain Holden, and she flushed all over. *That probably wasn't the best way to say hello to Dad's boss.* Particularly when she'd brought her ship all this way. Tilly groaned and rolled over to put her face into the pillow. This was awful. She could feel all her old awkwardness coming back. It was like the past few days hadn't happened. A couple of hours ago, she'd been on the brink of a whole new life—a job, a place to live, a friend to meet in the evenings. And now here she was, back with Granna and Quinn and Dad, turning back into Sills again. Turning back into Sylvia, that clumsy, misplaced, overgrown kid who was always saying the wrong thing and doing the wrong thing and missing the mark and getting things wrong.

But I don't want that, she thought. *I don't want to be that girl anymore. I want . . .*

But she wasn't sure yet exactly what she wanted. Staying on Zymne, she knew, had been completely unrealistic. There was never any chance of that happening. Her mother's prominence, and the risk that Tilly posed to Federation security if she was running around unprotected, meant that she would be found. It was just a matter of time. But a couple more days of freedom would have been nice. She would have liked to prove that she could earn her living, make her own way. She would have liked to have sat with Natalia and chatted. But no. She was back where she started.

Tilly rolled onto her back and locked her hands behind her head. She closed her eyes and listened. Just beyond the door, she could hear her father and her grandmother talking.

"Iain, my dear," Granna was saying warmly, "it's very good to see you again."

"Always lovely to see you too, Adèle," said Dad, and then he gave a quiet laugh. "I'm sorry that it's such a crazy situation . . ."

"I hope this hasn't caused too much difficulty for you with your captain," Quinn said. "Will the ship be able to get back on schedule?"

Tilly heard her father give a sigh, and a wave of guilt

washed over her. She already knew she'd caused significant disruption, and she'd been willing for that to happen to be able to get away. She just hadn't planned on the disruption being *starship*-sized.

"Don't worry about that," Iain said firmly. "Holden's very laid-back and most of the time I'm no trouble at all." Again, his quiet laugh. "Of course, when it does happen, it's probably the biggest interruption to its schedule the ship has had in years. Still, that's life with Siobhan for you. Everything's always on the biggest imaginable scale."

Tilly rolled onto her side, propping herself up on her elbow in order to listen more closely. Her parents' marriage always intrigued her. She had never really had a chance to look inside: she'd been too young when they'd split. To be honest, when she thought about it, she had never really understood what had brought them together. Mom was so outward focused; Dad was so inward looking. Mom acted; Dad deliberated. Mom loved cities; Dad loved hills. When she tried to imagine them meeting, dating, falling in love, Tilly drew a complete blank. She was pretty sure she knew what had forced them apart, though . . . She sighed. Trouble, that's what she was. *Starship*-sized.

The grown-ups carried on talking, about where the ship was heading next, about where Granna and Quinn and Tilly would disembark. After a little while, Tilly heard a tap on the door, and her father looked in.

"Hey," he said with a smile. "Do you need anything?"

Tilly shook her head.

"Comfortable?"

"Sure," she said. "It's nice here."

"You like it?"

She shrugged. One starship was much like another. "I guess."

Iain looked at her thoughtfully. "If you're up to it,"

he said, "we should speak to Mom. We've put her off long enough."

Tilly groaned and rolled over again, hiding her face once more in her pillow. *I'm not up to it*, she thought. *I'll never be up to it.*

She felt her father sit down on the edge of the bed. Gently, he put his hand on her hair, and stroked it. "Hey," he said. "I'll be right here throughout."

That'll be a change, she thought bitterly, and then felt bad. They'd all agreed he should take this posting. She'd agreed, and she'd wanted him to take it. She just hadn't banked on the past year being so full of *Mom* . . .

"I know Mom can be . . ." Iain gave a short laugh. "Well, she can be Mom. But I'm here, Granna's here—Quinn would chuck himself in front of you if all else fails."

That made her smile into the pillow. Good old Granna. Good old Quinn.

"So that's three on Team Tilly—I like the new name, by the way, makes me feel important, though probably best you make sure you're not following orders meant for me."

That made her giggle. She rolled over to look at him, and he smiled down at her lovingly. She felt a rush of reciprocal love. It was really nice, having him here, right next to her. She took hold of his hand.

"Yep," she said, "I'm *right* on top of following orders at the moment."

"Yes, well, it's okay for you," he said. "Yindi Holden can't court-martial *you*. Anyway, Team Tilly—three of us."

"I think technically Quinn only counts as a half."

"Two and a half, then. Is that enough to face Mom?"

She sighed. He was right—they couldn't put it off any longer. "I guess," she said. "Can I freshen up first?"

"Put your armor on, eh? Sure." He watched as she rolled off the bed. "Tilly," he said, his voice quiet, "I'm going to say this to you once, and once only, and then I'm not going to bring it up again."

His tone was so serious that she stopped what she was doing to look at him. His expression was serious too. Tilly felt dreadful. This was nearly as bad as facing Mom. Actually, she thought, realizing her mouth had gone unaccountably dry, this might be *worse* than facing Mom, because Dad hardly *ever* told her off.

"This was a bad idea," Dad said softly. "It made a lot of people very frightened, and it's caused a lot of people a great deal of trouble. And if someone had worked out who you were, and had been less than friendly, it could have caused a great deal more trouble—"

Causing trouble, she thought. *That's all they're worried about. Having their nice well-ordered lives disrupted . . .*

But Iain wasn't finished. "But I don't care about the trouble. I'd have mutinied and taken over the ship if that's what had been needed to get you back."

She flushed. She believed him. He came over and took her by the hand.

"What matters is that you could have been hurt or harmed. And that almost scares the life out of me, kiddo."

She leaned forward, putting her head against his shoulder. He put his arms around her, and hugged her, hard, and planted a kiss on the top of her head.

"I think I have a good idea why you did this," he said, "and I have a lot of sympathy for you. But please, Tilly, for the love of all that's holy—promise me that you won't do anything like this, ever again."

She started to sniffle, and before long it had turned into a good old, big, no-nonsense cry. Because although she had, in the end, done *just fine*, she had also been scared, and lonely, and far from home, and constantly aware that the whole idea had been absolutely, thoroughly, and com-

prehensively *dumb* and that it could have ended spectacu-
larly badly. So she had a good cry on her dad's shoulder,
and then he wiped the tears away from what she was sure
would now be an *impressively* blotchy face, and they sat on
the bed and gave each other small smiles.

"Dad," she said, "I'm *really* sorry. I will *never* do anything like this again. I promise."

"Good," he said. "That's all I wanted to hear. Thank
you for your apology. I accept."

Tilly wiped her hand across her eyes. "I bet I look just
great," she said. "Just right for talking to Mom."

"You get yourself washed and tidied up," he said, and
squeezed her hand. "Put your armor on, come on out, and
let's ride into battle together. The honor of the name of
Tilly is at stake."

When Tilly came out of her room, Adèle and Quinn smiled
to see her. "Well," said Adèle. "Are you ready to talk to
your mother now?"

"I guess . . ." Tilly said faintly. She felt Dad's hand on
her shoulder and she took a deep breath. *Remember how
well you did*, she told herself. *You did just fine.* "Yes," she
said. "I'm ready."

"That's the spirit," Quinn called from his seat on the
far side of the room. *Lucky old Quinn*, thought Tilly. Ever
the spectator. Tilly went over to the comm, sitting right in
front of it. Dad sat next to her. Adèle was to one side. They
waited for the signal to come through.

"I think she's coming from a meeting," Dad said.

She's always coming from a meeting, thought Tilly. She
put her hands flat on her knees and took another deep
breath. *Don't let her scare you*, she thought. *Don't let her
make you do anything you don't want to do . . .*

At last, the signal came through—and there was Mom. Tilly stared at her for a moment or two. It felt like years since she'd last seen her. It felt like a lifetime ago. They stared at each other.

"Well, Sylvia," Mom said eventually. *"What do you have to say for yourself?"*

And, despite all Tilly had promised herself about how this conversation would go, that faint hint of disapproval made her curl up inside, and the tiniest of voices came out.

"Sorry, Mom."

But the problem was that the tiny voice had never really had the desired effect on Siobhan. For some reason that Tilly had never been able to work out, it only annoyed her more. *Maybe it's not the voice,* Tilly thought. *Maybe it's everything about me . . . Just not right. Wrong.*

Mom was tapping the table in front of her. *"Sorry? Is that all? Do you realize how much trouble you've caused? Do you realize the size of the security operation that's been mounted?"*

But, then, out of nowhere, another voice whispered in Tilly's head.

Maybe it's nothing to do with me at all . . .

"Police and security on at least two worlds," Mom was saying. *"Your poor sister terrified out of her skin in case there'd been a kidnapping and she was next on the list. Not to mention your father's starship pulled days—no, I bet weeks—off schedule just to come and pick you up, like you were on a play-date or something—"*

"Siobhan," said Iain mildly.

Mom stopped speaking.

Tilly blinked. *Huh? How did* that *happen?*

"Tilly knows," said Iain quietly. "She's sorry. Everything's turned out okay. Why don't we move on from what's happened and focus on what we need to do next? Work out what's best for Tilly?"

Her mother threw up her hands. *"Tilly, Tilly, Tilly. Why is everyone calling her that all of a sudden?"*

"Because," Iain said sternly, "that's what she asked me to call her. And I'm respecting her request."

Tilly winced, waiting for the explosion or, worse, the icy sarcasm. But, wonder of wonders, her mother didn't say a thing. She looked at her ex-husband with a mixture of affection and exasperation, and she tilted her head, as if to acknowledge he had a point. Iain looked calmly back. *Wow,* thought Tilly. *How does that work? Dad, if I'd known you had special powers, I'd have asked for my share!* Because it was plain as the nose on her face that Dad was not intimidated by Mom. He was simply *not afraid of her at all.*

Is that a thing? thought Tilly. *Is that even* possible?

"Well," said Siobhan, in a quieter voice. *"Names are a hard habit to break. I can't promise I'll get it right every time."*

Apparently so.

"Okay," said Dad. "Let's talk about what we need to do next."

Siobhan was already busy with her notes. *"I've been in touch with the starbase nearest to you. There's a ship coming through in three days that can pick up Syl . . . Tilly and Granna and Quinn, if you can get them there. They can be back on Earth by the start of next week. It'll mean a couple more days off your ship's schedule, Iain—do you think your captain would be all right with that?"*

"I think I can swing it."

Tilly frowned. *Okay, so that's what's happening, is it?*

"I've spoken to Stavath back at the school on Talaris," Mom said, and her expression looked pained. *"Quite a long conversation, in fact. We've agreed that it's best if Tilly doesn't go back."*

Tilly thought about that for a moment. Was she disappointed? On balance, she decided, no, she wasn't. She hadn't fit in there. She hadn't been interested in most of the program it offered, and she hadn't been able to do the things she cared about. She didn't want to go back. Would she miss any of the friends she'd made? She thought about that too. No. They hadn't been interested in her for herself. They'd mostly been interested in her for Mom. She wouldn't miss them. The people she would have liked to get to know—from the engineering club—she had dropped them. You didn't come back from that. Besides, she thought dryly, it sounded like the school wasn't keen to have her back. She couldn't exactly blame them.

"It's been quite a bad time for them," Mom was saying. *"It looks like their security has let them down. I think you should write Stavath, Syl . . . Tilly. To apologize."*

Dad turned to her. "Okay, Tilly? Seems fair."

Tilly nodded slowly. Yes, it was more than fair. She hadn't thought about the embarrassment she would have caused the school. She sighed. Another complication.

"So what we need to do next," Mom was saying, *"is find another school. It's a big ask, given the circumstances, but I've been looking at a few closer to home, and I think there's one that might be willing to take you, Syl— I beg your pardon, Tilly."*

She was really trying, wasn't she? But as for her suggestion: "I don't want to go back to school," Tilly said quietly.

Both her parents turned to look at her.

"Tilly—" Mom started.

Dad lifted a finger, and Mom stopped. "Go on, Tilly," he said.

"I wasn't happy there," Tilly said, looking at Dad. "I didn't like the program. There wasn't enough science. There wasn't enough of the kind of thing I like to do, that I'm good at, and too much of the kind of thing I just don't care enough about—" She stopped, and glanced at her mom, taking in her expression. "I'm sorry, Mom. It wasn't right for me. I want to be with family—"

"But Tilly," Mom said. *"You can't stay with Granna forever. It isn't fair on her and Quinn. And we need to find a school that's going to offer the right program if you're going to get into the diplomatic corps—"*

"Mom," said Tilly. "I don't want to be a diplomat."

There was a silence. Tilly felt the ground open up before her. And then Dad took her hand. She looked at him. He was smiling. *Good girl*, he mouthed. *Well done.*

She looked at Mom, but Siobhan's expression was unreadable.

"Siobhan," said Dad. "Did you hear that?"

"Yes," said Siobhan. *"I heard."* She sighed. *"Okay. Well, that's about as clear a statement as it's possible to make. Can I ask, Tilly, what it is that you want to do instead?"*

Astromycology, she thought immediately. But she wasn't going to say that, not to Mom. She knew what Mom would say, and she couldn't bear to hear it derided.

"I don't know," she said slowly, and she saw exasperation begin to appear on Siobhan's face. Quickly, she said, "But I think that's okay, isn't it? I mean . . . I like math, and I like science, but I just don't know what I want to do with them yet. And it turned out that I was really good at fixing things."

Mom frowned. *"Fixing things?"*

"When we arrived on Zymne," Dad said, "it turned out Tilly had gotten herself a job in a factory as an apprentice mechanic."

"A mechanic," said Mom flatly.

"I was tempted to let her stay," said Dad mischievously. "The money wasn't bad. They loved her on Zymne, Siobhan. They were sorry to see her go."

"I see," said Mom. *"So,"* she went on, after a short

silence, *"math and science programs. All right, there are some good schools around specializing in that—"*

"Mom," said Tilly. "I don't want to go to a boarding school. I didn't fit in. I didn't like sharing a room—it was too stressful. I got angry with my roommate and she moved out."

Dad's eyebrows shot up. "Wow, Sills," he said unhappily. "You *did* get stressed."

Siobhan sighed. *"We're going around in circles. Tilly, it's going to have to be a school somewhere. Won't it help if the subjects are closer to your interests?"*

"Siobhan," said Iain, "you've heard her. She doesn't want to go back to a boarding school, and I have a feeling that if you make her, she won't stay for long. It's not working—"

"That's all well and good, Iain, but do you have a better idea?"

"Yes," Iain said. "I do, as a matter of fact."

Siobhan eyed him suspiciously. *"Why do I get the feeling I'm being set up?"*

"I wouldn't dare," Iain lied. "But I think this is a good idea. The *Dorothy Garrod* has a couple more research stops to make—when we get back on schedule, that is," he added, with a wink at Tilly. She flushed, but she wasn't upset. "Anyway," he went on, "then we'll be back in Federation space for the foreseeable future. Staff are going to conferences, presenting their research, that kind of thing. I'm giving the keynote at the big xeno conference back on Earth in a few months—"

Siobhan smiled. *"Iain, that's great! I'm really pleased for you!"*

"Thanks, Siobhan," he said with a fond smile. "But the point is, I've cleared this with my captain, and Tilly is welcome to stay on board. With me." He turned to her. "What do you think, Tilly? It's about time we hung out together."

Tilly stared at him, taken completely by surprise. Adèle, who had been sitting quietly and watching while the children sorted this out between them, moved swiftly into the gap. "I think it's a *marvelous* idea. Tilly—what do you say?"

Tilly hesitated. Anything was better than going back to school, that was for sure. But a starship? She wasn't too sure about that, but, on the other hand, she would love to spend some proper time with Dad.

"Yes," she said. "I think I'd like that."

Dad smiled. "There," he said. "That's settled." He gave his daughter's hand a squeeze. "Welcome aboard, Tilly."

There was some more conversation, sorting out some of the details, but Tilly let it all wash over her. She felt exhausted. It was crazy, she thought. It was just over a week since she'd run away, found herself in all kinds of difficult situations, and none of it—*none* of it—had required as much courage and energy as telling her mom that she didn't want to go back to school. But she'd done it. She'd done it. Tilly sat back in her chair, and found herself wishing, bizarrely, for a cup of Salla's strong and possibly not entirely nonalcoholic tea.

She'd done it. But the question now was: What's next?

When they had deposited Granna and Quinn at the starbase, and sent them on their way back to Earth, Tilly moved out of the guest quarters they had been sharing, and into her dad's quarters. There was a small spare room that was now her bedroom. Some of his books were on the top shelf in her room and there was a stack of his papers on the dining table.

"Dad," she said, one morning over breakfast, "have I moved into your office?"

"What?" He looked at her blearily over his coffee cup. He was awful at mornings.

"Some of your books are in there. And there's these . . ." She gestured toward the end of the table.

"Don't worry about those," he said. "They'll be gone by tonight."

"But have I taken your office?"

"I was using that space," he admitted. "But to be honest, Tilly, my notes were getting out of hand. They needed organizing. You've done me a favor."

She wasn't entirely convinced by that, but she thought it was nice of him to put it that way. Still, it was true that he had a dedicated office space elsewhere on the ship, and she had to sleep somewhere. But she was conscious that there were adjustments going on all around. She had her own adjustments to make, not least the idea of being on a Starfleet ship. The thing was—and she would *never* say this to her dad, never— Tilly had her doubts about Starfleet. At the back of her mind, she held Starfleet partially responsible for taking Dad away.

Sure, Dad was very committed to his research, and when your subject was xenoarchaeology, you were bound to spend a lot of time away. You couldn't exactly dig up alien cultures back on Earth, could you? Okay, everyone was alien to someone, but it didn't count if it was your home planet. So part of the issue was that time away was baked into what he did—just like with Mom. After the divorce, he had always made time for her. They had always spoken, at least once a week, wherever he was. And when he took research leave back on Earth, she split her time between him and Mom. But then, just over a year ago, he was offered an assignment on the *Dorothy Garrod*. They'd sat around and talked about this—Tilly and Mom and Dad—about whether he should take it, because it was going to mean at least a year out of regular contact. He hadn't been sure, but Tilly and Mom had pressed him to go, because it was such an amazing opportunity, Tilly insisted. Huh. That hadn't worked out so well, had it?

Dad being away was one reason she'd been living with
Granna. But Dad being away had brought Tilly much more
under the scrutiny of her mother. Tilly could see now that
was where the problems had started. Mom left to make decisions on her own, imposing her will on Tilly, without Dad
mediating. Tilly thought about the effect he'd had on that
conversation, how Mom had listened to him, even deferred
to him. When he was there, the whole dynamic changed. It
all worked better. And then Starfleet had come along with
their once-in-a-lifetime opportunity, and Dad had warped
off, and Tilly and Mom had gotten into the pattern of rubbing each other up the wrong way. Thanks for that, Starfleet!
Thanks a whole bunch!

So Tilly harbored some long-standing prejudices toward
Starfleet, although part of her knew that wasn't entirely fair.
But it was easier to blame Starfleet for Dad's absences than
the alternative. In her secret heart, Tilly feared that the reason that her parents' marriage had broken up was nothing
to do with two career-minded people pulling in different
directions, but was something she had done. What that was,
Tilly couldn't for the life of her have said, but she couldn't
shake the feeling that this was true. At the very least, she
thought, a kid should have been enough to keep them together—wasn't that the *point* of kids? Something to *share*?
Something to bring you *together*? She would have died before she said any of this to Mom, of course, and she'd never
mentioned it to Dad, either. Tilly knew he felt bad enough
already, spending so much time away.

One problem with the *Dorothy Garrod* was that, although there were a couple of families on board, all the children were much younger than her. The oldest was twelve,
and while he was a nice kid, and into math, he was, well—
twelve. Tilly's seventeenth birthday wasn't far away now.
Hanging around with a twelve-year-old wasn't something

she wanted to do (and he wasn't into the idea either). The other children on board were even younger than him. Sitting in class with the other kids wasn't fun. Instead, she, Dad, and the ship's teacher, and with surprisingly less input from Mom than Tilly had expected, sat down together and came up with a self-study course for her. Tilly was fine with self-study; she was happy to work at her own pace and had never had difficulty being motivated to work, particularly when the subjects were of interest to her. They made sure there was more of the kind of things that mattered to her on her syllabus. But she did miss company. She missed chatting about her studies to someone who was at the same level and working through the same problems. Dad was good to talk to, obviously, but that was more like teacher and student. Besides, he had his own work to get on with. They had some companionable evenings at the dinner table, working together, but she did miss others of her own age. *Enough to go back to school? No.*

The people closest to her in age were the cadets. But the gap between sixteen and early twenties was at least as big as the gap between sixteen and twelve. They seemed so *grown-up.* Tilly had led, she was coming rather ruefully to realize, a pretty sheltered life. One short adventure on a cargo ship and a frontier world might have been massive to her, but in reality the whole business had lasted only a week. One evening some of the younger cadets invited her over for pizza and vids and she told the story of her week "on the lam," as one of them called it. She made a good job of telling it, too, but then they started talking about their own exploits, and she realized how narrow her experience was in comparison. They had seen many frontier worlds, experienced many different cultures and species. She was slightly in awe of them.

No, she didn't quite fit in on the ship. She was an outlier. She wasn't a kid anymore, no doubt of that, but she wasn't in the same league as these capable young cadets, brimming over with confidence and with tales of far-flung worlds and fascinating work. Her dad, aware of this, said in passing one evening, "You know, Tilly, you will find your tribe one day. I promise. Look at me. What kind of kid wants to spend his summers poking around ruins? And yet Nana and Granddad—every year, they let me choose where we would go."

Lucky you, thought Tilly sadly.

"Do you know what your ruins are yet, Tills?" He'd started calling her that, halfway between his old nickname for her and her new name. She let him get away with it—nobody else, mind.

"Well, yes," she said. "Mushrooms."

He nodded. "Yes," he said. "I thought you were going to say that. But you don't need to be so self-deprecating about it, Tills. Astromycology. That's what you mean. You may as well say it. Once I stopped saying ruins and started saying xenoarchaeology, I felt much better about it. If people want to know more, they can ask." He grinned. "So. About these mushrooms—"

She threw a cushion at him.

"We've never talked about the attraction, Tills."

She took a deep breath and tried to explain. "It's about patterns, okay? It's about how things are connected, when you don't expect them to connect." She shrugged. "I guess this is why I like tinkering with things, you know? Opening things up and fixing them. Seeing how things connect . . . wires and circuits and the rest of it. But there's everything else too. Everything *behind* all that. Seeing how it all connects."

He was nodding. He understood this. "That's behind most kinds of serious study," he said. "That's what I'm doing, most of the time. Trying to work out how things connect. But I think you're talking about something more fundamental?"

"I think I am . . ." She gestured around. "There's something deeper going on. There's something there, I know it, I feel it. Something that unifies quantum and regular mechanics." She started to blush. "I don't know. I'm probably getting it all wrong. I usually do."

But he was taking her seriously. "I have to admit this is all beyond me," he said. "But your teachers seemed to think what you were doing was good. Maybe we just need to find the right people for you to talk to."

"You know," she said tentatively, "if there's anyone working on this kind of thing on board the *Dorothy Garrod*, I'd love to talk to them."

"Mushroom science department, eh?" Dad shook his head. "Not that kind of ship, unfortunately. We're mostly woolly-minded social scientists round here. Not surprising when you think who the ship's named after . . ."

Tilly nodded. She had looked up Dorothy Garrod when her dad had taken the assignment. ("Ah," she had said, when she read about her archaeological exploits, back when women didn't have the *vote* on much of Earth, if you can even *believe* that. "Okay, she sounds pretty cool. If you have to be on a Starfleet ship, Dad, you can be on that one.")

"So, no," said Iain. "No mycologists on the *Dorothy Garrod*, and definitely no astromycologists."

She sighed.

"But, you know, some of what I do when I'm not in the field is data analysis. Statistics."

She perked up at the sound of that. Statistics were good. Statistics were patterns.

"We've got some pretty smart people round here doing that kind of work," Iain said. "I've had to drag my figures over to them plenty of times. Is there something you're working on? I could have a word with some of the statisticians. See if they know anyone or anything. Everyone's keen on interdisciplinary studies, you know."

"On what now?" Tilly said, wrinkling her nose.

"Different disciplines, different subjects, working together. Swapping ideas and perspectives. It's Starfleet's mission statement, when you think about it. Let's have a chat with them and see what they're up to."

She nodded. She'd like that. Swapping ideas and perspectives. Connecting people and ideas together. Was that really what Starfleet was about? Perhaps there was more about Starfleet than she'd realized.

The biggest surprise, after a week on board, Tilly realized, was just how *relaxed* everyone was on the ship. Partly, she suspected, that was down to Yindi Holden's laid-back style, but partly it seemed baked into the setup. These were a bunch of smart and talented people who were mostly interested in doing good work and finding out about the good work that their colleagues were doing. It was, she realized, kind of what she'd wanted from her engineering club. Hang out, talk about interesting stuff, work through a few puzzles or problems together . . . Was that what Starfleet was, when it came down to it? One massive high-school science club? Why had no one ever mentioned this before? More importantly, where were they hiding all the astromycologists? Surely there were some out there. If Starfleet could manage to turn her dad's weird obsession with alien ruins into a respectable profession, surely it could manage to do the same for her?

Easily the best thing about being on the ship was hanging out with Dad. They had always gotten on well. There were no conversations about clothes, or hair, and absolutely no attempt to make her hold conversations over the dinner table in a language with massively overwrought subjunctive verbs or some other hellish complication. In fact, there wasn't a dinner table, as such, not least because Iain never quite managed to sort through the stack of padds that took up half of it. Instead, Dad would rustle up some food and then they would sit down in front of an old vid. *Wow*, thought Tilly as she ate spaghetti carbonara that they'd coaxed out of the food slot, and watched *The Man Who Fell to Earth* for the third time, *imagine what Mom would say if she could see this!* She thought about restaurant dinners and room service with Mom, or Granna's dinner table, with clean white linen and nice cutlery. And she put her feet up on the table in front of her and thought: *Is this what families do?*

There were walks on the holodeck too. Iain liked hill-walking. Not mountaineering, he said. Hillwalking. That was good enough for him. Tilly thought a lot about this too. Mom—Everest or nothing. Dad—happy with a hill. Was *that* what the problem had been? One afternoon, after they'd bagged Tilly's third summit of a Munro, they sat and watched a pretty spectacular sunset spread out across the Cairngorms, and Dad said, "Tilly, I owe you an apology."

She looked at him in surprise. "Hey," she said. "I thought *I* was the one that hacked her school tracking system and put the security forces of at least three worlds on high alert."

"Pshaw," he said, and waved his hand. "Water under the bridge."

"What do you mean, then?"

"I mean . . . I hadn't realized how bad things had got between you and Mom. We don't need to hash it over now, but I did want to say sorry. I know I haven't been around much the past year, and I know we all thought it would be okay, but it wasn't. It wasn't fair on you, Tills. I'm not going to say I can make it up to you, because I can't. Lost time is lost time. But I'm sorry that it didn't work out, and I'm really glad you're here now."

Tilly gave him a hug. She was glad too. Against all expectations, life was pretty good right now. Still, she just wished there was more for her to do.

10

Yindi Holden didn't miss much that happened on her ship, and, besides, she had decided to take a personal interest in her lieutenant's wayward teenage daughter. Leaving aside the chaos the whole exploit had caused, the sheer bloody annoyance of having to pull the ship off its schedule, Holden thought it had taken some guts to pack up and leave the way Sylvia Tilly had done. Other kids—they were out-and-out troublemakers. They pushed the boundaries as far as they could and looked you in the eye as if to say: *What are you going to do about that, huh?* What did you do? You grounded them, took away their privileges, and gave them an earful. This kid was, by all accounts, hardworking and overachieving. But for some reason, according to the story Iain had told her in that short and agonizing meeting they'd had before she'd turned the ship toward Zymne, this bright kid had hacked her way out of a security-obsessed school and turned herself into a working mechanic in the space of a fortnight. Holden knew as well as anyone how badly this could have turned out: she would never forget how white Iain Tilly had gone when she'd called him into her ready room to tell him his daughter was missing. But since everything had turned out okay, and Iain was now clearly looking at the funny side of the past few weeks, Holden was happy to join him there.

Iain's kid, so far as Holden could make out, seemed to be some kind of brilliant eccentric. That was okay with her. Holden liked brilliant eccentrics. It was why she captained a Starfleet science vessel—she had a whole ship of brilliant eccentrics. She had a whole *gutful* of brilliant eccentrics. But life wasn't easy for that kind of person, particularly during their teens, with such a high premium put on conformity and fitting in. Holden had a feeling this kid of Iain's could thrive in the right environment, and she had a feeling that the *Dorothy Garrod* could provide a lot of what she needed. But she knew they weren't there yet. She knew Tilly spent a lot of time alone during the day, studying by herself, checking in with the teacher periodically. She knew she spent most of her evenings with her dad. And here was another of Holden's . . . not *problems*, not exactly, but concerns.

Because Holden had a selfish reason for keeping an eye on things. Iain Tilly was quietly turning into one of her ship's success stories. His style wasn't flashy, and he wasn't pushy, but *shit*, the man knew how to put in the hours, and all that work was starting to pay off. Holden had been watching Iain Tilly's publications over the past few years and she was keeping a close eye on the work he was doing right now. At their fortnightly research meetings, she always paid particular attention to what he presented. She wasn't versed in his field, but Holden had a doctorate of her own in applied xeno-narratology, she read broadly and intelligently, and she knew that Iain's work was building momentum. Holden was certain that over the next few years Iain was going to write something major, something that would change his field. It was one of the reasons she'd invited him on board in the first place.

The problem? Single parenting would quickly put the brake on all that. Those long quiet evenings spent at his desk exploring his data and finessing his arguments would turn into movie nights and hanging out with his daughter. Which was great (not to mention, by the sound of things, probably well overdue), but Holden was worried that if Iain lost his groove right now, he might never get it back. It takes a village to raise a child, Holden knew, and her sense was that when that child was a smart, sensitive, and, okay, more than slightly neurotic teenager, then it probably takes a pretty substantial village. More like a small town, or a decent-sized *conurbation*. Iain was only one man. Even Tilly's mother, who by all accounts was some kind of superwoman, had needed support, hadn't she? The grandmother, the step-grandfather, eventually a boarding school. If Iain got some backup, he'd be able to carry on working. But Tilly didn't need a babysitter. She needed stimulation. She needed *friends*. People who were interesting, and interested, and ready to take her on her own terms. If only, Holden thought, Iain were surrounded by a bunch of clever, interesting people who liked to talk at length about their intellectual pursuits.

Hey, guess what? He was! He was surrounded by a ship full of brilliant eccentrics.

Holden's job, as she saw it, was to make this ship work for everyone. To create the kind of environment where everyone would flourish. You didn't get that by ignoring the fact that people had responsibilities and families, not to mention sudden crises and changes of circumstance. That was what was happening to Iain right now; and, to be fair on his ex-wife, it did sound like it was his turn to step up and take on some direct care of Tilly. These things happened in life, and part of Holden's job was to make the *Dorothy Garrod* the kind of place that supported its people. Sure, you could pretend that all that personal stuff didn't exist; you could expect your team to live like medieval monks at one of those weird old universities—but think of the talent that got wasted! Think of what was lost! All you had to do was adapt to circumstances and put the support in place.

So, Holden was set on making this situation work, for everyone. Support Iain's work. Help the kid find her feet. Get the whole team on board. She'd done it before, she'd do it again. She had an idea of what might work, but she wanted to be sure. She had a few quiet words with some of her team, and then she sent Tilly a message: *Swing by my ready room tomorrow. Fourteen hundred.* And then, on a whim, she sent a short video message to Earth.

"Madame," she said. "I'm Iain Tilly's captain. We met when you were on board the *Dorothy Garrod*. Can I ask a few questions?"

Adèle replied within the hour, and she was a mine of information. Holden smiled. She knew that Adèle would be a good mate.

Tilly received the captain's message with some trepidation. Her immediate thought was, *Oh dear, what have I done now?* When she showed the message to Dad, he said, "Oh dear, what have you done now?" Her heart sank.

He must have seen her expression, because he patted her on the arm. "Tills," he said, "I'm joking. You've met her. She's nice. She probably just wants to get to know you. Find out how you're getting along."

Oh no, thought Tilly. *Not another parent-teacher conference.* "Are you coming too?"

"Well, I've not been invited," Iain said with a laugh. "There's not much in the way of protocol on this ship, scandalously, but my standards are such that I certainly wouldn't turn up at the captain's ready room without an invitation. You're old enough not to need a chaperone. And why do you want your old dad hanging around anyway?"

So not a parent-teacher conference . . .

"Do you think I really am in trouble?" Anxiously, Tilly ran through everything she had done over the past week. Not much, to be honest. Got on with her studies . . . Got briefly obsessed with molecular gastronomy and then found out that gels were a bore, so switched to baking bread, where at least there was *yeast*. Ate a lot of bread. Got fed up of eating bread. Had the yeast done something when she wasn't looking? That stuff could take on a life of its own. Could yeast do something to a starship? Worriedly, she said, "I can't think of anything *specific* that I might have done."

"Well, you haven't run off," Dad said cheerfully, "so I'm taking this week as a win."

Tilly punched him on the arm. "I'm never going to live that down, am I?"

"Not while I have breath in my body. The last thing I'll say to you, through cracked gums in a toothless mouth, is *Remember that time you broke out of school?*"

Tilly giggled. "All right, I'll go and see her."

"She's nice, Tills. Honestly. Unbelievably nosy, but really nice."

Tilly tidied herself up, even going so far as putting on some lipstick. She picked out some of her slightly better clothes. Nothing too flashy, nothing *Mom*, but something that you might wear for a day out with some friends' parents. *If you had any friends*, she thought with a sigh. At fourteen hundred on the button, she tapped on the door of the captain's ready room, and heard Holden's friendly call, "Hey, come in!"

Holden was sitting behind her desk, writing something. "Hiya, Tilly! Give me two seconds, gotta get this abstract finished . . ."

"Sure!" Tilly watched her with interest. Holden was in her early forties, she guessed, gorgeous long dark hair, and an overwhelming air of . . . *Energy*. That was it. She was energetic. You sensed an appetite for life, for living, great curiosity for everything around her. Not nervous energy, but controlled and focused. Holden finished what she was writing, snapped shut the screen, and hopped up from her chair. She tied her dark hair back into a ponytail, pulled on a University of Wollongong sweatshirt (she didn't seem to wear a regular uniform much, Tilly had noticed), and headed toward the door.

"Okay," she said, "let's show you the sights."

They sped down the corridor. Holden moved like lightning and covered ground quickly. Tilly bounded to keep up. "What was the abstract about?" she asked. "If you don't mind me asking."

Holden grinned at her. "Nobody minds talking about their work," she said. "Okay, it's an interesting one. I've been looking at oral traditions amongst the K'la'bisi. They've got some really interesting patterns in their storytelling. A lot of Earth cultures hang their stories around conflict, Tilly—you might not have noticed that, but now I've told you, you will. Man kills the monster, that kind of thing. But the K'la'bisi don't do that. Their stories build up their effects from accumulation and association. Partly it's because their stories are constructed almost like choral music—polyphonic, you know? Like a piece of Thomas Tallis." She glanced at Tilly to see if she was following. "Do you get what I mean?"

Tilly thought of the Elisurians and their melodic quadratic equations. "Yes," she said thoughtfully. "I think I do."

Holden beamed. "Good! Not everyone does. Their eyes have usually glazed over by now, to be honest. So that's what my abstract is about. Nonconflictual storytelling modes in contemporary K'la'bisian narratives. It's going to be a long article, if I get my way."

"It sounds really interesting," said Tilly. She meant it.

She wondered whether she could find out more, see how it all connected to what she knew about the Elisurians.

"You think so?" said Holden. She seemed pleased, and slightly surprised. "You should come to our research seminars, Tilly. We have them once a week. I'll be talking about all this in a couple of weeks."

"I'd like that," Tilly said.

Holden smiled. "Come see this." She led Tilly over to an observation port.

They stood there for a while, looking into space. "Starscapes," said Holden. "You can't beat them, in my opinion. They just shout excitement, adventure, really wild things. Did you ever want to live on a starship, Tilly?"

Tilly bit her lip. Should she tell the truth? She didn't want to offend Holden, who had been incredibly nice, all things considered, but she also didn't think that hearing the truth would offend. "Honestly?" she said. "No."

Holden grinned. "Well, I did ask! Why not?"

Tilly looked out at the stars. Since she was being honest . . . "I wasn't sure I liked Starfleet very much."

Holden burst out laughing. "Okay! Well, thanks for your honesty! And are we as bad as you thought we'd be?"

"No," said Tilly, shaking her head. "You're very different from what I thought you'd be."

"Good!" said Holden. They walked on. They poked their noses around the bridge, and then left them in peace. As they walked along, Holden said, "So you didn't like school, huh?"

"It's not that I don't like school," Tilly said. "I just didn't like *that* school. I *love* school!" That wasn't quite right. "Well, I love learning things."

Holden was nodding. "Yeah, it's not always the same thing. How are you getting on right now, though? How's the self-study working out?"

"Oh, it's great!" Tilly said with genuine enthusiasm. "I love working at my own pace. I've worked out this reward system. Every two hours I do on something I really don't like, I get to do an hour on something I really do like."

"Sheesh, you've got better self-control than me!" Holden laughed. "Every four hours I spend on something I like, I spend one hour *thinking* about doing something I don't like!"

Tilly smiled. She didn't believe that for a second. She was sure Holden would do whatever was needed to get her work done, including the boring bits.

"It struck me, though, that the downside of self-study is that you end up spending a lot of time on your own," Holden said. "Not much in the way of company."

"There is that," Tilly admitted.

"Yeah, I've struggled to think of a way around, I'll be honest," Holden said, with a frown.

"That's okay," said Tilly. She was surprised to think that Holden had been giving the issue any thought at all.

"Sorry there's no one here your own age," Holden went on. "We had a really nice family a few years back— their daughter was about your age. But that's no good to you right now, is it?"

"To be honest," said Tilly, "I've never really got on with people my own age." She gave a nervous laugh. "Must be why I ran off!"

Holden laughed too. "Yeah, you didn't hold back there making your feelings clear!"

They walked on for a while, companionably.

"I'm really sorry I messed up the ship's schedule," Tilly said, in a tiny voice, but she thought it was important to make sure that had been said. "I mean—really, *really* sorry."

Holden patted her arm. "All is forgiven. You know, I thought about putting you on bread and water for a few months, but—nah. Sounded a hassle." Then she gave Tilly a sharp, clear look. "Not everyone would have made sure to apologize, you know. Good for you, Tilly."

Tilly flushed with pleasure. *Jeez,* she thought, *I really want this woman to like me. Don't mess it up now, Tilly. Don't say anything stupid.*

"Your dad said you're into mycology?" Holden said.

Tilly took a breath. *Please don't let there be any mushroom jokes.* "Yeah . . ."

"I'm not gonna pretend I know the first thing about that, but I've got a mate at the University of X'lis on Casaris IV. He's doing something in that area. He's into toxins."

"Oh, *amazing*!" Tilly's fingers were tingling with excitement. "Gotta love a pathogen!"

"He's a bit of a weirdo, but aren't we all?" Holden said. "I'll put you in touch?"

Tilly's flush deepened in sheer delight. "I would *love* that. Captain, is that Byth Th'vaales you're talking about? Because that's the expert on toxins . . ."

"Wow, you do know your field!" Holden was clearly genuinely impressed. "I'll send him a message later. He might have a little project you could get involved with. Everyone wants an extra research assistant. Do some number crunching, maybe? That'll keep you busy."

Tilly wondered whether anyone would mind if she did a little dance right where she stood. She thought probably not, but decided against it.

"Toxins, though," said Holden. "I'm going to wake one day and find out he's a *mass murderer*. It's always the quiet ones." She grinned. "I'm only joking. He's nice. I wouldn't put you in touch with an actual mass murderer."

"I think my dad might get a bit worried if you did."

"I think you're probably right."

They walked on a while, Tilly glowing with pleasure.

"Must be nice spending time with your dad?" Holden said.

"Yeah, I've *really* missed him."

"I'm not surprised," Holden said. "Sorry I stole him."

Tilly smiled. "That's okay."

Holden grinned back. Then she said, "Hey, look where we are. Engineering." Holden checked her chronometer. "Dammit, gotta go and speak to the research directors in ten minutes. You okay if I head off?"

"Sure," said Tilly, feeling a bit sad that the company was coming to an end. But Holden wasn't quite done yet.

"Hey," said Holden, "while you're here, you should have a look round." She called over to one of the crew, who was tinkering away at a panel nearby. "Patterson! You've got a visitor!" She patted Tilly on the arm. "Gotta dash. Catch you later, Tilly!"

Tilly watched her bound off down the corridor. Holden hadn't gone four paces before she broke into a jog, loping off down the corridor. Tilly turned back to Patterson, who was a scruffy young man with a furrowed brow. Tilly smiled wryly to herself. She had the faintest feeling that she was being set up. "Hi," said Patterson. "Tilly, isn't it? Iain's kid?"

"That's me . . ."

"We like Iain around here. Iain's no trouble." Patterson eyed her thoughtfully. "Hey, I heard you're pretty handy—"

"I'm not bad," said Tilly.

"Okay. Well, come on in. You can meet the gang."

Tilly smiled. Yeah. She'd been set up, all right. *Other kids—blind date with someone's brother. Me? A blind date with a wrench.*

—

Setup or not, it was a turning point. Engineering was run by Etraxis, a kindly man ten or fifteen years older than her father, but the rest of his team—four of them altogether—were all in their early twenties. As well as Andy Patterson, the young human male whom she had met that first time, there was a human woman, Mei Domoto; an Andorian, Thritte Zh'iqyliq; and an androgyne from the little-known world of Ri'tis, called Nish. The only people on the ship who weren't social scientists, they had bonded into a tight group. Smart, funny, interested in what made things tick, impervious to nonsense—they had all the best qualities of engineers. Tilly fit like a glove. Not only was she technically competent, which was perhaps the thing they admired most, she had also a great deal in common with them: a similar sense of humor (mostly bad puns or jokes that depended on arcane information), and a deep pleasure in problem solving. And then there were the late-night board-game sessions.

Iain watched this with interest and no small degree of pleasure. "You've got a better social life than me these days, Tills," he said as she hurried out the door one evening.

She stopped, halfway out, and gave him a worried look. "Will you be okay? You won't be lonely?"

Iain was already by the table, fidgeting with his notes. There was a mug of beer standing there too. "I'll keep myself busy."

She was glad he was okay about it. This was what she'd wanted from her club at school—but a hundred times better, because these guys were already doing it, and they let her help with noncritical projects. She hadn't really thought much before about what went on in Starfleet, mostly resenting the organization for taking her dad away. But it turned out that there was a place for her kind of people. Maybe, she thought, there was more to Starfleet after all. If there was room for all these diverse people . . . All very different. All getting along quite happily.

Holden, watching all this unfold, patted herself on the back and tried not to feel too smug. It had been a good plan, even if she hadn't really concealed it from Tilly—but then why hide anything? What mattered was the result. And the result here was a happier, more-settled teenage girl making friends and discovering role models, and a talented researcher on the cusp of doing his life's work who now had three or four free evenings a week.

Free and readily available childcare, Holden thought. *The simple solution to many of life's ills. Life's all about connection, isn't it?*

About a month and a half into her time on the *Dorothy Garrod*, Tilly had her first real brush with danger. The ship had finally returned to its planned itinerary and had sent a small group by shuttle to the surface of Varetis, to visit a dig. Dad was assigned to the landing party. He was going to be away for five days, and Tilly had been secretly looking forward to it: staying up a little later than usual, maybe getting started later in the morning. But all good things come to an end, and Dad's shuttle was now heading back. Tilly tidied up their quarters and programmed her own concoction of curry from the food slot. Midafternoon, she got a call from Dad, on the shuttle heading back to the ship.

"Hey!" she said. "How's it been?"

"*It's been fantastic,*" he said. "*Wait till I show you some of the artifacts, Tills. I've got to take a closer look, but I think we're on our way to solving a big puzzle about their religious practices.*"

She smiled at him. His eyes were shining, like a kid's at Christmas. She loved seeing him like this. He was living his best life, wasn't he? He was where he was supposed to be.

Suddenly, she saw a light in the shuttle start flashing red. Dad stopped talking.

"Dad? What's that?"

He was frowning. "*Tills*," he said, "*don't worry. But I've got to go.*"

The channel closed. "What just happened?" she said, to the empty room. And then an alarm went off, sounding all around the ship.

She dashed down to engineering. The alarm was still going off. Thritte and Nish were there, looking busy and intense. "Are we okay?" she said to Nish. "Is there a problem with the ship?"

Nish shook zir head. "We're fine. The ship's fine."

"So what's going on? Is there a problem with the shuttle? With Dad's shuttle? There was a red light there and he cut the comm."

Nish was staring down at a screen. "Not sure yet, Tilly. I'll tell you when I know."

Patterson and Mei arrived. They huddled in a corner with Thritte and Nish, talking in hushed urgent voices. Tilly caught something about the power being down, and she felt her throat constrict. She went over to join them. "Please," she said. "Please tell me what's happening!"

"Tilly."

She turned and saw Holden standing behind her. "Captain, I just want to know what's going on."

"I know. Come over here. Let's let these good people get on with their job." She led Tilly over to a quiet corner, gesturing to her to sit down. "Okay, Tilly, there's no good way to say this—"

Oh god, thought Tilly, *Dad* . . .

"Your dad's shuttle has run into trouble. There's been a power surge, and some of the critical systems have been knocked out—"

Tilly's heart nearly stopped. "Is he okay? Are they okay?"

"He's okay—everyone's okay. But the life-support systems are breaking down—"

"Are we heading there? When will we get there? Will we get there on time?"

"Yes, we are. We'll be with them midafternoon tomorrow. And—to answer your last question—we don't know yet."

"We don't *know* . . . ?" Tilly's hand went to her mouth. She thought of Dad, stuck in the tiny shuttle, running out of air . . . "Is he going to *die*?"

Holden took her hand. "Tilly, everyone's working really hard here. Mei, Thritte, Andy, Nish—they're working on some calculations to extend the shuttle's power so that the ship can get to them in time."

Tilly nodded. "Those guys," she said, with a quivery attempt at humor. "My heroes."

"Mine too," said Holden. "Listen, you don't have to stay here. You can go back to your quarters if you feel safer there—"

Tilly shook her head. "No, not back there, not by myself . . . I think I'd rather stay here, if that's okay." She saw Holden glance over to where the others were hard at work. "You won't need to nanny me," she said. "I won't interrupt, and I won't get in your way. But . . . I want to be with friends." She held back a sob. "Is that okay?"

Holden patted her shoulder. "Of course it's okay. Mind

if I stay with you?" She gave Tilly a wry smile. "I'm kind of worried too. And there's not much a narratologist can do in a situation like this."

"Oh, please!" said Tilly. She really didn't want to be alone. They sat together, quietly, watching the others work, throwing figures at one another, testing their theories. She closed her eyes. She couldn't help picturing the inside of the shuttle, seeing Dad struggling to breathe. She shook herself and tried not to think about that. She started humming her way through some Elisurian verb arrangements. They had an oddly soothing effect.

Someone tapped her shoulder. Tilly's eyes shot open. Nish was standing in front of her, holding out a padd. "Tilly, could you take a look through this? We could do with another set of eyes, just in case."

Numbly, Tilly took the padd and read through. It was calming, to look through numbers. She had to concentrate, and that was restful. When she was done, she handed the padd back to Nish. She thought she'd seen a couple of places where they could be more efficient with the fuel, and she'd marked these up. Nish took the numbers to the others, and they got back to work. Five minutes later, Patterson looked up.

"Okay," he said, "I think we've got it." He called over to Holden. "Captain, we think we've got some fixes that can extend life support for a few more hours. But we're going to have to cut comms to conserve power."

Holden glanced at Tilly. "Do you want to speak to him first?"

"What? Yes! Yes, of course!" She dashed over to join the others.

"Tills?" There was Dad. He sounded—he sounded the same as ever.

"Dad? Dad, are you okay?"

"*I'm fine, sweetheart. How are you?*"

"Terrified!" she wailed.

"*As long as you've tidied up our quarters, you've got nothing to worry about. Hey, Tills, we have to cut back on comms now. Saving power. I love you, sweetheart. I'll see you really soon.*"

"Tilly," said Nish, "I'm sorry, they have to turn this off now."

"Daddy!" she cried, but the comm had been cut.

Holden's hand was on her shoulder, moving her back to her seat. "Come on, kiddo. We just have to wait now. It's not much fun, but I'll be here with you. I'm not going anywhere."

At some point, exhaustion took over, and Tilly fell asleep in her seat. When she woke, she saw Holden standing over her, holding two steaming cups of tea. "Peppermint," she said, handing Tilly one of the cups. "Good for nerves."

Tilly accepted the cup gratefully. The vapor from the tea was good; it seemed to help clear her thoughts. Holden sat down beside her.

"Any news?" said Tilly.

"Nothing yet. We're still making good time, though. Even if they stop dead, we should be able to get there in time."

Tilly frowned. There was a lot being covered by that "should." She sipped her tea and said, "Why do you do this? Why do you choose to live with this danger?"

"What do you mean, Tilly?" Holden asked. She didn't sound offended or upset—she simply sounded like she wanted to understand the question clearly, in order to answer it properly.

"I mean . . . you could all have nice safe academic posts

somewhere. University towns are always really pretty. But instead you come all the way out into space, and then things like this happen . . ." She realized that she was crying. Next thing she knew, Holden had her arm around her shoulder and was stroking her hair, soothing her. "It's okay," Holden was saying, "it's okay."

"It's not okay! He could *die*!" Tilly had a little cry, and then wiped her eyes and turned to Holden. "I'm really sorry," she said. "I just . . ."

"Normal reaction," said Holden. "But to answer your question . . . I guess, well, you know that some of us love to do fieldwork, and that's part of why we come out here."

Tilly nodded; she could see that.

"But the main reason we come out is because . . ." Holden shook her head and held up her hands. "We're explorers, Tilly. It's as simple as that, you know. We want to see what's out there."

"I wondered, sometimes," said Tilly, "whether people were just running away from things."

Holden gave her a sharp look. "Some people, maybe. They don't last long. Whatever they're running away from, it usually turns out to be something they've brought with them. No, we're heading *toward* things. You can't do that at a desk back home."

"And if what you're heading toward turns out to be dangerous?"

"It's who we are, Tilly," Holden said. "It's what we do."

Tilly sat and thought about that. The last she'd seen of Dad, he'd been grinning like a kid. Living his best life, she'd thought. Was this the price? Was it really worth it?

About an hour later, the *Dorothy Garrod* reached the shuttle. Tilly, realizing what was happening, sprinted down to the shuttle bay. Holden barely kept pace with her, and, when the shuttle was finally on board, it was all the captain could do to hold her back.

The first two crewmembers came off on stretchers. Tilly burst into tears. And then—there he was. There was Dad, walking off the shuttle, leaning on one of the medical staff but looking *okay* . . . Holden let her go. She ran over to him and threw her arms around him.

"Hey, Tills," he said. "I'm glad to see you."

"Are you all right? Are you okay?"

"More or less. I think." He breathed out. "That was a bad one, wasn't it?"

Yes, she thought, *but it's what you do.*

Suddenly, he was holding her tight. She realized he was trembling. "Oh, Tills," he said. "I'm glad you're here. I kept on thinking about you, back here. I thought, *She'll be so cross with me if I don't come back.*"

Holden gently disentangled them. "All right, mister," she said, "let's get you to sickbay and checked out."

It wasn't long before Iain was released from sickbay, feeling pretty sorry for himself but without any harm done. Soon he and Tilly were back in their quarters. Breaking one of Mom's strictest bans, Iain ordered beers for them both. He handed one to Tilly, and then flopped down on the couch, his feet up on a low table. "Well," he said. "That was a hell of a thing."

Tilly snuggled up next to him. His arm went around her shoulders, and they gave each other a big hug. Tilly, holding on tight, felt her father tremble, just a little, before he took a deep breath and made himself relax.

"Okay," he said. "What are we going to watch?"

They picked the stupidest old vids that they could think

of and ate the curry that Tilly had made the previous day. They didn't do their usual running commentary over the top of the film; they were both too tired and just glad to be together. Partway through their third vid, though, Tilly said, "Dad?"

"Yep?"

"Why did you marry Mom?"

Iain turned his head to look at her in surprise. "What a question to ask!"

She panicked slightly. "Is it okay for me to ask?"

"What? Sure! Just . . . isn't it *obvious*?"

"Well, you know, given it ended in *divorce*, I'd say . . . no."

"Oh, okay." Iain took a swig from his bottle of beer. "Well. Here's what happened. I was at the Academy. Post-graduate work—writing up my doctorate, in fact. Looking for postings. My roommate thought I needed a night out. You turn into a bit of a hermit in the final push. You forget to eat and dress and so on. Anyway, my roommate . . . Sean, you remember Sean, yeah?"

Tilly nodded; he was her dad's oldest friend. She'd met him a couple of times.

"Sean made me shower and shave and took me off to this party. God, I was miserable. I'd forgotten how to make small talk. I've never really been good at it."

Tilly smiled. *Yeah, I thought that was probably your fault!*

"I was hiding in a corner wondering how quickly I could leave and go back to stressing needlessly by myself in my room, and suddenly the mood changed. And the reason it changed was that this woman, who I can only describe as a *minor deity*, had just walked in."

A minor deity? Tilly stared at her dad. *Wow.*

"So I decided to hang around for a while."

Tilly turned to face him. She was fascinated by this story. "Don't stop! What happened? Did you go and talk to her? What did you say?"

"Go and talk to her? Of course I didn't go and talk to her!"

"So what *happened*?" Tilly wailed.

"I'm by the drinks table, remember. Everyone comes past the drinks table eventually. And eventually your mother did, and while she was reaching out to pick up a bottle of beer, she knocked it over instead."

Tilly gaped. "*Mom* knocked over a bottle of beer?"

"She was a little bit drunk."

Tilly gaped even more. "*Mom* was *drunk*?"

He smiled at her. "The hits just keep on coming, don't they, Tills? We weren't born at forty, you know."

"I know, but . . . *drunk*?" Tilly shook her head. "Mom. I mean. Wow."

"Just a little bit."

"Still . . . And *beer*. Not even *wine*."

"Anyway, it went all over my shoes." Iain began to laugh. "She was mortified. I didn't mind. I couldn't believe my luck. We started mopping up the worst of it, and she said, 'I've done you a favor. That's a terrible pair of shoes.' Oh, my poor shoes! I loved those shoes. They were so comfortable."

Tilly tutted. "So *rude*!"

"I know. Wasn't she appalling? Anyway, as we were cleaning up the mess we got talking, and it turned out that not only was she beautiful and stylish, if rude about shoes, but also that she was incredibly smart, and when I said *xeno-archaeology* she didn't do that thing that happens when you say *astromycology* . . ."

Tilly nodded vigorously.

"But instead she said, 'Hey, what an interesting field.

I went on holiday to Estrevis II last year.' Which, as you know . . ."

"I know. She said that?"

"Oh yes," he said with a fond smile. "There were little hearts dancing around my eyes by now."

"I bet."

"Anyway, she was nice enough not to ditch her date that evening, but she did take my details, and she contacted me the next morning, and we went shoe shopping."

Tilly fell back into her seat. "Mom took you *shoe shopping* for your first date?"

"I know. How much more Mom could that be?"

"That's, like, *peak Mom*."

"Yep. She picked a really nice pair of shoes too. I don't think I've had a nicer pair of shoes. And that was how we met."

"Wow," said Tilly. "Why have I never heard this story before?"

"Partly because it involves alcohol," said her father. "And partly because when I've tried to tell you in the past, you've freaked out and gone, *Eurgh! My parents were never young and in love, that's so gross!*"

She slapped him on the arm. "So you married her because . . . ?"

"Tills, I married your mother because she was and continues to be the sharpest, most focused, most brilliant, most *sparkling* woman I have ever met."

And then I came along . . . Tilly thought sadly.

"You know, Tilly, you do remind me of her an awful lot."

"Oh, stop it, Dad, it's like they *cloned* you—"

"No, really, I mean it. You're supersmart. You make your presence felt in a room."

"Not in a good way!"

"Eh, that's just practice. And also, when you get an idea in your head, you pursue it thoroughly and vigorously, until you're absolutely on top of it. Like the gels and the cooking." He laughed. "Your mom took up the same hobby once. She did exactly the same thing. I really enjoyed watching you do that."

Another little glimpse into their married life, Tilly thought. She hadn't seen much of that. By the time she'd been born, one of them was always away for work, while the other looked after her. And then he'd called the whole thing off. Mom was a minor deity in his eyes, apparently, and still he'd left. *What changed, Daddy?* she thought, but she was sure she knew the answer already. She arrived on the scene.

"Does that answer your question?" her dad said.

She nodded.

"I really love your mom, Tills," he said. "And you really remind me of her sometimes. But, you know, it's not about what you get from me or what you get from your mother. It's about who you are, yourself." He sighed and stretched. "I'm beat," he said. "Bedtime." He hauled himself up off the couch and held his hand out to pull her up. "I'm taking tomorrow off. Let's go for a walk, hey?"

"Great idea," she said.

A little later, he came and tucked her in, like she was a little girl. "Don't forget," he said, "your mother might seem scary, but sometimes she just needs to be told, clearly, and without fuss—*No.*"

She shuddered at the thought of saying that to Mom. "Can't I just send you in to do that for me?" she said in a pleading voice.

He kissed her on the top of the head. "Not forever, Tilly."

11

The *Dorothy Garrod*'s final destination, before the ship turned back toward Federation space and its crew went on the academic's holiday of writing-up and conferences, was the planet Vesnoy. Tilly had been reading everything she could: Dad had been particularly looking forward to this part of the voyage. An earlier exploratory vessel, passing this way, had discovered not only the world, which was uninhabited, but evidence of an unknown, long-gone civilization. Planetary surveys had revealed the existence of numerous lost cities and various building-complexes dotted along the edge of one continent. But this was the first time that a team would go down and look at the ruins firsthand. Dad was of course part of this team. He'd been excited about this landing party since signing up for the voyage (it was one reason he'd taken the posting). Excited for Dad meant reading even later into the night than usual and making long lists about what he wanted to do while he was down there.

Tilly, however, was not happy about him going away. She followed him around as he packed. "I don't feel good about this."

"Tills, it'll be fine." He sounded absentminded, like he wasn't quite listening and was halfway down to Vesnoy already.

"That shuttle trip was meant to be fine," she pointed out.

"Well, yes, okay, sometimes things aren't fine."

"But what if you *die*? What if you're *attacked*?"

"There are no people down there."

"There are *rocks*. You can cut yourself on rocks. You can get *gangrene*."

He laughed, and carried on packing.

"How can you be so relaxed about this?" she said. "After what happened. Aren't you even the tiniest bit scared?"

He took a proper look at her. "You're really worried, aren't you?"

"Er, *yes*."

He came over and gave her a hug. "There's really nothing to worry about."

"No?"

"No."

"Then take me with you."

He pulled back. "What?"

"If it's all going to be fine, if there's no danger—take me with you."

He shook his head. "Tills, I can't do that."

"So it's not really safe after all."

"It's not that, it's—"

"What, then? Oh, *please*, Dad. Please, please, *please*." She suddenly felt as excited about the trip as he did. She wouldn't mind so much, if she could keep an eye on him. Besides, they would have fun. "You've taken me on digs before."

"Nothing this remote."

"We've gone hillwalking in Scotland—that's pretty remote."

"Tills," he said in a pained voice, "Scotland isn't remotely remote."

"I've been *great* on digs before. I've come in useful. I've come in more than useful. I've been *indispensable*. You said that once—do you remember? On Metlis III. *Indispensable.*"

"I knew I'd regret that," he muttered. "Do you know, Tills—and I mean this in the nicest way—but when you get like this, you are exactly like your mother."

"Low *blow*, mister!" Then she turned on the wheedling voice. "Please? *Please?*"

"Oh, for heaven's sake . . ." muttered Iain. "I'll have a word with the captain. You know, all Holden and I ever talk about these days is you. It's like I'm your agent."

"But you'll still talk to her?" said Tilly.

"It would be nice if *I* were the more famous Tilly round here. Fat chance."

"But you'll *talk* to her, huh? Yeah? Agreed?"

"Yes," said Iain, "against my better judgment, I'll talk to her. And if she's okay, you can come. But you must never, *ever* tell your mother."

She put her hand against her heart. "Tilly's honor."

Holden, weighing the balance of the safety of a minor on an uninhabited planet accompanied by four experienced officers against having to listen to Tilly complain, came to much the same conclusion as Iain about which battles she was willing to fight. Which was why the following morning found Tilly with her father and three other crewmembers on board a shuttle heading down toward Vesnoy.

"Remember, you're here to watch," Iain said as they went on board. "Not to talk."

So she did watch, and she enjoyed their camaraderie, and the easy way they discussed their work and shared their ideas. She had a brief moment of wondering whether this was a good idea when the shuttle pulled away from the *Dorothy*

Garrod, but none of the others seemed to be worried, so she tried to make herself relax. She reminded herself that shuttle accidents could happen anywhere—on a trip to Talaris, for example, or a straightforward transport between Earth and Mars. Space travel was dangerous, wherever you were. One thing she was sure about, though: she would never again take for granted the courage of the people in Starfleet.

As the shuttle made its way down to Vesnoy, Tilly tinkered with her latest project. Right now, she was working to optimize some of the functionality of the universal translators. They weren't great at a whole subset of languages with certain conceptual differences. Those Elisurian melodics, for example. And Holden's K'la'bisian—there was a lot of nuance missed. The work was so absorbing that she didn't realize that the shuttle was getting ready to land. Her dad came to sit next to her. "Hey," he said, "I've got something for you."

He was holding out some kind of armband, which he strapped around her upper left arm.

"What's this?" she said.

"This is how you get to come out of the shuttle and onto the surface with us," he said. "It's an emergency transporter. Any sign of trouble—tap this, you'll be back on the ship in seconds."

She looked at him. "You're not wearing one."

"No."

"But—"

"This is the deal, Tills," he said. "Holden insisted. Up to you. Put this on—or stay here on the shuttle."

"Okay," she said. "But I still think you should have one too."

Vesnoy was certainly a lot more remote even than Scotland. Chillier, too. They were working in a narrow valley between two rocky ridges, and the wind whistled through, howling like some strange beast. Tilly didn't mind. After so long on board ship, she was loving every second of being outdoors. There was a bright pale sun, which was one better than Zymne. They'd picked the spot for the dig very carefully, after sifting through the planetary survey data, but of course there was no accounting for weather. Dad was in his element. On his knees, messing around in the soil and the stones, looking happy to be in the fresh air, wind tousling his hair. Tilly didn't judge. After all, she was the one into mushrooms. She had seen this before from him, hundreds of times; hour after hour of careful, meticulous study—and then a sudden burst of excitement, when he was ready to commit to what he'd found.

She left him to his poking around and spent some of the morning on the other side of the dig. One of his colleagues, Jameson, had found some mosaics, and they were so interesting that Tilly couldn't tear herself away from them. The best part was when they extrapolated from what they had—which sometimes wasn't much—to generate holo-images of how the mosaics must have looked in their glory. "Now," said Jameson, "what do you make of these?"

"Eeuw," said Tilly. "They're *gruesome*!"

"They certainly are," said Jameson. She sounded very cheerful. "Sacrifices, maybe? I wonder if these here were animals, or whether they're what the locals looked like."

"*Human* sacrifice?" Tilly caught herself and blushed. "You know what I mean!"

Jameson laughed. "Easy mistake to make. Yes, I know what you mean."

Tilly shuddered. "I'm kind of getting the feeling that this place wasn't very nice."

"No," said Jameson. "And you've noticed how some of the stones are black?"

"I meant to ask about that. Doesn't that usually mean there's been a fire?"

"Yep. I'm starting to think that maybe this place didn't have a happy ending." Jameson shook her head. "Shouldn't jump to conclusions. Plenty more to find out first." She peered along the valley. "But I bet if we poked around up there, we'd find some fortifications, defending entry to this place, and probably some bodies . . ."

"Tills," Dad called over. "Come and take a look at this."

She went to join him at the trench he'd been working at. "What have you got?"

"Bones," he said, rubbing his hands together with relish.

"Ooh," she said, equally delighted. "Gotta love a skeleton."

"Okay, indispensable one, what can you tell me about these?"

She looked over the jumble of bones that he had uncovered. "They've not been arranged, have they? I mean, if someone is buried for a funeral, they're usually all nice and tidy. Arms folded, or scrunched up, crouch position . . ."

"Good! You *do* listen!"

"But these—they've sort of been thrown in here . . . Are they universal, Dad? Burial practices?"

"It's a pretty good rule-of-thumb."

"Poor old bones," murmured Tilly, "chucked into a pit. That's horrid."

"I agree," he said, more soberly.

"Dad, are those skulls?" She was pointing at something that would definitely be a head on a humanoid. Guessing from the jawbones, the mouths seemed unusually large. "Do they have *holes* in them?"

"I think so, Tills, yes," he said. "I think they've been stoved in."

Again, Tilly shuddered. "It's kind of sad here, isn't it?"

"Do you feel that too?" Iain was frowning. "Like something happened here . . ."

"Shouldn't jump to conclusions," Tilly said piously. She glanced over to where Jameson was working, back by the mosaics. The rest of the landing party—two other crewmembers—had gone to join her, and they were all looking down at something and talking excitedly at once. Tilly tried to catch a glimpse of what was causing so much debate, and then something moved at the corner of her eye, up on the ridge. She looked up and saw . . .

"Dad," she said, grabbing his arm. "There's someone up there. Up on the ridge."

He turned to look. Tilly saw a thin figure, easily over six feet tall, wearing what appeared to be a long and rather shapeless gray robe. Definitely not Starfleet. She tried to make out distinguishing features. She saw a smooth, pale, oval face; no hair . . . There was something uncanny about this.

"Okay," said Iain, "we need to be careful now." He gestured to his colleagues, and they too looked up to the ridge. Tilly saw them tense, move into a more cautious mode. "Tills," he said, "I might be sending you back soon—"

The figure shifted forward. It raised its arms, half-height, palms of long-fingered hands outward, as if to push the landing party away. Tilly saw the cruel curve of its closed mouth: wider, much wider than any human mouth would be. This opened, and Tilly gasped as the maw seemed to take over the whole of the alien's face, which became a huge hole into nothing.

And then the alien *screamed* . . .

The noise was excruciating, like the scrape of metal, but loud, and made scarier by the fact that something *alive* was producing such a terrible sound. Tilly slammed her hands against her ears. Dad too seemed to be in pain. *Oh jeez*, thought Tilly, *this is the noise something makes before it* kills *you* . . .

But the worst hadn't come yet. As Tilly watched, the stones around Jameson and the others began to shudder, almost as if responding to the alien's command. And then, suddenly, a great hole opened up under them, a huge cavity sucking the rest of the landing party down, down into the soil. Down amongst the bones. Tilly watched in horror as the hole began to seal over, folding them underground— and then she felt the ground beneath *her* feet begin to tremble . . .

"*Shit!*" yelled Iain.

Tilly knew what was going to happen next, and she knew she couldn't do anything to stop him. Dad leaned over and tapped her armband—and then he and the hungry Vesnoyan valley and its awful screaming alien were gone. She was standing in the transporter room of the *Dorothy Garrod*, and Holden was hurrying toward her.

"Tilly, what the *hell* is going on?"

Holden marched her toward engineering. Later, Tilly would realize that Holden was trying to debrief her but that she wasn't really making much sense. "Is Dad okay? Have you heard from Dad? One minute they were all there, and then they were underground, and—*have you heard from Dad?*"

"Tilly," said Holden, her voice calm but clear, "I need you to slow down—"

"That thing started screaming at us—oh my goodness, that noise!—and the ground opened up . . . I told Dad this was a bad idea! I told him it wasn't safe!"

They reached engineering. Holden maneuvered her into one of the seats. The team gathered around to hear what she had to say. Nish handed Tilly a glass of water, which she gulped down. "Deep breaths, Tilly," said Mei, and Tilly obeyed. Then she was able to tell her story. "We were digging. Dad found some bones—"

"Cool," said Andy. He shot a quick look at his captain. "Sorry."

"And we were talking about them. The others were all together on the other side of the site. I saw someone on the ridge—"

"Someone?" said Holden, her eyes sharp. "Alien?"

"Well, yes, because they opened their mouth, and . . ." Tilly shivered, thinking again of that terrible sound. "They *screamed* . . ." She began to cry. That awful, terrible sound. "Oh, Captain? Have you heard anything from Dad?"

"Not yet," said Holden. "You know we'll tell you the second we hear—but you've got to carry on with your story. If you tell us everything you saw, that's more we know about what happened, and more clues to help us work out what to do. What happened next?"

"So the thing was screaming," Tilly went on, "and it was like the ground opened up. Jameson and the others— they all fell inside this *hole*. And then it sealed up—"

Her friends were already on the move. "We can try to extend the range of the scanners," said Thritte. "See if we can pick up life signs under the surface—"

"I might be able to boost the range of the communicators," said Mei.

Holden nodded to Tilly. "Carry on."

"And then the ground by us—by me and Dad—started to shake, and Dad hit this thing on my arm, and I was here again."

"Okay, Tilly," said Holden. "That was great. You're doing great." She glanced at Etraxis. "Is that something you can work with?"

"It will have to be," he said, and went off to join his team.

Holden knelt down next to Tilly. "Okay," she said. "I'm going to leave you here for a while, Tilly, because I need to go to the bridge now, but try to stay calm and—"

Suddenly, the comms channel blared. What came out was noise—hideous, senseless noise. "Holy shit!" yelled Andy. Tilly put her hands over her ears; everyone else in engineering did much the same. "This is it!" she cried. "This is what the alien screamed!"

The sounds scraped on. Eventually they stopped, and everyone in the room breathed a sigh of relief. Thritte said, "It *hurt*!"

"It's like having to listen to Schoenberg run backward through a blender," said Andy.

"It's bloody horrible," said Nish.

"Tilly," said Holden. "Is that what you heard down on Vesnoy?"

Tilly nodded. The worst was that although she couldn't make out words, the underlying message was clear. Anger. Threat. Violence. She hugged her arms around herself. "They *hate* us," she said. "Oh, Captain—where's *Dad*?"

Holden patted her arm. "We'll find him." She stood up and issued crisp orders to the comms team to get to work on deciphering the message. Meanwhile, the engineering team continued trying to find a way to contact the missing crew. Tilly sat quietly, but her mind was ticking over.

It was Patterson's mention of Schoenberg that did it. Tilly's mind started wandering to music and harmonies and making all sorts of connections. There would be a pattern here, she knew, if they could just discern it somehow . . .

After ten minutes, she jumped up. "I've got it!" she cried. "I know what's going on!"

Holden's eyes narrowed. "Tilly, you need to sit down—"

"No, Captain, please—I think I know what's going on—"

"Really, Tilly, this isn't helping—"

"Captain, I can talk to them! I know I can. Please—let me go back down and talk to them."

"Tilly!" said Holden. "No way!"

She dashed over to the captain and grabbed her by the arm. "Please!" she begged. "I know I can do this."

"If you take her away," said Etraxis, "we have more chance of making a breakthrough here. Because it will be quieter."

Holden was shaking her head. And then a message came through from the bridge. "*Captain, we've been scanning the surface. There's a planetary defense system—*"

"Impressive for an uninhabited planet," muttered Holden.

"*Captain, it's being marshaled toward us.*"

"Well, shit," said Holden. "Of course it is."

"We can defend ourselves for a while," said Etraxis. "But at the end of the day, we're just a science vessel. Who knows what firepower they have at their disposal."

Tilly took a deep breath and then tried again. "Captain," she said. "I can talk to them. I know I can. Please—let me go down."

Holden looked at her and then at her engineering team. "For what it's worth, Captain," said Etraxis, "she's a smart kid." The rest of the team nodded their agreement. Tilly looked at them gratefully. *My guys*, she thought. *My team. My tribe*.

Holden closed her eyes, put her hand up to her brow. "Iain's going to kill me," she muttered. Then: "Okay, kiddo, get yourself down to the transporter room."

Ten minutes later, Tilly and Holden were on the surface of Vesnoy, back at the site of what had been the dig. There was no sign of any of the landing party, and practically no sign of the work they had been doing. "It all caved in," explained Tilly. "Everything went under."

Below their feet, the ground began to tremble once more. Tilly looked up at the ridge. The alien had come back. It stood there—tall and gray and almost featureless. Then it opened its huge mouth and screamed.

"*Shit!*" said Holden. "It's even worse close up! Okay, Tilly—whatever you've got in mind, it's time to give it a go."

Tilly steadied herself. She was sure this would work—no, better than sure. She *knew* this would work. The languages were so similar . . . She focused her mind, tried to clear it and calm it, and then launched into the speech she had prepared for the school's mock-summit. Elisurian melodic quadratic equations. And this time she didn't have to worry about the hat . . . She stood, and she sang her heart out, tweaking the words as she went along, singing a speech that explained who they were and where they had come from. From the corner of her eye, she saw Holden's horrified expression: *Oh god, what have I done? We're going to die* . . . But she kept on singing and singing and singing . . .

And the alien stopped screaming.

Tilly paused for a moment. Then she sang, *"Hello?"*

The alien sang back—a few notes, nowhere near as harsh this time. *"Hello,"* it sang. *"Your accent is terrible."*

Tilly laughed. *"I know,"* sang Tilly. *"Sorry about that."*

The alien laughed too. Beside her, Tilly could see Holden, waving around her tricorder. Tilly kept talking to the alien, just chatting, really: *We just dropped by, didn't know anyone else was here, sorry if we disturbed you, is everyone else okay, gosh I'm really glad to hear that because one of them is my dad, no that's okay but if you could let him go soon I'd be really grateful* . . . It was a good thing, she thought, for perhaps the first time in her life, that she had the gift of the gab. Soon Holden's tricorder had acquired enough language for Holden to try her own tentative "Hello?"

The alien turned to the captain. *"Ah. You're quick learners. That's something in your favor, at least."*

Holden lifted her hand in greeting. "We love to learn. Any chance we could get to know you better?"

And that was that. First contact. *Official* first contact. Tilly had been the first to speak to them, of course.

"Tilly," said Holden about fifteen minutes later, when the release of the landing party had been agreed, and an invitation to come on board the *Dorothy Garrod* had been accepted. "What the *hell* happened back there?"

"It's a project I did a while back," Tilly explained. "Elisurians. You won't have heard of them. Really *minor* planet. Probably because they talk in melodic quadratic equations." She smiled. "Schoenberg. There's structure. It just isn't always what you expect. And the universal translators—they struggle with this kind of thing. I've got an idea about that, though. You'll like it."

Holden began to laugh. "You're a bit of a marvel, aren't you?"

Tilly smiled. "Could you put that in writing and tell my mom?"

So that's first contact, she thought. *Beats cocktail parties.*

It took a day or two for things to settle down. The ship had to move from exploratory mode into first-contact protocols, which, as Iain explained, when he was back in their quarters, were much more cautious and concerned with avoiding disclosure of advanced technologies or inadvertently intervening in local politics. It turned out that there wasn't much that they could do to surprise the Vesnoyans. A long-lived and ancient species, they had at one point had their own star-spanning empire in this part of space, but their empire contracted, and the last Vesnoyans, very old and wise, had retreated to their home, cutting themselves off from the rest of the galaxy. That had been centuries ago. They'd avoided contact since, until the *Dorothy Garrod* arrived.

Holden invited a small party of them on board to tour the ship. Tilly, slipping into engineering at the right moment, caught a glimpse of them as they passed through. They seemed . . . *polite*, she thought. Happy to listen to what Holden had to say, willing to walk around the ship if it meant a gesture of friendship, but keen to get home. Holden, busy with their guests, nevertheless didn't miss that Tilly was there, and she raised an eyebrow at her as she went past.

Oh dear, thought Tilly. *Have I pushed my luck?*

That afternoon, back in their quarters, Iain, sitting on the couch, gestured to her to sit down next to him. "So," he said. "I gather you somehow found yourself in the thick of things on Vesnoy."

"In my defense," said Tilly, "it was at the captain's invitation."

"Are you quite sure about that?" said Iain. "I heard you nagged her into submission."

"I guess . . ." She gave him a bright smile. "It all worked out okay, didn't it?"

Iain put his head in his hands. "Oh, Tills. This is becoming a habit, isn't it?"

Uh-oh, thought Tilly. *This sounds like what Mom would call an "emerging issue."*

Iain sighed. "It's quite hard to be annoyed with you, given that everyone on board is singing your praises and saying how we wouldn't have made first contact without you." He made a face. "Actually, it's quite easy to be annoyed with you, Tills, but any attempt to discipline you is made harder by the fact that colleagues keep on coming up to me to say how proud I must be and that you deserve at least a commendation." He gave a short, slightly bitter laugh. "Ha! It's the 'at least' that gets me."

She flushed with pleasure. *Go on, Dad, admit it. Part of you is proud.*

"You don't do things by halves, do you?" said Iain.

Tilly mumbled something.

"Anyway," he said, "you're grounded."

"Huh?" she said. "How long?"

"I haven't decided yet," said Iain. "Maybe your thirties." He eyed her thoughtfully, and then, wearily, pushed a hand through his hair. "Oh, Tills," he said. "What am I going to do with you?"

The communicator beeped softly. Iain went over to answer it. The captain spoke. *"Tilly—"*

"Yes?" said Tilly.

"I think," said Iain, "that she means me."

"Oh yes! Sorry, Dad."

"Could you send your daughter to my ready room, please," said Holden. *"Now."*

"Yes, Captain," said Iain.

Tilly bit her lip. "I thought I was grounded," she said.

Her father pointed toward the door. "Don't push your luck."

When Tilly entered Holden's ready room, the captain was busy at her desk. She looked up and nodded, but didn't invite her to sit. So Tilly stayed standing, shifting nervously from foot to foot, watching the captain finish whatever task was keeping her busy. Holden, she noticed, was wearing her uniform—no sweatshirt, nothing informal. She looked incredibly professional and pretty scary. Tilly swallowed. *I really am in trouble this time.* She flushed. It wasn't entirely fair, she thought. Okay, so she had kept on until Holden had let her go down, but ultimately Holden had *let her go down* . . .

Eventually, Holden finished what she was doing. She looked up at Tilly, her expression unreadable. "Okay," she said. "Ms. Tilly."

"I'm really sorry," said Tilly quickly. "I can't say how sorry I am. I know I shouldn't have gotten involved. I know I should have gone back to my quarters or something. But I was really scared about Dad . . . I couldn't stop thinking about him . . . And then I realized that I knew how they were communicating—it was the Elisurians that did it, you see, and that seminar you gave on K'la'bisian narratives—"

Holden's eyes narrowed.

Oh no, thought Tilly, *she thinks I'm blaming her. Or, worse, trying to suck up to her* . . . She gabbled on. "But I knew the translators couldn't cope, and . . ."

Holden was drumming the desktop with her fingertips. Tilly ground to a halt.

"Finished?" said Holden, shifting forward.

"I'm sorry," said Tilly humbly. "I'm really, really sorry."

Holden sat and looked at her. "What did your dad say?"

"He's *really* pissed with me. You wouldn't believe how pissed."

"Oh yeah?" said Holden.

"He's *grounded* me!" Tilly said, and she wasn't able to stop her voice from brimming over with outrage at this affront.

"Right," said Holden. Did her lips just twitch? Tilly wasn't sure.

"What are you going to do with me?" said Tilly. Tiny voice. Tiniest of voices.

Holden folded her arms. "Well, you're grounded, aren't you?"

Tilly looked at her, puzzled. Was that it?

"I might suggest to your dad we try *shackles*," said Holden. "You know, a ball and chain or something? But that's really his business and you'd probably work out some complex mathematical formula to disintegrate *metal* or something. And—well. It's not like I didn't let you go down there in the first place, and it's not like I didn't allow you to come down with me after."

"There is that," agreed Tilly.

"So. Since we're all square when it comes to . . . well, let's say *bending* the rules . . . I'm going to make you an offer."

Tilly frowned. An offer?

"I know from speaking to your grandmother that your plans for the immediate future aren't settled yet," said Holden.

Tilly goggled at her. Holden had been talking to *Granna*? The thought of that back channel was more than slightly alarming.

"Yeah," said Holden with some satisfaction. "That's got your attention. People talking, Tilly. So, you've no fixed plans yet for when the ship gets back to Federation space."

"Um, yes," said Tilly. "I guess."

"But your mother's still talking about some school—?"

"I don't want that," said Tilly quickly.

"Thought not," said Holden. "Anyway, stop *yapping* for two seconds, will you, and I'll tell you what I have in mind."

Tilly nodded and kept quiet.

"Okay. Here's the deal. You can stay on board here, on the *Dorothy Garrod*, working alongside the engineering team and completing a course of study that we'll put together for you. If you do that well over the next few months, and if you manage not to break any more rules or be in the wrong place at the wrong time or *suborn* me into making stupid decisions, then I'll sponsor your application to Starfleet Academy."

There was silence.

"Oh, good," said Holden. "That's shut you up."

"Starfleet . . ." said Tilly.

"I'm going to be honest, Tilly," Holden went on, "your track record so far is a bit, um . . . *spotty*? Great grades, *terrible* insubordination issues."

Oh, thought Tilly, *those wretched issues.*

"But. On the plus side—you broke the security at your own school . . ."

That's on the plus side?

"You managed to keep going on your own for several days. You got a job offer and a place to live within a day of arriving on Zymne. You kept your head while your dad was in trouble on that shuttle. And, most of all . . . Well, you just averted a fairly decent-sized crisis. I think that probably all adds up to initiative. And guts. Oh, and smarts. Let's not forget the smarts. But . . ."

Tilly knew what she was going to say. She sighed. "Playtime's over."

"You got it. It's time to start working hard, Tilly. Really hard." Holden leaned forward in her chair. "What do you say? Do we have a deal?"

Tilly could hardly believe her ears. *Starfleet?* She would never have imagined it. And yet it seemed so obvious now, so *right* . . . "Oh gosh, oh wow . . . I'd . . . I'd love to! More than anything." She clapped a hand over her mouth. "Oh. I've got to talk to Dad." Then she blanched. "Oh no. I have to talk to *Mom*."

Holden smiled. "You go and do that."

—

Iain took the suggestion in his stride. "I wondered if we were heading that way," he said.

Tilly frowned at him. "Really?"

"Mm. Well, you've fit right in around here, haven't you?"

"So you wouldn't *mind*?" Tilly said.

"What's there to mind?" Iain said. "I'd love to have you around the place for the foreseeable future, surely that goes without saying. But most of all, Tills, what I want is for you to find out what's going to make you happy and to start doing that. Really doing it. Using all your talents, the way you want to use them. I want you to be happy. And I think this has got a good chance of being the thing that makes you happy. Why would I mind?"

She shrugged. "It's just . . . Starfleet was always your thing. I was supposed to be doing the diplomacy thing."

He gave her a sideways look. "I think we all know that's not going to make you happy."

"And then . . . Dad, is it always like this? Red alerts and crises and that kind of thing?"

"Not always," he said. "Not on a ship like this, at any rate. Anyway, would that be a problem? We're all trained not to panic. But you didn't panic anyway."

"I guess not," she said.

"Not to mention being the reason we got through the whole last thing," he added—scrupulously, she thought, given how out of line she'd been. She blushed.

"I had a good idea, Dad. Everyone listened and let me get on with it." She smiled. "I suppose they didn't have to do that."

"Well, why wouldn't they listen to you, Tills?"

Nobody ever has before, she thought. "I don't know . . ."

"You're smart, you have good ideas. You don't waste

people's time." He stopped and corrected himself. "Actually, you have, over the past year, wasted a lot of people's time, but you seem to be reforming in that respect."

"Yeah," she said, "never living that down. But, Dad, what will Mom say?"

He frowned. "I honestly don't know."

"Will you talk to her?"

He looked at her. "No, Tills. I think this has to come from you."

"Will you sit next to me while I talk to her?" She remembered how much more reasonable Mom was with Dad there. "Please?"

"I'll be right across from you," Iain said.

Tilly spent some time that night thinking about what she was going to say to Mom. Starfleet! She would never have thought of this before, but now that she had, it seemed so obvious. Where else did all the brilliant eccentrics end up, if they wanted to make a difference? Mom had always been big on that, making a difference, and Tilly wanted to, she really did, but not through receptions and networking and small talk. She knew that kind of thing suited other people down to the ground. She knew that was how *they* made a difference. But it wasn't right for her.

The past few months . . . She'd seen so many different things. She'd seen life outside the Federation, even if only briefly, heard different stories—Salla's, and Natalia's, and then Orlotz's of missing his daughter while trying to make a living on a cold, hard world . . . She had a new appreciation now of her privileges, her good fortune in being born into the Federation. She knew she was never going to take that for granted. And she knew, now, that she was capable of doing a great deal. She *had* managed by herself, even if only for a few days, and she *hadn't* gone running back when things had gotten tough. She'd stuck it out and found a place for herself. She knew too the kind of things she was good at—solving technical problems, using her knowledge and her smarts to fix things, solve things. She'd done well here on the *Dorothy Garrod*, even as she'd pushed her luck. What she needed was a place that would nurture these talents, make good use of them.

But Starfleet? Tilly couldn't help but laugh to herself. She'd always been so suspicious in the past. But it hadn't been what she'd expected, not at all. Holden—laid-back and approachable, but sharp as nails and nobody's fool. Her friends in engineering, who had welcomed her, and trained her, and been prepared to listen to her not because of her mom or even her dad, whom they really liked, but because she—Tilly—had something worth listening to. This whole ship, working together, not just during a crisis, although they excelled in that, but in the everyday support they gave one another—the interest they took in one another's lives and work. A big high-school science club, but populated by adults, the best of all possible worlds. Against all the odds, she'd found, well, her *tribe*. Her team. She'd always been the odd one out at school, but now she was starting to see that it didn't have to be that way. She didn't have to be alone. As for the danger? Okay, that was scary, but she'd *coped*. She hadn't panicked. No, Starfleet wasn't anything like Tilly had thought. And, besides, she had always known in her heart that it wasn't Starfleet that had made Dad leave. No, that was something else entirely.

The next evening, Tilly sat down for her weekly conversation with her mother. Iain, as promised, sat across from her. As the signal went through, Iain stuck both thumbs up. *You can do it*. They'd talked together about how she would manage herself and her emotions. Deep breaths. Don't get upset. Look at him, if she needed moral support . . .

Siobhan looked gorgeous. She *always* looked gorgeous. Tilly thought about what Dad had said. *The sharpest, most dedicated, most brilliant, most* sparkling *woman I have ever met . . . A minor deity.*

How did you take on a goddess?

Siobhan, Tilly realized, was talking about a new school she had found. *"Look, it's got a more focused science curriculum,"* she said. *"And it's on Earth, so you could board in the weeks and come to New York or Paris at the weekends . . . We could see more of each other . . ."*

"Mom," she said. She had to say it twice. "*Mom.*"

Siobhan looked up at her. *"Yes, sweetheart?"*

She glanced at Dad. He nodded. "Mom, I'm not going back to school."

Siobhan fell back in her seat. *"Sylvia!"*

"It's Tilly now, Mom," she said. Her mouth felt ash dry. *Am I really saying these things?* "This school—it sounds great, it really does. But I'm not going. I've . . . I've grown past that now."

"You're sixteen *years old! You should be in school—"*

"Mom . . ."

"You've wasted months now—"

"Wasted?"

"We've got to get you back on track!"

"Mom! *Listen* to me!" *My voice sounds weird*, thought Tilly, before realizing what was different. It didn't sound tiny. "Listen! I'm not going back to school. I'm not going to go into the diplomatic corps—"

"Oh, okay," said Siobhan. *"So what are you going to do? Live in Dad's spare room for the rest of your life?"*

Tilly glanced at her dad. He looked like he was about to intervene. She shook her head at him, ever so slightly. *I can do this.* He nodded. *Okay.*

"No," Tilly said firmly. "I'm going to stay here, and I'm going to work hard on the subjects I love, and in a year or so, Captain Holden is going to sponsor my application to Starfleet Academy."

There was a pause. Then Siobhan looked past her. *"Iain? I know you're there. Did you put her up to this?"*

"*Mom!*" Tilly was shocked. "This has nothing to do with Dad!"

"Forgive me for not finding that very convincing."

"Mom, listen. This is important. You're a diplomat, and I know you wanted me to do the same. But I've come to realize—not all diplomacy takes place at cocktail parties—"

"Is that what you think I do all day?"

"Of course not, Mom! I know what you do—I've seen you in action often enough! But this work—the kind of thing Starfleet does—it's diplomacy too, isn't it? A different kind—on a distant world, in the middle of danger sometimes. It's important, in the moment, but it's still diplomacy. Mom, I'll still be doing what you want—just not the way we thought I would be."

She was sure this would win Mom over. But Mom wasn't listening. Mom *never* listened. *"Iain, I want to talk to you now."*

"Why talk to Dad? This is *my* choice! My decision! Mom—this isn't your life! This is *my* life! I can't turn myself into you. Surely everyone can see by now that isn't going to happen? And I can't try any longer. It's wearing me down! I know I can do this—"

"Iain!"

"Don't talk to him!" Tilly said. "Talk to me! This is about *me*! Not you, not Dad—me!"

"*You're* sixteen, *Sylvia! You don't know what you want! You've been on a starship for, what—three months? And now you're talking about Starfleet as if it's all you ever wanted! I'm your mother. I'm supposed to stop you from making mistakes. So is your father, for that matter—Iain! Where are you?*"

This is weird, thought Tilly. She glanced at Dad. He nodded. *Keep on.*

"Mom, listen to me. I've done well here. I've been working hard. I've made friends. I feel . . . I feel happy. Even when things have been rough, I haven't felt panicked or stressed or anything like that. This is *good* for me—"

"*Sylvia! Stop talking and listen! This isn't going to happen—*"

"Mom—"

"*No, you've had your say. Now it's my turn. Do you know how much trouble you've caused this year? Do you have any idea how hard it's been? And then your dad swans in, takes you flying around for a bit, and suddenly it's all,* Oh, Starfleet, how marvelous! *Well, listen up, miss, because this is what's going to happen. You're coming home. You're going to school. You're going to work hard, and you're going to aim for the diplomatic corps—*"

"Seriously," Tilly said, "are you even *listening*? Because I don't know how much clearer I can be. I am *not* going back."

But Tilly wasn't her dad, and whatever trick Iain had up his sleeve, his daughter hadn't yet acquired it. More than that, Siobhan was used to having her own way where her daughter was concerned, and that was a very hard habit to break. Siobhan lost her temper for real.

"*You ungrateful little . . . Honestly, Sylvia—yes, Sylvia, I'm not indulging any of this any longer—do you have any idea how appallingly you've behaved? How much trouble you've caused me, your dad, Granna—not to mention the school, Federation Security, and your precious Starfleet—*"

"Siobhan, stop."

Tilly realized that Dad had come around the table. His hand was on her shoulder.

"I'll come back to you in a minute, Iain. Sylvia, do you know how hard I work to make sure you've got all these terrific opportunities? And what do I get back? Oh, the sulks and the backchat have been bad enough, messing around instead of working, but for you to sit there, after all you've done, and talk to me like that . . . It's not good enough, Sylvia! None of it! It's not good enough!"

"Siobhan!"

Tilly nearly jumped through the roof. She had never heard her father raise his voice in anger before. Quietly, she began to cry. *Is this what happened?* she thought. *Is this why he left? Did I do something wrong, and then they quarreled, and then he left?*

At least Mom, blessedly, had stopped talking.

"Okay, Siobhan," Iain said, his voice much calmer. "Everyone's upset, so I think the best thing to do right now is finish up this call—"

"Did you put her up to this, Iain?"

"I didn't," Iain said, a slight edge to his tone, "and when you're calmer you'll know better than to say something like that. We'll talk later, Siobhan, okay?"

The call ended. Tilly heard her father mutter, *Shit!* Then he turned to her. "I'm really sorry," he said. "I wouldn't have let you talk to her by yourself if I'd thought she was going to react like that. Don't worry, I'll talk to her—"

"Why did she *say* those things . . ." Tilly cried.

"I think she's scared, sweetheart," Iain said. "She knows, you know, that the ship was in danger at Vesnoy. Both of us were here. You, most of all. And then you say you want to do this kind of thing full-time? When you ran away—"

"Oh, please can we forget I ever did that!"

"We can't, sweetheart. We'll never forget how that felt. When you ran away, we were all terrified. That you'd been taken, that you might get hurt . . . She's scared for you, sweetheart, that's all."

"She shouldn't have said those things . . ." Tilly wept.

"No, she shouldn't."

" 'Not good enough,' Daddy! Is that really what she thinks of me?"

"Of course it isn't! Of course not." He sighed. "I'll talk to her. I'll sort it out."

"I'm not going back," said Tilly.

"No," said Iain. "I think that's perfectly clear."

The next morning, Holden received a message from Ms. Tilly. It was pretty formal. *Please could I make an appointment to see you at your earliest availability?*

She shot back: *Sure. Thirteen hundred?*

Tilly arrived promptly. Holden invited her to sit, but Tilly said she was okay standing. She looked different somehow, Holden thought. A little older. Maybe . . . a little sadder? She wondered what had happened.

"Do we still have a deal?" Tilly said.

Holden raised her eyebrows. "Sure! Have you talked to your mom and dad?"

"Yes," said Tilly, but didn't elaborate.

Holden didn't press her. She would find out the story in due course. If there was going to be a problem here, she knew Iain would have the sense to confide in her.

"Okay then, Tilly—we have a deal." Holden stuck out her hand, and Tilly shook it.

"Playtime's over," said Tilly.

"Well, not all the time," said Holden with a smile. She watched the girl head toward the door and, on some instinct, called back to her. "Your route here may have been unorthodox, you know—but I think you're doing really well. Good on ya, Tilly."

The girl turned back and gave her a smile. Holden watched her go. Praise, she thought—it cost the giver nothing to say, but it reaped the receiver huge dividends.

The *Dorothy Garrod*, near the Getrexi system

Dear Ms. Keith,

You said in your letter that I should keep in touch and let you know how things were going. That was really kind of you—I should think you would be glad not to have my name popping up in front of you too often! But if you don't mind, I'll take that invitation at face value, and I will write, when I get the chance.

I'm aiming for Starfleet. Wow, that looks momentous, written down, and it's not something I ever thought I'd write. I have always been a little suspicious of Starfleet. It always seemed a bit too good to be true, and with a rotten tendency to make one's father disappear for months at a time. Well, that last bit is true (although that's changed for the better) but it turns out that the first bit is sort of true too. It's really good. I didn't think I'd like living on a starship, and I wasn't sure I'd like the people, but I was wrong on both counts. Turns out starships are great places to live (if a little scary, sometimes) and the people are the best.

Some of them are even interested in astromycology, or else are nice enough to pretend.

So wish me luck. Hard work ahead. But I think I can do it. I think I'm good enough. Let's find out.

Your grateful (if errant!) former student,
Tilly

The *Dorothy Garrod*, four days out from the Netur system

Dear Risera,

I imagine you never thought you'd hear from me again, and I hope it's okay for me to write. I kind of took off without saying goodbye, after all . . . !

I don't know if you heard anything about my adventures. All told, I was "on the lam," as my friends here call it, for about a week. Pretty eventful week. Maybe I'll get the chance to tell you about it one day.

Because the real reason I'm writing is that I wanted to apologize. You were really kind to me when I arrived at school. You went out of your way to make me feel welcome—helped me to make friends, showed me the ropes, took me out for that great dinner with your supercool parents. And in return I got all your stuff and put it in a big pile on your bed. I am embarrassed and ashamed writing that. I am really, really sorry. I was stressed, and unhappy, and I made a massive mess of things. I am SORRY.

Okay. That's done. But the thing about apologies is that you can only offer them, not force someone to accept them. Even if I've apologized, you're not obliged to accept. So if you haven't already deleted this message unread (AND WHO FRANKLY WOULD BLAME YOU??), then I wanted to say that maybe it would be fun one day to meet up, and swap stories, and find out what's been happening to each other. Boy, do I have a tale to tell, and I'm sure you have some stories too. The short version of mine? I'm aiming for Starfleet. Engineering track. Makes sense, I guess?

Okay, that's the short version. Maybe we'll be in the same place at the same time one day, and you'll hear the long version. In the meantime, I hope you're doing brilliantly. GO REDS-AND-YELLOWS!

Your difficult roommate,
Tilly

P.S. Granna sends her love.

The *Dorothy Garrod*, in orbit around Vulcan

Dear Salla,

I wonder if you remember me. I stowed away on your ship, and you stopped your captain throwing me out of an airlock. Ring any bells?

I hope you're okay. I hope you're a day closer to your happy retirement and to long days of peace in the sunshine. I suspect, now, looking back, that you knew pretty early on who I was, and didn't give me away. That choice of yours made all the difference to me. It changed my life. So thank you, from—

Your grateful stowaway fixer,
Tilly

The *Dorothy Garrod*, near Earth

Dear Natalia,

I have thought long and hard over whether or not to write you. There is no obligation for you to write back, unless by some chance you would like to.

We met, briefly, almost a year ago. We made friends—or started to. And then . . . Well, life caught up with me, I guess, and my family arrived, with a starship, and I went back home.

I think maybe you remember me now.

Since then, my life has changed completely. I'm now preparing to enter Starfleet Academy. But I think a lot about my time on Zymne (less than twenty-seven hours altogether). I think a lot about how kind you were to me. How fair you were. That had never really happened to me before. You were the first person, ever, to take me on my own terms, and judge me for my own worth. For that, for your kindness and offer of friendship to a stranger, I am and always will be grateful.

Your nearly friend,
Sylvia Tilly

Coda
Summer

A year later . . .

Summer always meant Granna's house in the Midi, and this year was no different. Granna and Quinn and Tilly, the same as every year. This year, though, Dad had come. Mom wasn't there, of course. Busy. Mom was busier than ever these days, if that was possible. They'd spoken since Tilly's arrival on Earth, but they hadn't met in person yet. Tilly was resigned to the meeting, although she couldn't say she was looking forward to it. Dad had promised he'd be there.

So far it had been a good holiday: lots of lying in the sun reading, some swimming, a few excursions to local vineyards. Iain had brought some writing with him, but he hadn't done much. Mostly he and Quinn had played croquet. Weird game, Tilly thought, even as her mind thought about ballistics and how you could mathematically achieve the best shots.

Tilly and Risera had met in Paris for lunch earlier in the week. It had been a nice meeting. Risera had caught her up on news of friends from school; Tilly had filled her in on her adventures. They'd laughed a lot and promised to stay in touch. Risera looked amazing. She was getting real poise now. But still, Tilly couldn't imagine being back in that world of bells and classes and homework. She imagined Risera felt the same way about Tilly's choices. Who would want to be on a starship, without anyone their own age, hanging out with some engineering geeks? *Me*, thought Tilly with a smile. She'd had a few exchanges with Keith over the year and she was glad about that too. Keith had been kind, and she'd liked Tilly. Salla had written once, the short sentences of someone who didn't like to correspond. *Good to hear from you. Take care of yourself. Keep on fixing.* Natalia had never replied.

Granna emerged from the house, bearing a tray. Champagne, with two glasses, for her and Quinn. Two mugs of beer. "I *would* like to propose a toast," she said, handing the beers to her granddaughter and her ex–son-in-law. "But how does one toast with beer?"

Iain and Tilly clinked mugs. "See, Granna? Not so hard."

"To Sylvia Tilly," said Dad. "Starfleet's latest recruit."

Tilly flushed. The acceptance letter had come through this morning. She took a swig of her beer. Mom hadn't been in touch about it, not yet . . .

"So, Tilly," said Quinn with a smile. "Chief engineer before thirty?"

Tilly thought about the recommendation that Holden had written. One of her interviewers had told her, privately, that it was among the best they'd ever received. "Oh no," said Tilly. "I'm going to be a captain."

"Watch out, Iain," said Quinn. "You're going to end up saluting her."

But Iain was smiling at her. "That's my girl," he said.

Epilogue

The lights were on now in the cabin on board *Discovery*. Michael and Tilly, sitting together on Tilly's bed, were wrapped in blankets. There had been no sleep that night. In their hands, they each held an empty cup. Hot chocolate. For comfort.

"Well," said Tilly. "I said it was a long story."

Michael stared down into her cup. "Your quarrel with your mother . . . ?"

"Yeah," said Tilly. "That was something else, wasn't it?"

"Did she ever apologize?"

"Apologize? Mom? Not likely!" Tilly shook her head. "I mean . . . she didn't stop me coming into Starfleet, but I know it's not what she wanted." She shrugged. "We don't really talk about it."

"That's a shame."

"It's okay. You get used to it."

"And what about your dad?"

Tilly frowned. "What do you mean?"

"Well," said Michael slowly, "it sounds to me like you never did ask him what you wanted to ask him."

"Ask him what?"

"Ask him why he left."

There was a silence. "I know why he left."

"Are you sure?"

"I wasn't good enough," Tilly said.

"That doesn't sound like it was the reason to me," said Michael firmly.

"Well, what else would it be? He was *besotted* with Mom. I think he still is, to be honest; he gets this *look* sometimes when we talk about her, or when they're talking, and you think, *Hoo-boy, that's a man in love*. And then I arrived, and the next thing he's moved out—"

"Tilly," said Michael gently, "that's not how it works."

"Then how does it work?" Tilly shot back. "What other reason would there be?"

"I don't know," said Michael. "All kinds of reasons. Maybe you should ask him."

"Maybe I will . . ."

There was a silence. Michael stared meaningfully at the communication console.

"What, you mean now?" Tilly stared at her. "Have you seen the time—"

"No time like the present, Tilly. Particularly when you can't get to sleep." Michael got up and padded over to her own bed, wrapping herself under the covers. "I promise I won't listen."

Michael lay for a while, eyes shut. *Do it, Tilly*, she willed her friend. *It'll help* . . . After a while, she heard Tilly groan, and mutter something to herself, and then she heard the soft pad of feet going over to the communicator . . .

Dad was on sabbatical on Earth right now. Visiting professorship at Cambridge. Finishing up his current book. Everyone was talking about it. The last one had been *major*. Tilly smiled to see his face. There was a little silver in his hair now, not much, just a reminder that everyone was getting older.

He smiled to see her. "Hi, Tills," he said. "Hey, what time is it there?"

"Late."

"I thought so. Hey, big day tomorrow. Why aren't you asleep?"

Tilly glanced over the room. Michael was pretending not to listen. "I . . . I fell to thinking . . ."

"Oh dear, no, terrible idea—"

"Dad," she said. "Why did you leave? Was it something I did? I just need to know. What did I do?"

He looked at her, completely bewildered. "What, you mean the *Dorothy Garrod*? The tour was up, Tills. You were heading to the Academy anyway—"

Tilly shook her head. "Not that. Mom. Why did you leave me and Mom? Was it me?"

Dad was staring at her, his mouth open. "Sylvia," he said, "what are you talking about?"

"I just . . . remember when I told Mom I wanted to join Starfleet. She really lost her temper—"

"I remember," Iain said, with feeling.

"And *you* lost your temper too. You never do that."

"Well, not often, no—"

"And it was because of me. And I guess I always thought, on some level, that it must have been something to do with me. Because you two got together—and I know you still love her—and then I came along, and then you broke up. So I guess I just need to know—was it me that drove you away? I know I was difficult, I mean, I know I *am* difficult, and I guess that wasn't much fun—"

"Tills," he said. "Shut up a minute and let me say something."

"Sorry," she said. "You know what I'm like."

"I know." He leaned back in his chair. He looked absolutely blindsided.

"Dad, are you okay?"

"Yes, I'm fine, I'm worried about you . . . Tills, have you *really* thought this for all this time?"

"I guess . . ." Tiny voice.

"Damn," he said. "That's awful. Tills, I had no idea . . ." She shrugged.

"But to answer your question—no, of course it wasn't you. You were so small!"

"But Mom . . . You called her a 'minor deity,' you don't leave someone when they're a minor deity—"

He blinked. "Did I say that?"

"Er, yes . . . ?"

"To you?"

"Er, *yes*."

"Wow," muttered Iain, "I must have been pretty drunk." *Well, not drunk*, she thought, *but pretty exhausted*.

"Tills," he said, "you didn't drive me away. Mom didn't drive me away; nobody drove me away. It just didn't work. Me and your mother—it didn't work. It was never going to work. She needed somebody who was going to completely support what she did. And . . . I wasn't that person. Look at me, Tills! Do I look like one half of a power couple?"

Tilly gave a small smile. She loved Dad, and there was no doubt of his significance in his own field. But . . . no. Really. No.

"All those parties and receptions and embassies. The constant mindless smiling. I could see it all unfolding ahead of me. I could see that it was only ever going to be more and more like that, more and more intense. The worst thing was, I was never sure I was saying the right thing."

Tilly shuddered. She could sympathize with that. It didn't suit her. But she'd never thought, really, that it might not have suited him, either.

"I knew it would only get worse," Iain said. "Your

mother needed someone completely in synch, someone who took that way of life in their stride, who thrived on it. And that wasn't me. It was awful. I could see the disaster unfolding ahead of us. At some point, I was going to start resenting it—all the scrutiny, all the intrusions, all the demands. And then, at some point, I knew, she would lose patience with me, and she'd regret ever meeting me, and I couldn't bear that. I couldn't bear her regretting me. But I couldn't ask her to stop. Could you imagine asking her to stop?"

"Like asking the sun to stop shining," said Tilly. *Or stop burning.*

"Something like that," said Iain. "Oh, Tills. It was never going to work. I'm a quiet soul. I like to be out there, poking at some ruins, and then back at my desk, sifting through the data."

She smiled. She recognized that.

"I knew I could lose all that. Worse than that, I could see that I was going to try to bend myself out of shape to try to make myself good enough for her and . . . Well, that's not a great idea. I couldn't do that."

No, thought Tilly. *No, you can't.*

"You didn't do anything," he said. "It was just . . ." He shook his head. "It was never going to work."

Tilly sighed. "But Dad," she said. "What about *me*?"

"Oh, sweetheart. I know. I know it was hard. But the other way around would've been worse."

She wondered about that. For him? Definitely. For her? She frowned. *Jury's out,* she thought.

"There's one thing I'd definitely take back," said Iain. "Your mother persuaded me it was better for you to have a steady home life rather than traipsing around on a Starfleet vessel. And, well, I felt so bad about going, so I kind of capitulated there. Let her take the lead. And looking back, I can see now that I shouldn't have. That school she sent you to! It was never going to work . . . I should have pushed for you to be with me more often, and I shouldn't have let her have her way so much. I can see that now. That was a mistake, Tills. I'm sorry."

Tilly wiped her eyes. "Yes," she said. "That would've been nice."

"And going away on the *Dorothy Garrod* when I did . . . Well, I guess we all thought that would be okay. But it wasn't, was it? You and Mom, you need a third person present. I should have been there more, Tilly. And I'm sorry that I wasn't."

Tilly sat for a while, thinking. It was going to take a while, she thought, to work through all this, to make it part of the story of her life. She still felt sad, and scared. "Dad," she said. "About tomorrow . . ."

"What about tomorrow?"

"Do you think . . ." Tiny voice. "Do you think I'll be good enough?"

He gave her his most loving smile. "Oh, Tills," he said. "I think you're going to be *amazing*."

Michael Burnham had, of course, heard every word. She heard Tilly and her dad say good night, with much love, and then she heard Tilly sniffling. Next she heard the rattle of their empty cups, and then Tilly muttered, "Oh for heaven's sake, just do them in the morning." She heard Tilly put the cups down and get into bed. Tilly turned off the lights, and, not long after, Michael heard her gentle snore.

Michael smiled to herself and settled down to sleep. *And you are*, she thought. *Sylvia Tilly—you are going to be amazing.*

Acknowledgments

Huge thanks to Kirsten Beyer, who has made this project so much fun from start to finish. Grateful thanks also to Margaret Clark for her support and cheerleading during writing, and to Ed Schlesinger and John Van Citters for their help. Thanks as ever to James Swallow for being such a mensch.

And thank you of course to Mary Wiseman for bringing Tilly so fabulously to life.

At home—love to Verity, who is so patient when Mummy goes off to do her writing. And all my love and thanks to Matthew, who holds the fort and somehow makes everything possible.

About the Author

Una McCormack is the author of seven previous *Star Trek* novels: *The Lotus Flower* (part of *The Worlds of Star Trek: Deep Space Nine*), *Hollow Men*, *The Never-Ending Sacrifice*, *Brinkmanship*, *The Missing*, the *New York Times* bestseller *The Fall: The Crimson Shadow*, and *Enigma Tales*. She is also the author of four *Doctor Who* novels from BBC Books: *The King's Dragon*, *The Way Through the Woods*, *Royal Blood*, and *Molten Heart*. She has written numerous short stories and audio dramas.

She lives in Cambridge, England, with her partner of many years, Matthew, and their daughter, Verity.